BLUNT IMPACT

Forensic scientist Theresa MacLean is puzzled by the questionable death of a female construction worker at a Cleveland building site. A witness to the death – a young girl nicknamed Ghost – may be able to help. Ghost says the woman was pushed by someone she can only identify as the Shadow Man. Soon Theresa finds herself in a race against time to protect Ghost from an unknown killer before he is able to find the little girl and silence her for good.

* available from Severn House

BLUNT IMPACT

Lisa Black

Severn House Large Print
London & New York

This first large print edition published 2014
in Great Britain and the USA by
SEVERN HOUSE PUBLISHERS LTD of
19 Cedar Road, Sutton, Surrey, England, SM2 5DA.
First world regular print edition published 2013 by
Severn House Publishers Ltd., London and New York.

British Library Cataloguing in Publication Data

Black, Lisa, 1963- author.
  Blunt impact.
  1. MacLean, Theresa (Fictitious character)--Fiction.
  2. Women forensic scientists--Ohio--Cleveland--Fiction.
  3. Murder--Investigation--Fiction. 4. Detective and
  mystery stories. 5. Large type books.
  I. Title
  813.6-dc23

  ISBN-13: 9780727897244

Severn House Publishers support the Forest Stewardship Council™
[FSC™], the leading international forest certification organisation. All
our titles that are printed on FSC certified paper carry the FSC logo.

Printed and bound in Great Britain by
T J International, Padstow, Cornwall.

*To my parents
because I can never thank them enough*

NOTES AND ACKNOWLEDGMENTS

There are, so far as I know, absolutely no plans to raze the Administration building.

I also invented the temporary aluminum forms for concrete pouring that Sam Zebrowski may or may not have been scrapping.

And to my great agent, Vicky Bijur – thank you for not giving up on me.

ONE

The dew had barely settled on the body when Theresa approached the site, camera and basic crime-scene kit in hand. The skeletal landscape of concrete and steel spread before her, populated with men in hard hats with too-bright lights who used noisy equipment without apparent concern for sleeping neighbors or that one of their own had just been found dead. But then, completion date penalties were completion date penalties and there weren't too many residential units in the heart of downtown Cleveland anyway. Theresa took a deep breath full of concrete dust and went to find her cousin.

The construction area took up the entire city block between Rockwell and St Clair and showed a remarkable lack of security for a place that would eventually house burglars, drug dealers and killers. The wide gate in the chain-link fence gaped open and Theresa traveled around unencumbered save for the chaotic maze of trucks the size of tractor-trailers, large metal storage sheds and piles of steel beams that towered over her. The men working there continued to work and did not question her presence. She found one of the (few) advantages of passing forty to be the ability to pass a group of construction workers without eliciting a single comment. They stared, yes, but she told herself that was due to the 'Medical Examiner's Office' stenciled across the back of her windbreaker.

Moving through a hard hat area without a hard hat did not seem to concern them, but it concerned her. She stopped every few feet to glance upward at the building's frame, reaching impossibly high into the air. At times it seemed to her that humans were searching the air the same way they'd explored the earth, one foot at a time.

For the most part it formed a simple rectangle, but a shorter stack of floors extended off the west side and then another, shorter still, its levels split from the first stack. In the main section the series of beams and concrete platforms stretched up at least thirty floors and would get higher, but nothing seemed to be falling off at the moment.

Theresa climbed up a short hill of dirt to the foundation, then balanced on the edge to scrape the wet Ohio clay off her shoes. It joined other dried and half-dried clumps along the sharp concrete edge. Spring in Cleveland stayed plenty damp.

'They're over there,' someone said. A wiry, dark-haired man carrying a beam that looked longer than he was gestured toward the interior, where her cousin spoke to more men in hard hats. She thanked the man but the words were drowned out as a jackhammer started up somewhere in their quadrant. He smiled anyway, watching her go.

Her cousin, Frank Patrick, worked as a detective in the homicide unit, which made her wonder why he had responded to an industrial accident. She found him with a man of medium height and medium complexion, whose curly brown hair was already beginning to part ways with itself at the top of his head. He wore an ID badge on a lanyard around his neck and his slight paunch would grow to a full-blown pregnancy in the next ten to twenty years. Despite that he appeared fully capable of picking her up with one hand.

'This is Chris Novosek,' Frank greeted her. 'Project manager.'

The man nodded at her. 'Thank you for coming.'

I'm a single forty-one year old with an empty nest, she thought. What else do I have to do? Besides, it's my job.

She nodded back.

Novosek seemed calm, but as if he had to work on it. 'When are you going to move her? It's not right, her just laying there like that.'

'I understand,' Theresa said as gently as she could manage while still having to shout the words over the jackhammer. 'We'll be as prompt as we can.' A lot to promise when she had no idea of the situation beyond that a construction worker had apparently fallen from a significant height. She followed tall, sandy-haired Frank, noting that while his navy suit jacket had begun to pill at the cuffs he had finally bought some new pants. He kept the department-issue mustache, of course, trimmed to perfection.

A slab large enough for a small suburban home spread across the ground at the north-east corner

11

of the building. It had a few spines of rebar sticking out of each corner, but no other clues as to its purpose. The body lay almost exactly in its center.

Theresa stepped the six inches down to the slab, checking where she put her feet. Blood had squirted upon impact like water from a burst balloon, and drops were everywhere. Several people had crossed this space before her and mixed the drops into the dust and dirt and some of last fall's brown leaves. The noise and activity behind her faded from her notice.

The dead woman was slim, in her late twenties, dressed in well-fitting jeans, a long-sleeved blue T-shirt and scuffed athletic shoes. All her limbs were still attached but fingers, feet and her right arm were flung at angles which seemed to indicate that the bones were no longer connected to each other. She faced the sky, brown eyes open and staring. A crown of blood radiated outward from her head, and Theresa knew that although the woman didn't look that gruesome at the moment, when they tried to move the body the back of her skull would probably come apart into shattered pieces of bone and shredded brain tissue. That would have killed her instantly, even before the broken ribs cut open her lungs and heart and liver, before the femur and its artery snapped open, leaving all her blood to pool on the perfectly level concrete slab.

Theresa looked up. Nothing above them but the cobalt sky, and slightly to the side, thirty-odd floors with no walls. 'No one saw anything?'

'If they did, they didn't pick up a phone.'

Across East Sixth street stood an office build-ing, which might have been largely empty after regular business hours, and an alley that, oddly enough, bore her name: Theresa Court. To the south sat the historic Cleveland public library which she knew closed at six. In-between the two and catty-corner to the construction site was the Federal Reserve Bank, a beautiful building she still couldn't look at without a shudder. They would work bankers' hours, but might have video cameras ... would almost certainly have video cameras.

Frank followed her line of sight. 'Yeah. We thought of that too. Angela's over there now, cap in hand. She's a lot better with the Feds than I am.'

'Never would have suspected that.'

'Ha ha.'

The Convention Center took up the block to the north, almost certainly empty on a week night. To the east across the grassy lawns and the fountain of the mall towered the Marriott Hotel, but the victim's fall would have been hidden from the view of any guests by the construction site itself.

The woman had died alone, with no one as witness.

TWO

Earlier that morning

Ghost slid her window open, slowly and carefully. She kept the wooden tracks waxed with a piece of paraffin left over from when Nana made jelly, a trick she'd heard on some household hints TV show her grandmother always watched. She eased her slender body over the sill and out on to the roof, damp with dew, then shut the window almost all the way. She wore her backpack even though school wouldn't begin for another five hours – no sense coming back for it. She'd find plenty to do and she knew from past experience that once she woke up there was no point to staying in bed. Nana said that children needed their sleep, but Ghost didn't. Besides, her mother's car had not returned to the driveway and looking for her gave Ghost an excuse to continue the search.

She crept along the shingles, having perfected the most noiseless path among them until she could both leave and enter her own home without making the slightest sound. At the edge she stepped down on to the heaviest branch of the maple tree in the yard, using two other branches as banisters. The leaves made a slight

14

rustle, but between wind, squirrels and rats the trees always rustled. That wouldn't alarm anyone.

From there she dropped down in the yard, quietly opened the gate and trotted down to the sidewalk. A deep breath. Free. She liked her house, loved her mother and grandmother, yet Ghost still felt this euphoric happiness only when standing alone out in the dark air, adored these dead hours of two and three and four sliding into five, when the world was quiet and still and the city glittered like a kingdom in a fairy tale. She could have thrown out her arms and done a quick twirl, but she didn't, having grown too old for little-girl behavior. She turned to the north and set off, as silent as her namesake and nearly as pale.

Most of the houses were unlit, their inhabitants slumbering, but several had the shifting blue glow of a TV set dancing behind drawn curtains. Rusting cars sat in tiny overgrown driveways next to dented garbage cans. Next door the Walker place had two lights on and no less than five people milling about, in, out, sitting on the step and bouncing up to talk to people who stopped their cars before driving on. Near as Ghost had been able to determine, no one ever slept at the Walker house. She kind of liked that about them, that they had learned to appreciate the night like she did. One of the younger boys noticed her walking along the sidewalk and lifted a hand. She waved back and continued on.

Ghost set off a few dogs with her passage but the two outside ones had grown accustomed to her and merely lifted a head or an eyebrow. Nearing the intersection she saw two young women on their porch, smoking and griping about some unnamed enemy. One nursed a baby, the other drank from a can. Between that house and the one next to it there ran a narrow, over-grown passageway to the neighboring street, but Ghost never took it at night. Besides, she wanted to go in the other direction.

From her street she headed straight into downtown. No traffic to worry about; when a car did come by she ducked into an alley or a doorway, sort of a game but with a purpose. Her mother and Nana had told her over and over again to *never* get in a car with someone she didn't know, no matter what they said, so she wanted to avoid the situation if possible. Also, the car might belong to a cop and for some unknowable reason they didn't care for eleven-year-old girls roaming the streets in the dark hours. They had caught her once, shortly before her tenth birthday, and taken her home. Nana and Mom had yelled for hours, she'd gone with-out dessert for weeks, and worst of all some woman from the government had come three times afterwards, looking around the house and asking Ghost weird questions like did Mom and Nana ever make her uncomfortable (no), was she happy (yes) and did she have good friends at school (Ghost wouldn't call them *good* friends, but she'd said yes anyway). It had convinced Ghost that if she wanted to continue these bouts of freedom, she'd have to get a lot better at keeping them to herself. So when Mom or Nana

16

found her bed empty she'd claim to have walked to school, leaving out exactly what time she had left. Neither her mother or grandmother ever woke before their alarms clanged loud enough to prod the neighbors. So the idea of Ghost leaving for school while they overslept remained utterly believable.

She encountered no one save two rats and a stray dog until she passed a bar closing up for the night, its clients now shoved out on to the pavement, blinking and stretching as if they'd been asleep for hours. Ghost paused at the corner of the building and studied each one carefully. None looked familiar. She skirted around the group and walked on.

She passed two more closing bars, paused to look in the window of an all-night diner where the lone cook lifted a hand at her, just as the Walker boy had done. She waved back, made a quick visual survey of the three men slumped about the place, and continued on to the construction site.

The spring air brushed gently at her warming cheeks as she nearly stepped on a homeless man, curled up on a piece of cardboard. Her shoes – a little big for her, Nana believed in growing into things – merely brushed the edge of the flattened box but the man sprang up instantly, growling a warning. Ghost skittered away, though her pounding heart quickly settled down. He had changed his corner. He usually sat at Prospect and Twenty-First.

She was only a block away from her mother's workplace now, but if she were honest about it,

Ghost wasn't concerned about her mother. Her mother had probably stayed with a friend (she often did) and would be home by the next dinner time.

The huge empty frame of the new building sat about two miles from Ghost's front door. Next to the fenced site sat a large open area, with grass and sidewalks and a water-filled fountain with the statue of a man rising out of waves and reaching toward the sky. They called this park a mall but it didn't have any stores. Its lights let her see her mother's car, parked in a rutted, sparse area. Ghost walked toward it, then stopped. Something about the car's dark interior, a visible black pulsing behind the glass, made her hesitate, and she approached the vehicle with a dragging step. No sound, not a flicker of movement. If anyone sat in the car they were utterly still.

She drew up next to the passenger side window and looked in. The slanting light from the park area opposite her passed through the interior, illuminating the emptiness.

Ghost let out a breath she hadn't known she was holding. She had come to the site just for something to do, not because she really expected to find her mother there. Her mother might be there very late, after a date or dinner with a friend, or very early, before the work started, but at this terribly wee hour neither explanation really made sense. Unless Mom had fallen to the same impulses that drove Ghost.

The building, while still only a collection of beams and flooring, dwarfed everything around it. It would span a city block and have forty-one floors when completed, her mother had told her more than once, and even now it thrust upward until it seemed to brush the night-time clouds. Ghost figured you could see the whole city from up there, all the streets and sidewalks and cars and people. Her mother always said that she felt proud to be part of its construction, of smoothing out concrete floors that would stand there until the next century. But Ghost had figured it out. Ghost's mother didn't spend her days walking over beams hundreds of feet off the ground just to do a job. She used that eagle's nest viewpoint to look for Ghost's father.

Ghost left the car and turned back to the site. The double gates were closed but not locked, and her tiny frame slipped through the gap without even snagging her backpack. She'd been there more than once during her night-time excursions.

No sign of her mother, no sounds or voices. Perhaps she had gone home with a friend and left the car here. One time Ghost and her mother had left their car at a cousin's house and drove with them to a birthday party in Pennsylvania, so something like that could have occurred here. In any event there was no way to find her mother in the floors and floors and floors of dark building in front of her, unless her mother made some noise or Ghost shouted. And Ghost felt as strangely reluctant to shout as she had been to approach the car. As if the darkness were a living thing; it ignored her for the moment but could turn violent if disturbed.

Besides, Mom probably wouldn't be too pleased to find Ghost here. Not pleased at all. They'd clamp down on the rules, and worse, maybe think about trimming the maple tree. Better to stay hidden.

Better yet to just leave, but instead she moved further toward the building. *What is she doing here in the middle of the night?*

The site spread out before her, a huge and unusual playground. She took ten steps, jumped up on a wooden spool of pipe or wire, then jumped down again. Perhaps if – then she heard a sound, like a scrape of a shoe against concrete, and automatically leapt into the sheltering shadow of a garbage can. Crouched against the greasy object, she tried to look in all directions at once.

Silence again. The office building across the street sat nearly dark, with no activity in its few lit windows. A car drove by at least one street over. A door slammed somewhere over by the hotel. With the sound bouncing and moving all over, the scraping sound could have come from anywhere. Ghost waited until her insides calmed down and no one emerged, then stood up and rushed into the shadow of the building proper.

For the first time she thought that there might be someone present who was *not* her mother. That worried her for a moment or two, but there were two exits to the site. If a person appeared in one direction she would simply take the other. Anyone who found her might shout, but they wouldn't chase. Ghost was tiny and had been told that from a distance people couldn't be sure

20

if she were a boy or a girl. She wasn't worth chasing – not yet. That would change in another year or two.

She did not hear any more sounds and thought it unlikely that grown-ups could stay quiet that long. Unless they were watching television, adults were always making noise. So Ghost felt free to move into the building proper, a pitch-dark area of large and comfortingly inanimate objects. She walked into a few of them before her eyes adjusted to the dark. The workers kept huge metal boxes to store all their stuff, plus there were cardboard boxes and stacks of pipes and big plastic buckets of things. First she stubbed her toe on one of those, then her other foot knocked into something that slid and clattered. The beams from outside slanted into the area creating varying sections of dark and light but the clattering object rolled five inches into a light one – a screwdriver.

It looked like her mother's, with black and red stripes along the handle, so she decided to take it home to make sure. Her mother took her tools very seriously, and if Ghost borrowed one she had to wipe it off and put it back in the basement exactly where she'd found it. So she knew her mother would be upset if she lost one. And if it wasn't her mother's, she could just bring it back.

Ghost dropped the screwdriver into her backpack, which didn't have much else in it – school was not the place to carry anything of value – besides a piece of pencil, a pen that wrote in splotchy ink, a few papers from her classes yesterday including one page of homework she

21

had been supposed to fill out for math class. She'd watched television instead. Ghost didn't care much for math.

She crossed the entire building to the stairwell, a black hollow that wound up and up and up. Ghost always pooped out around fifteen or so, but some day she would make it to the top floors and be able to see every single street for miles around. She plunged into the hole of nothingness, not afraid of the dark. The shadows had always been her friends.

But then she heard another sound, like a cross between a scrape and a thud, and thought it came from one of the upper floors. Then a voice, just a few words, quiet and not angry.

There must be someone there after all.

THREE

Theresa straightened up, already unzipping her camera case as she asked Frank, 'You have an ID?'

'Samantha Zebrowski. Twenty-nine, unmarried. Licensed for cement work. The first guys on the job found her, about five thirty this morning. They got here about five, entering from the south entrance – gate was open, they assumed the project manager was here – and didn't see her until they started flicking on the halogens.'

Theresa wondered why construction workers

always started so early. Aside from avoiding rush hour traffic, she couldn't see the advantage of trying to function in the dark. 'She worked here?'

'Yeah,' the project manager, Chris Novosek, answered, and Theresa turned toward him.

'What did she do?'

'Cement finisher. She could also work on spreading. She's been here since the project started. Wasn't bad at it.'

She wondered if he had a lot of female construction workers, but couldn't think of a reason to ask. 'So she would be working on the upper floors?'

'Yeah.'

The man was upset, she could see, but not abnormally so. She couldn't blame him. The job and its workers appeared to be his responsibility, and seeing the young person tossed down like an unwanted toy would upset anyone. 'She has some sort of safety equipment she's supposed to use up there?'

'Yeah, of course. They all use a fall harness if they're doing anything within ten feet of an edge. But nothing like that was scheduled for today. She should have been in the center of thirty for the rest of the week.'

'She's not dressed for work anyway, is she?' The woman's pants were a deep indigo, and unfrayed. A woman wouldn't risk getting a good pair of skinny jeans full of concrete.

He shook his head. 'Everybody has to have steel-toed shoes.'

Theresa persisted. This was important. 'Maybe

23

she kept her shoes in her box and changed when she got here.'

Chris Novosek snorted. 'Nah. Nobody does that.' He had blue eyes under the brown hair, something like Theresa's. There were a lot of blue eyes in Cleveland, from all the northern European ancestors who had come to the city during the Industrial Revolution.

'So why ever she was on this property, she wasn't here to work,' Theresa said.

'Therein lies the rub,' Frank said. 'If it wasn't part of her job duties, then it's not covered by OSHA, Worker's Comp, union rules – do not pass Go, do not collect two hundred dollars. On top of that, this is – or will be – a county building. That necessitates the crossing of T's and dotting of I's.'

'That's why you're here,' Theresa said.

'That, and because business is slow. Which is what happens when your population dips seventeen percent in the past ten years. The chief has to justify his guys or we'll get transferred to vice. Or worse, traffic.'

Theresa knelt again, pulling on a glove and touching the woman's stomach. The bones crinkled and shifted, making a sound like a bag of potato chips, but the muscles were beginning to stiffen. The cool night and lying on the cold concrete would cause the rigor mortis to progress more slowly, making it very difficult to determine whether the woman had died before work started that morning or if she had returned to the site during the night, for reasons of her own. Why come there at all? What had she been

24

looking for?

Theresa glanced at her cousin.

'They knocked off at five thirty yesterday,' Frank said, anticipating her thoughts. 'Everyone is fairly sure she left with them, everything normal, no beefs with anyone, no arguments. We're going to have to keep everyone off the upper floors until I can examine them, try to figure out where she went over.'

Chris Novosek made some desultory complaints, but nothing too stringent, and he and Frank went off to make that happen. Theresa could have examined the floors first and then worked on the girl, but decided that removing the poor broken body trumped completion date penalties. Whether there had already been workers on the upper floors became a matter of some debate, with no one admitting to it while not exactly denying, either.

Theresa spent the next hour photographing, measuring, documenting everything about the body and its landing spot. Samantha Zebrowski had two red marks on the left side of her face which could have become bruises had she lived long enough for the blood to pool along its broken vessels. She might have struck the edge of a lower floor on the way down, or they might have come from someone's fists. Her hands showed no signs of defense, however, and no small injuries that might have occurred from clinging to a beam or platform before the final plunge, at least not so far as Theresa could determine, since the right had been soaked in the blood pool. The left had bounced up on to the girl's stomach and remained clean. Cement work was hell on skin, and Samantha's palms and fingers were heavily calloused. Her cell phone had also survived the fall, stored in her front pants pocket, cushioned from the shock of impact by the woman's body, something Theresa would not have believed was possible if she hadn't seen it with her own eyes. But perhaps it was not that surprising; cell phones were designed to withstand a teenager throwing them across the room.

Samantha's beat-up Skechers were thoroughly scuffed, and none of the damage appeared particularly new. The back half of the body had been soaked in the pooling blood but the front half did not show any inconsistent smudges or stains.

Theresa looked up from her work now and then. She could feel eyes upon her, even when she couldn't determine the source of the stares. The dead girl's co-workers ran the gamut in terms of reactions. Some came for a quick peek with appropriately sorrowful expressions, then removed themselves and did not return. Some skirted around the concrete slab until they could get a good look at the gore, turned slightly green, and likewise disappeared. Some stood at the edge of the cement and watched Theresa's every move without the slightest hint of sorrow; in fact, body language made it clear that all they lacked for an entertaining morning was a lawn chair and a cold one.

Two black men, however, didn't fall into any of these categories. Young, buff, with nearly matching bandannas, they stood back and yet watched every move, and spoke only to each other, often with a sharp shake of the head and deep scowls of consternation instead of regret. Theresa absently theorized that they had come from some island community where a death on the job was a bad omen for all and the presence of a dead body an invitation to a curse. But their faces and dress seemed as American as apple pie and TiVo, so she gave up on that. Every person had their own and intensely personal reaction to death, and Theresa did not fool herself that she had yet seen them all.

After copious photographs and the arrival of the body snatchers (technically called the ambulance crew, though their patients were never transported to a hospital), Theresa was finally ready to turn the body on its side.

Rigor mortis had set in, putting the woman's death at some time in the wee hours. The mild temperatures and the additional coolness of the concrete slab would have delayed the process.

The skull came apart with the first movement, leaving pieces on the slab. The small intestine, which lay in surprisingly clean coils next to and slightly under the abdomen, peeked out from under the T-shirt. Theresa photographed as best she could, noting items in the girl's back pockets but leaving them in place. They would have to be carefully removed and dried of the saturating blood and she didn't have time or room to do it there.

She and the two men moved the body and its pieces to a clean sheet as best they could and from there into a body bag. Theresa sealed the bag with evidence tape and a zip-tie, as if some nefarious person might steal into the back of the ambulance en route, open the bag and alter or remove some piece of evidence without alerting the crew. Downright silly, some of the hoops she jumped through in the name of security.

Without the body to command one's attention, she took a fresh look at the bloodstained concrete, circling around to find the outermost reach of the impact pattern. It seemed to exist in a fairly oval shape, radiating out from where the victim's head landed, but Theresa continued to find dark red specks trailing off to the south. Nothing organized enough to be a splash pattern or shoe prints. When she got her face down to the specks via a contorted position that might garner extra points in yoga class, she could swear that the stains weren't stains at all, but flakes. Flakes of dried blood. She collected some with a swab before moving on.

Most of Samantha Zebrowski's blood had dried by then – perhaps a strong wind?

But then she reached the end of the concrete slab and any further flakes were lost in the packed dirt and patchy grass surrounding the building.

And shoe prints began.

Theresa stepped out on to the mud, now hard, though it would have been softened during the damp night. The prints traveled in a vaguely south-south-east direction, fading out and then beginning again, or so she guessed, since the trail led through a minefield of boot prints, shoe prints and tire tracks that ranged from bicycle to Sherman tank-size. More than once a crate or small trailer or piece of machinery presented a fork in the path and she had to guess at one, then go back and choose the other. But as she reached the second dumpster along the eastern fence, she found where they led.

And she couldn't believe it.

Huddled in the gap between the two metal squares, knees drawn up to her chest, sat a little girl. And the girl was covered in blood.

FOUR

Earlier that morning

'Time to go, Ghost had decided. She would have to take in the view another night. If the sounds came from her mother, Ghost didn't want her to know that she had snuck out of the house so early. And if they came from some other person, she didn't want to meet them. Ghost turned from the stairwell and walked, quickly but carefully, back the way she'd come.

She'd gotten to the other end of the foundation when something occurred to her. The gate had been open when she'd arrived. It had always been chained shut before (though she could slip through the opening under the chains). So the people on the site had come in through that gate

29

and would most likely leave through that gate. If she wanted to avoid an encounter, she should take the other exit.

Terrifically pleased with herself over this show of logic, Ghost stepped off the concrete foundation and down the small hill at the side of it. The smaller East Sixth gate remained placidly locked on the other side of a flat concrete slab protruding off the side of the main building, a span of patchy grass, three huge cardboard boxes on wooden pallets, a pyramid of long pipe, and three dumpsters, parked parallel along the side of the fence. Ghost felt pleased with herself for this observation as well. Parallel and perpendicular were the only two concepts in math she *had* managed to grasp, perhaps because they only involved pictures and no numbers.

All of these areas, unfortunately, were well lit by a bright security light on a high pole. If the people on the upper floor looked out, they would see her walk to the gate.

Circling outside the light's reach, Ghost took some tentative steps, hugging close to the other objects on her route. She skirted behind a bulldozer and along a small trailer. Two more cardboard boxes and she finally stood far enough away from the building to be able to see the interiors of some of the lower floors.

She scanned these for movement, listened for sound. Nothing.

Another ten feet brought her to a large truck-like thing with a scoop on the front. She touched it gingerly, as she had the bulldozer, as if they were sleeping animals that might wake up at any

30

moment. If they did she would have much more to fear than being grounded by Mom and Nana.

But the machine sat cold and quiet, and Ghost sprinted five more feet to the side of one of the dumpsters. Almost to the fence, about as far away as she could get from the building without leaving the site.

Way, *way* up high, two dark shapes moved against the dark interior. They hovered at the edge of the building, moving cautiously along the open space. When Ghost squinted the people became fairly clear, lit from behind by the security lights along the mall and from her direction by the security light on the pole. Two people, touching each other, but not in a friendly way. One seemed to be holding the other with one hand, arm out as straight as a pipe. The one being held clutched at the other's wrist and kept buckling at the knees.

At least they seemed too occupied with each other to notice her. Ghost breathed out, but decided not to make a run for the gate until they went away. The shadow of the dumpster would keep her hidden.

One of them said something; Ghost couldn't make out the words but heard the voice, low and almost sweet. The other said something harsh and fast like a scream. Like a woman screams. Like her mother screamed.

But that couldn't be her mother. Her mother had long hair, black and silky down to her waist, and if that were her backing toward the open edge of that high-up floor until she became easier to see with every step, her hair would be

31

swishing over her back. It wasn't, so she wasn't.

Ghost knew she should breathe out in relief about that, but didn't.

She also knew they should be getting away from the edge, but instead both people moved closer until the one being held had backed right up to empty space. Ghost couldn't figure out what they were doing, other than talking – at least, one talked, a slow, steady stream of words. Ghost couldn't make it out and didn't try, just wished they would go away. The East Sixth side entrance was twenty feet away and chained, but she had gotten through it before. But if she ran for it now they would see her. Patience, Mrs Dressler always told her class, is a virtue. Ghost didn't know the definition of virtue but had figured out the saying meant that sometimes it was better to wait for stuff. It somehow made you stronger to wait for stuff. And usually she was good at it.

This was different. Something bad was going to happen and she didn't want to see it.

The one person pushed the other over the edge.

The long hair trailed her body as the earth pull-ed her down to it. Arms and legs waved wildly but the empty air wouldn't hold her up.

Long hair.

Ghost wanted to close her eyes but she didn't, because closing her eyes had never done her any good. Maybe if she watched, something would catch her mother. A trampoline or a swimming pool or a tree full of leaves that she could grab on to – *catchhercatchhercatchher—*

All at once Ghost felt aware of every single

32

thing around her. Her skin tingled with aware-
ness as she watched her mother fall. The wind
was there but not strong enough, it whispered
instead of moaned. Summer bugs, already
hatched, formed a light cloud around the street
light along East Sixth, nowhere near as bright as
the security light whose rays caught and illuminated the gleam of her mother's face. The man
on the building looked down at his handiwork,
the front of him illuminated by the street lights
and the back of him disappearing into the gloom
of the inner building as if he were part of it. A car
horn bleated from a block away, the rest of the
city going on as usual without the slightest
idea—

Ghost's lungs began to ache from not breathing, as if she could possibly think about breathing when her mother—

The woman hit the ground.

The impact seemed to shake the earth all the
way over to Ghost, making the dirt underneath
her quiver as if with electric shock, and the
sound – both a thud and a crunch and the snap of
a bunch of broken bones all at once. All the
sounds were ordinary in their way, but taken
together in one quick cacophony they turned into
something alive and more horrible than anything
Ghost had ever heard.

Time seemed to stop, the bugs stopped buzz-
ing, the distant cars receding to their own reality.

Ghost looked up. No one. She did not see the
other person, could not even be sure what floor
they had been on. No movement broke up the
darkness or gave a flicker of reflected light. It

was almost as if the other person – the one who pushed – had been swallowed up by the deep murk of the building's interior as if he were part of it.

She moved out from beside the dumpster, across the patchy grass, up on to the flat concrete slab and toward the person lying there without hesitation. It would not be her mother. It could not be her mother.

Even though it was her mother's hair, her mother's face, her mother's scuffed shoes and her favorite jeans and the silly friendship bracelet of colored string that Ghost had made for her in art class months and months ago.

This didn't make sense. Her mother worked up on those high floors every day. She wouldn't have fallen. Nobody would have pushed her—

But her eyes were open, so maybe she'd be okay. Ghost knelt down and shook one shoulder. 'Mom,' she said, calmly, in an even tone, the first sound she had made. 'Mom.'

No response. Her mother didn't even blink.

Ghost kept shaking. 'Mom. Mom. Mom. *Mom*—' her voice rising in timbre and level until she was screaming, her throat rasping and the frantic shakes causing the growing puddle of blood to splash and fling itself about—

And then suddenly the monster, the shadow man, appeared next to her. She looked up but the security light blinded her until he seemed to be only a fuzzy black outline of head and arms and legs, artificially elongated until they could surround her, both her and her mother, and pull them into the center of his darkness.

He spoke to her, in a sibilant hiss of incomprehensible sounds. A star flashed at her from inside him and she turned her face away.

She would never remember what happened after that.

FIVE

Theresa stood for a moment startled into utter paralysis. Whatever she had thought she might find, this child was not it.

'Honey.' Theresa dropped to her knees and began to pat the thin arms and shoulders. 'What happened? Are you all right? Are you hurt?' The blood had soaked the girl's pants from the knees down until they were as stiff as thin cardboard. Dried. Obviously the source of the flakes. Heavy smears coated her forearms and hands, marked her cheeks and dark blue polo shirt. None of it wet. Any injuries had since clotted.

Unless this blood wasn't from her at all. Of course it wasn't; the kid would be passing out if she'd lost that much—

The girl gazed up at Theresa and spoke, grim, hopeless, shell-shocked: 'Where are you taking her?'

'Who?'

'Mom. Where are you taking Mom?'

The implications of this struck Theresa completely dumb. How—? Why—?

Worry about that later. What seemed obvious right now: this child had either found her mother's body or witnessed her actual death, was now in shock and required immediate medical attention.

'Where are you taking her?' The child's voice rose a note or two, and at least the effort brought the first tinge of pink to her bloodless cheeks at the same time a tremor ran through her body. *'Where are you taking her?'*

'To my office,' Theresa blurted. 'We're going to take her to where I work. We'll take really good care of her there.'

The girl blinked, and something in her expression changed. She seemed to see Theresa clearly for the first time. 'Your office?'

'Yes. It's where we take care of people who are hurt like your mother's been hurt.'

The girl's eyes narrowed, just a millimeter. 'She's dead, isn't she?'

Theresa's voice caught in her throat. She had never had to do this before. Dealing with families and the loved ones left behind had always been Frank's job, not hers. The worst news she'd ever had to deliver to Rachael involved her cat. But this little girl deserved the truth, quickly and cleanly. 'Yes, she is.'

No response at first, and Theresa used the pause to dial frantically. Then the girl's eyes filled with tears. 'I want to go to your office too. I want to go with her. I want to go with her!'

'You'll see her again, honey, don't worry about that. You will. Right now I – Frank, I'm over by the dumpsters, get over here *right now* – I need to know your name. What is your name?'

The child whispered: 'Ghost.'

It took some gentle prodding but Ghost allowed herself to be shed of her backpack and wrapped in a blanket, then set in the back of Frank's police car. Frank shut the door and took a few steps away before conferring with Theresa. 'I made some calls. Apparently she lives with her mother – Samantha – and Samantha's mother. Victim advocates are understaffed as usual and are tied up with a shooting in Solon. We could call Families and Children if you think she's in shock.'

'I don't know! Children in shock are not my field – or if she's trembling because she's chilled to the bone after being out here since "early", she says. I don't know if that means since long before dawn, maybe back to the wee hours,' Theresa told him, the little bit she'd managed to learn spilling out of her. 'But if Samantha committed suicide she changed her mind about taking her daughter along because Ghost says she was definitely on the ground when she saw her mother fall.'

'She saw it happen?'

'Every agonizing moment, it sounds like. And she is definitely going to need medical attention. Her responses are reasonable but she's still trembling and zoning out.'

'Okay, okay, slow down. We'll get her help, but let's get her home to her grandmother first and get that blood washed off. That's probably the best help we can provide.'

'And she says her mother was pushed.'

'*What*?'

Theresa nodded emphatically. 'Pushed.'

'By who?'

Now Theresa added, without emphasis: 'A shadow.'

'A shadow. Terrific. Well, what's she supposed to think when her mother drags her out of bed to come witness her suicide?'

'I'm not so sure. She says she didn't come here with her mother. She walked.'

'So she gets up in the middle of the night and walks unaccompanied halfway across the downtown area of a major city in, again, the middle of the night, just in time to watch her mother plummet to the earth. Excuse me if I find it much easier to believe that her mom wigged out.'

'Maybe.' Theresa sighed. She returned to the car and opened the rear door, taking the little girl's blood-crusted hands in hers again. 'Ghost, this detective – he's my cousin – is going to take you home to your grandmother, okay?'

'I want to go to your of—'

'I know, but your grandmother is really going to need you right now, so we need you to go there first. Don't worry about your mother, you will have time to say goodbye to her, but right now you need to see your grandmother.'

The girl turned white – again – and her words sounded as if her throat had closed up. 'She – Nana – *I don't know how to tell her*!'

Theresa squeezed the tiny hands, imagining the horrors the child must now be enduring at the thought. 'Honey, you don't have to do that. We'll tell her. You don't have to. That's grown-up stuff.'

A gasping breath, only partly of relief. 'Will you come with me?'

This stumped Theresa. She should stay with the crime scene; talking to relatives was not her job, handling bereaved children was not her job, keeping a construction project locked down while she comforted the next of kin was not her job. But she couldn't send this tiny, bloodied child off locked behind a metal grate while contemplating how best to break the news to her second mother – 'Yes. Yes, of course I will.'

In those wee hours of the morning, when he descended from his aerie and the machinery for the zip lift cut off, he had heard the wailing. He hadn't intended to take a ground-floor look at his handiwork – the view from above having been too sharp and clean to diffuse – but followed the sound across to the east side of the darkened building. Not that it worried him. Nothing could worry him at that moment. The night flowed over his body, infusing each pore, the front of his pants wet from that glorious moment when he'd let go of Samantha, when his fingers unclenched from the mass of her hair and she floated backward into space, one last tendril licking at his hand in a final supplication. In vain, of course. He had no intention of letting her live, of letting her escape the void he had reserved for her.

The act had been incredible.

It had been even better than he had imagined,

and he couldn't wait to do it again.

So when he saw the child weeping, pale, delicate, bathed in the whitest light, it seemed completely appropriate. An angel had descended to grieve for poor broken Samantha, for the sultry body and the doomed, bitch's soul, its keening a song from another dimension. Or perhaps it represented Samantha herself, the good, innocent, childlike part of her now separated from the weak flesh and formed into a pure but small being on the brink of escape to heaven. The two of them made such an exquisite picture that he watched in fascination for a moment before moving closer. He had to see this angel for himself. Or demon. A demon would also be small and might weep for a bitch.

He got up close, reached out to touch her, even more enraptured by the child/angel/demon than by Samantha's broken corpse, but the thing gave a shriek straight out of hell and disappeared into the night. It moved like a rabbit, so fast you couldn't comprehend it. Nothing human moved that fast.

With one last look at Samantha, he turned and walked towards home.

It wasn't until much later that he began to wonder what had happened to the screwdriver, and whether or not the angel might have been more than a euphoria-induced hallucination.

SIX

Frank's partner, Angela Sanchez, returned in time to join them, without – as she quietly discussed with Frank as they drove – much to show for herself. The Federal Reserve had had the only surveillance cameras in the area; not surprisingly, they were angled to protect the Fed and gave her a terrific view of the sidewalk and the streets outside the eighty-nine-year-old building and nothing else.

'No ATMs?'

'Not a one. Go out one block and we're ringed by them. But on those four pieces of street, nothing.'

Frank turned on East Thirty-First. They were only a mile and a half from the construction site. Ghost hadn't said another word during the trip, only stared at the back of the seat in front of her. But Frank noticed that she did not let go of Theresa's hand.

The next half-hour proceeded every bit as painfully as Frank would have expected. Ghost's Nana, Betty Zebrowski, sobbed and clutched the child for several minutes until the girl's wails subsided, then sent her upstairs to shower and change clothes. 'Immediately,' she said and the order seemed to calm the girl, assure her that

41

adults were once more in charge. Theresa went upstairs with her, leaving the two detectives to obtain some badly needed background.

'Her name's really Anna,' the woman began. 'When she was little she used to like to sneak up on us, and she was pretty good at it. Scared the life out of me once or twice while still in kindergarten. You couldn't believe such a small child could be that quiet. Sam said she walked like a ghost and we let the name stick. Shouldn't have done that, I suppose. It's no sort of name for a girl.'

Betty Zebrowski was fifty-four, widowed, and wheelchair-bound. She remained on the ground floor of the elderly bungalow that matched its unassuming neighbors on the outside but had been well-maintained on the inside. The dining room had been turned into her bedroom and a half-bath turned into a full one. 'Sam did that for me, even the plumbing,' she added, one of many statements that brought choked-back tears and a hand to her mouth.

Frank and Angela perched uncomfortably on a worn blue couch, their knees almost touching a low coffee table scattered with issues of *Cosmo* and Walter Drake catalogs. The house appeared comfortable and relatively tidy. No doubt any moment Mrs Zebrowski would offer to brew some coffee for them, but Frank had learned long ago to keep the questions coming. It staved off the hysterics of grief, sometimes. In quick succession they learned that Samantha had come home as usual after work the evening before, had had dinner with her mother and daughter,

42

then gone back out. She had not mentioned a specific date, just 'out'. She had her favorite bars and bistros and would often run into friends there. Nor was her mother much concerned when she woke up to a silent house. Sam would occasionally stay out overnight 'with friends', as she explained with a curl to her lip that showed she knew exactly the gender of said friends. She was not so sanguine about Ghost having already left as well, but: '—she does that. She's supposed to take the school bus, it stops right at the corner, but she sneaks out of her room to walk to school. I don't know why she does it, Lord knows her mother and I have flat-out yelled at her often enough. She's not supposed to even be in the yard unless one of us is watching. This neighborhood isn't what it used to be.'

Frank nodded, having noticed the activity at the house next door, and the baseball bat propped behind the front door. Mrs Zebrowski looked liked she could have played a mean game of softball in her day.

'But she's like her mother, I guess,' the woman went on. 'There's only so much you can do.'

'She had this backpack with her.' Angela held it up.

'That's for school.'

'Just some homework papers, a pen and a screwdriver.' The detective held up the tool.

'That would be Sam's. Her initials scratched into the handle – yes. Ghost imitated Sam all the time with the tools and the fixing stuff. I had hoped that would be all she'd imitate.'

'You conflicted with Sam a little bit over her –

43

lifestyle?'

The woman gave a rueful smile, adjusting her chair's position with a flick of the wrist, the way a person might recross their legs. 'My daughter lives – lived – a little more carefree than girls in my day. I always thought, especially after her father died so young, that she was looking for something she never found. But I don't want to give you the wrong impression – she was a wonderful mother. She always took good care of Ghost. She took good care of me.' Again, the voice cracked on the last word.

'Do you have any other children?' Angela asked. 'Is there anyone you'd like us to contact?'

'My son, but I'll call him. He moved out to New Mexico years ago and never came back.'

'How long have you lived here?'

'Since I married. The neighborhood wasn't much then and it's not much now – there's good people here, but there's bad ones too. After my husband died so young I couldn't afford to move. Neither could Sam. Her work was too sporadic and, well, she wasn't much of a saver.'

'She's always lived here with you?'

'Yes.'

'She never married?'

'No.' A frowning regret passed over her face. 'She was only eighteen when she had Ghost. Told me the father shipped off to the Army before she knew she was pregnant and then got killed in a training exercise. That's all I could ever get out of her on that score.'

'Did she have a boyfriend?'

'Nothing steady, not at the moment. Her last

44

serious boyfriend, I think that was almost two years ago now. He moved out of state. How did she fall off that building?' the woman suddenly asked, an unexpected sob escaping her. 'She loved that building.'

'Did she often go there on her own, not during working hours?' Angela asked.

Betty Zebrowski considered this. 'I think so. She's mentioned it once or twice, walking by it at night when she's out with friends. She loved her job. It sounded awful to me, like hard labor and then so high up sometimes, but she just loved it.'

Angela got to the heart of it. 'Did she seem upset about anything lately? In her work life, her personal life?'

'No. Not at all.' The woman wiped her nose, then looked up sharply. 'Why?'

'We're just trying to figure out why she was there. And how Ghost – Anna – wound up there as well. You say they didn't leave the house together.'

She wasn't about to be deflected. 'Sam was happy. Sam was *perfectly* happy. We may not be living in clover but we have what we need. She was young and healthy and loved her daughter.' She stopped short of saying *she would not have killed herself*, and Frank couldn't blame her.

But Betty Zebrowski had been an honest woman all her life and wasn't about to qualify that now. 'But I have no idea why she would have gone there, and even less how Ghost would.'

* * *

45

Theresa browsed Samantha Zebrowski's accoutrements as she listened to the water run in the hallway bathroom and wondered what on earth to say to a child who had lived through such trauma. What could possibly help when years of therapy might only blunt the worst of it? She had helped Ghost choose fresh and comfortable clothes and made a quick check that the bathroom had all the necessary supplies before reminding the girl to wash her hair as well. Theresa hated to leave her out of her sight but knew that had she been eleven she would have rather died than undressed in front of a stranger, even a female one. So she took the opportunity to do her job, as in getting a clearer picture of the victim's mental state.

Samantha's bedroom seemed only slightly arrested in time, with denim pants and shiny tops draped over the bedposts and chair, a bright comforter tossed across the mattress and a collection of purses hanging from the back of the door. Theresa scanned the surface, opened a drawer or two before realizing that, unless Frank had specifically asked Mrs Zebrowski for permission to look around, this would probably be an illegal search. Though she wasn't searching for drugs or alcohol or a despair-filled journal in order to charge anyone with a crime, but simply to get a better idea of why Samantha Zebrowski would have thrown herself off a building. Or why she had gotten drunk enough to fall off the building. Because despite what Ghost had said, Frank must be right. Samantha had taken her daughter out in the middle of the night, either to witness her suicide or include her in it, or for some reason that would not make sense to anyone other than Samantha Zebrowski.

But she didn't open any other drawers. Enough remained on the surface to keep her busy: jewelry, make-up, postcards from girlfriends on vacation, a parking ticket, an overdue notice from the library and a receipt from Netflix, a short stack of Ghost's homework papers with distressingly low grades, a recipe for dill dip, a flyer from something called PETI which had been used as a receptacle for a discarded piece of chewing gum. Nothing that screamed 'disturbed mental state'. Frankly, it seemed an older version of her daughter's bedroom – cluttered with the clothes and the shoes and the old magazines and the costume jewelry of a struggling but utterly normal family.

Theresa checked again on the bathroom – water still running, a soft clunk like a bar of soap hitting the floor. She resumed her survey.

The mirrored vanity table had only a few new item categories. An overflowing ashtray, two crystal bowls with beads and key chains, and a news clipping about the groundbreaking ceremony for the new jail. It mentioned a 'searing controversy over this use of public funds'. There were four photos of Ghost ranging from infancy to what must have been a year or two prior, snapshots taken both indoor and out. Theresa recognized the living room in one, Cedar Point in another. A fifth photo showed Samantha with two other women about the same age, and a sixth obviously dated back to the victim's school years. Sam could only have been about fifteen or sixteen, her date about the same. The framing suggested a school dance.

'That's my father,' Ghost said from the doorway.

Theresa jumped, feeling guilty that the absence of shower sounds had not alerted her. 'Oh. Where is he now?'

'Nana says he's dead. He joined the army and got blowed up in an accident there, but he was brave and good and the angels are taking care of him now.' She said this as if by rote, arms wrapped around her midsection, wet tendrils clinging to her cheeks. 'Mom said he was dead too, most of the time.'

'Most of the time?'

The girl perched against her mother's bed, her face dazed and empty. 'This one time I was up really late 'cause it was summer and I didn't have to go to bed for school, and she came back from going out with friends and laid on the couch where I was watching TV 'cause she said she was really tired. I asked her what happened to my father – I guess I just wanted to hear the story again. But she said, "I lost him." So I asked where she lost him and she said, "Downtown."' Ghost ended there and waited for Theresa's reaction.

Which she had a hard time producing. 'Lost him?'

'Yeah. So I don't think the soldier that got blowed up was really my father, or if he was, he didn't get blowed up. I asked her about it the next day, but she wouldn't answer me. And Nana gets all funny when I ask about it too.'

Theresa finally settled on a response. 'What do you think that means?'

Ghost shook her head, solemnly. 'I don't know.'

'Ghost, do you have any idea why your mother went to that building this morning?' Or why she took you along, Theresa thought but didn't ask.

'No. I don't know why he pushed her, either.'

'The shadow?'

'Not a shadow,' Ghost corrected. 'The shadow *man*.'

SEVEN

They left Ghost damply wrapped in the arms of her grandmother. Angela would stay behind to await the child protection team while Frank and Theresa returned to finish processing the scene. But before Theresa could escape, Ghost grasped her wrist and said, 'I want to come to your office.'

'That's not necessary. You can trust me to take good care of your mother.'

'I want to go there.'

'You need to stay here with your grandmother right now. Besides, by the time you get there your mother will probably have already moved on to the funeral home, where you and your family members and friends will have a ceremony to

49

say goodbye. So you don't need to worry about coming to my office.'

The child let her finish before saying, 'That's not acceptable,' in a tone so clipped it seemed chilling and comic at the same time.

'I'm so sorry, Ghost. I know this is really really hard for you.'

'Don't argue with the lady, Ghost,' her grandmother told her. 'We'll talk about it later.'

The girl obeyed this apparently familiar refrain, but not before shooting Theresa a steely glance to let her know the matter had not been settled.

Now she and Frank compared notes.

He turned on to Rockwell. 'She says the shadow was a man?'

'That's what she said.'

'But no details? Height, weight, hair color?'

'Too dark.'

'Terrific. I'm assuming you have a reason to believe he isn't just the product of a traumatized child trying to rationalize why her mother would commit suicide right in front of her.'

'That's still possible, I suppose. I'm no child psychologist. But she didn't waver from her story: that she saw the man struggle with her mother and then push her over the edge. After she ran to her mother's body, suddenly he was there. She looked up but only saw a dark outline – black cloth points, she said. It sounded like he wore a hoodie. I'm thinking that the security light at the north-east corner of the slab blinded her, so his face and chest were lost in the darkness. That would make sense. So yes, she's sobbing and terrified half out of her mind, but she gave plenty of details, which indicates a true memory and not a fabrication. Unfortunately they're not helpful details. Plus she looked up and to her left most of the time.'

'Accessing visual memory.'

'Yes. But not auditory. Apparently he didn't say anything to her.'

'But even if she truly believes she saw a man, that doesn't necessarily mean she did.'

'True.'

'And then this guy just leaves her there. His only witness?'

Theresa shrugged.

'Terrific.' He pulled into the lot, easing around the milling construction workers. 'She say what floor Sam was on?'

'Just "way up high".'

He peered through the windshield at the structure. 'To an eleven year old, that could be anything above three. We've got our work cut out for us. You really think this isn't the suicide of a drunk, melancholy party girl? That a shadow man pushed her?'

'At this point,' Theresa said as she swung herself out of the front seat, 'it makes as much sense as anything else.'

They found Chris Novosek, who still looked slightly green. 'She's eleven?' he asked them without preamble. 'That kid's eleven? I knew Sam had a daughter, but I would have thought a younger one ... Can we open back up? We have a lot to do and I can't keep them all busy down here.'

'Sorry,' Frank said absently, then gestured at the ten-foot fence topped with barbed wire. 'It was cloudy last night, but you have lights. And they found the place open this morning? Any sign of forced entry?' Keep the questions coming.

Novosek shook his head. 'Usually I get here first and open the gate. Only two keys – me and the construction superintendent, who's in Aruba for two weeks. I ran late today because my wife didn't slide the pot into the coffee-maker all the way so I woke up to dark roasted all over my kitchen floor.'

'Then how'd Sam get the gate open?'

The guy looked at them and Theresa would swear he told the complete truth when he said: 'I have no idea.'

'You don't have a hide-a-key somewhere?' she asked.

'Lockbox. No one has the combination except me. And the guy in Aruba.'

'There any security here? A guard? Cameras?'

Novosek snorted again. 'No and no. Gang boxes have been broken in to at least twice, guys had their tools stolen. Vehicles have been vandalized by kids who want to take a backhoe for a joyride. I've scheduled a copper pipe shipment so we can put it in the same day it arrives because if we don't it will disappear overnight. The project is government-funded. We're lucky we have the fence.'

Theresa asked him, 'Can you think of any reason she would come back here on her own time?'

'No.'

'She might have come back for something she forgot to take home? Maybe wanted to show the site to a friend?'

'How would I know that?' he asked, but reasonably.

'Does it ever happen?'

Chris Novosek began to fidget, shifting around like he wanted a cigarette. 'Look, Sam was all right. Yeah, there's only three women on this job, but she wasn't some sort of raging, um...'

'Feminist?' Theresa supplied.

'Yeah. She worked hard and was a perfectionist about her edges, which most guys aren't. She was fun and joked around. Did she like being surrounded by guys all day? Yeah, probably. Why not? She's young and – she *was* young,' he corrected himself, visibly swallowing, and tilted his head to see past Theresa as if to make sure the corpse was still out of earshot, 'and goodlooking, and got plenty of attention here and liked it. Just flirting, though – most of these guys are married and the rest are nothing but talk. If she hooked up with anyone I would have heard about it, and I didn't. If my crane operator got a bunion I'd hear about it. These guys can't work without talking at the same time.'

'So you don't know of any red flags in her life or work?' Frank asked.

'Not a one.'

Theresa was trying to read between his lines. 'But she might consider this a romantic place to take a boyfriend?'

'Or meet one?' Frank added. 'Show off her

53

work, give them a ride in the hoist?'

Again that glimpse toward the dead woman. *She might*, he was clearly thinking and trying not to admit. 'I don't know. I've never heard of her doing that, or anyone else. They spend eight hours a day here. The last thing they want to do in their spare time is come back.' Again, that hesitation, as if he were thinking: *But they might*. A construction site aroused the senses. So much raw power and noise, not to mention the outsize ego that made humans alter their surroundings and form a tower that reached into the sky in clear defiance of the law of gravity.

'How was she on the job?' Frank asked. 'Did she follow all the regs? Did she get careless, ever?'

'They all do,' Novosek admitted with a rueful shake of the head. 'Fool around, think safety equipment is for geeks. That's the hardest part of this job, truth be told. Looking out for safety slows me down more than anything, but I'm pretty strict about it. But if they make it past thirty they get smart and start looking out for themselves a little more.'

'Anything change in her personal life recently? Is it possible she didn't fall, but jumped?'

A new wave of horror rolled through Novosek's face. 'No! I mean – why would she? She was young, had a good job. No way.'

If he'd been a callous man he would have went with the idea. The construction company could not be held liable for a suicide. But he insisted that, like Samantha's on-the-job romantic life, if something had gone terribly wrong for her he would have heard about it.

'You had a more personal relationship with her?' Frank asked, his face a study in innocence.

Novosek didn't take offense at the implication. 'I don't have a personal relationship with any of them. I can't – I'm the boss. I have to lay guys off when work is slow. I have to give them stuff to do when they're just standing around because you have to keep everyone busy or they'll slack off even when they don't have a reason. I have to fire people. It's tough to do that when you consider them a real friend. No, Sam just wasn't real good at hiding her feelings. She was a talker. There's time to kill while the stuff is mixing, and she'd talk. And the way she looked, guys would listen.'

'And yet she wasn't dating any of them.'

'I think she went out with Jimmy Malone once or twice. That would have been three or four months ago, now.'

'They broke up?'

'His wife found out, made him quit. He signed on with a job in Independence.'

'Oh,' Frank said.

Theresa said, 'We're going to have to look at the floors. To figure out which one she was on when she fell.'

Novosek nodded. 'What floor do you want to go to?'

'The one she fell from.'

'How do you know which one that is?'

'I don't. So let's start at the fifth and go up from there.'

'Terrific,' Frank muttered.

'We have a zip lift,' Chris Novosek told them. 'A construction elevator. It doesn't have any walls, though, just a platform.'

Frank turned a bit green himself. 'A little exercise will not kill us.'

'But why take the chance?' Novosek said, and led them across the ground floor to a two-by-four enclosed structure that functioned as a huge dumb-waiter. No walls, only hip-high cable railings and a control box dangling from a post, held by a grinning man in a hard hat and a Marlboro belt buckle. Evidently Novosek felt he got enough exercise during the day.

Theresa stepped in after him. Frank did not move, but looked at them, at the platform, at them again.

'No way,' he said, 'in hell.'

Novosek hit a button on the control box, and the platform began to rise. Theresa shifted her crime scene kit to the hand holding the camera bag as the sight of her cousin's upturned face was cut off by the second floor. With nothing else to hang on to, she wrapped her fingers around Chris Novosek's arm. This made both him and the other man smile but she had long since passed the point in life of caring to look tough, or cool, or unflappable. Theresa could walk up to a badly decomposed corpse without batting an eye, and everyone knew it. That was as tough as she needed to be. So on an open platform about to move fifty feet into the air, she had the good sense to hold on tight to Chris Novosek's rock-like biceps.

On the fifth floor she immediately went toward

the eastern edge of the building. She had expected a vacant space, but found a surprising amount of stuff present and had to skirt around stacks of impossibly long pipes and shiny metal braces, five-gallon buckets of joint compound, cardboard boxes three feet square with pipe ends and fittings, and one sturdy table made of two-by-fours with a slanted top which held a set of dog-eared blueprints. Here and there were rusting metal boxes the size of a refrigerator turned on its side, with spray-painted labels like 'Coastal Duct Pro' and 'Amer Pipe'. One had been opened to reveal a confusing jumble of tools and power cords. It seemed that the building and every single item in it was heavy, rough and covered with grime. Obtaining fingerprints would be well nigh impossible.

She took this in, trying to detect a recent disturbance in an area that appeared to be nothing *but* disturbance and movement and activity, a controlled chaos.

The open edges of the building were framed with a railing of two-by-fours; the crude structure didn't seem to be able to hold in a kitten but no doubt was as solid as everything else around her. Nevertheless, she approached gingerly, scouting every inch of the floor even while at the same time she kept an eye on the great open space before her, drawing ever closer. But the dirt and dust and bits of paper and scattered materials did not reveal any fresh scars, no signs that the victim had been there, struggling with someone else or even only herself.

Neither did the sixth floor, the seventh, or the

eighth. They gave up on the lift and took the steps to each new level. Frank caught up with them there, a bit red-faced but refusing to pant.

'You need to lay off the cigarettes, cuz,' she told him.

'You need to—' he began, but a coughing fit overtook the rest of the sentence.

They continued upward. The amount of items present thinned with each subsequent floor. After seven no ductwork had been laid out, and after eleven, no buckets of joint compound. By seventeen even the pipes were dwindling and the edges of the building were left open, without even a railing of two-by-fours. Theresa asked about that.

'That's why there's no work being done up here yet,' Novosek told her. 'The floor is poured and left to cure. When it's solid enough then the railing will be put up and work can begin. Until then we can deliver materials to the center and guys are not to get within ten feet of the edge. OSHA rules.'

So Samantha would have been working on the very top floors – the more likely place for her to go, as long as they weren't still wet. But Theresa continued her methodical check of every floor. Better to start from the beginning than have to go back.

By nineteen the wind had begun to pick up, pushing and prodding at her body as if gauging its ability to send her over the edge, an invisible cat making desultory swipes at a mouse. Theresa asked Novosek what working construction was like, in a city where the temperatures could, and

58

did, range from ninety-eight in the summer to twenty below in winter.

'Rough,' he told her as she combed over another empty level. 'The weather does suck. It's more or less a young man's game. By fifty guys are just beat. But I think it's one of the few occupations where someone who doesn't particularly like school – like me – can still make a good buck and advance reasonably. I started out in high school laying pipe.'

'Your guys here are good?'

He waited for her by the stairwell before they continued up, considering this question. His body seemed to hum with strength but his face showed uncertainty. 'They aren't angels. Construction workers have a reputation, and for the most part they live up to it. You can get a lot of sketchy kind of guys, but in this economy it's an employers' market. I could get the best because they're available. This is probably the most clean-cut crew I've ever had, and the most experienced. Guys with no experience are the most nerve-racking to work with, because it's easy to get hurt here if you don't know what you're doing.'

'And Sam did.'

'She knew. Whether she did it or not is another matter. Like I said, the young ones...'

They took another flight of steps.

By twenty-one, Novosek asked what she was looking for.

'Signs,' she said.

On twenty-three, she found them.

EIGHT

Workers had delivered an open box of metal fittings and the long but thin steel beams that made up interior walls all over the building, but the rest of the floor remained bare. The sun, now fairly high, slanted into the building and caught each mote in the floor's layer of concrete dust weighed down by lake effect moisture. Swipes and smudges appeared, shapes that could be footprints or could mark the sloppy landings of large birds. Theresa caught them on camera, then proceeded, the two men behind her.

The marks in the dust were not suspicious in themselves, of course, since workers had no doubt inspected the concrete floor and delivered the few materials present, but the way they made a meandering path to the eastern edge raised the hairs on the back of Theresa's neck. The dark spots she found on an interior pillar, even more so.

'What's that?' Novosek asked.

'Looks like blood,' Frank panted.

Theresa photographed. There were three small dots on the two-foot square concrete post, and another one at its base.

Novosek snorted. 'That? It looks like dirt. How can you tell?'

'I see a lot of it,' Theresa understated, and followed the trail. She found another dark stain, about the size of a pea with a tapering tail, five feet away. They could belong to a construction worker with a paper cut, but she kept thinking of the bruises on Samantha Zebrowski's face, which might or might not have come from an intermediate collision on her long trip down.

The man who had operated the lift – somewhere between floors fifteen and twenty she had learned his name was Jack – found this much more fascinating than his boss did. 'You want blood, there's some on thirty where I jammed my spud wrench into my side the other day. Put a good gash in it – want to see?' He patted his left hip, from which hung the nasty-looking tool. A normal monkey wrench at one end, tapering to an unnervingly sharp point at the other.

But since Samantha Zebrowski hadn't been stabbed, Theresa politely declined the invitation to view his flesh and continued photographing.

'Hey,' Frank said, loudly. 'Ten feet, remember?'

'I'm civil service,' she pointed out. 'OSHA doesn't care. Stay there. I don't want any stray shoe-prints.'

'There's going to be stray shoe-prints all over this place,' Novosek pointed out. He had picked up a plastic bottle before their trek and now swigged something that looked like Gatorade.

Theresa wished she had some, and she didn't even like Gatorade. 'Then there's no sense in adding more.'

But nothing else sprang into sight. No blood-stains, no stains of any kind. Disturbances in the dust that could have been workers coming to see how well the concrete had hardened. Over the side, the eastern edge of Samantha Zebrowski's landing zone came into view.

Chris Novosek offered to set up a safety harness for her. Frank observed the ten-feet rule, OSHA relevance or irrelevance, but bounced on his feet in agitation.

Theresa didn't have a daredevil bone in her body. She didn't approach the unrestrained edge of a two-hundred-odd-feet-high platform because she liked to flaunt conventional safety rules, but because she needed to see. Without a railing she sought out the exterior pillar, a solid rock of security. But just as she put her hand up to serve as a brace, she saw another dark smudge on its poured cement surface.

She photographed it, then pulled on a fresh latex glove, leaned that hand against the pillar, and looked down.

From twenty-three floors up the city became an abstraction, an artist's canvas of structure and color, each buff hue leading into the next in a patchwork of life and achievement. Up here the struggle, the inhumanity of each to the other became abstractions as well and Theresa thought only of the vibrant pulse of the wind as it skimmed over her skin and its promise of utter freedom, terrifying and thrilling in equal measures. It made the brain dizzy, both physically and emotionally. Was that why Samantha Zebrowski had fallen?

Theresa felt her own knees sway. She straightened up and took a half-step back.

The only buildings high enough for their occupants to have a glimpse of Samantha's plunge were the PNC Bank and Erieview Tower, both directly east, both office buildings and unlikely to be occupied at night.

Samantha Zebrowski's final resting place lay directly below, the dark and drying blood marking the spot. A wall would eventually encircle this slab, currently represented by sticks of rebar. The woman would have been impaled had she not landed in the center.

Theresa retreated, to her cousin's audible sigh of relief, but only to take more photographs. Then she approached the edge on all fours, which felt much more secure even if it looked ridiculous. But she got a good look at the floor, collecting a few fibers and a piece of plastic, and dizzying shots to illustrate the distance between where the female construction worker began and where she stopped.

The concrete pillar closest to where the woman went over sat to Theresa's right, and she stood to examine it more closely. The rising sun made this difficult, slanting directly into her eyes and turning the inner surface of the pillar to a deep shadow and the outer surface, when she leaned out to take a look, to a blinding mirror. She let her eyes adjust, while her cousin made loud and dire predictions for the next few moments of her life.

Three dark red smears marred the pristine cement surface. They could have come from Samantha's right hand, any smears on those fingers now lost during its soaking in the pool of blood. Because the victim injured herself first in an inebriated fall, then tried to scoot to the outside of the pillar before throwing herself to the ground? Because she changed her mind just as she took that last step into space? Because she hadn't meant to take that last step, maybe was trying to climb around the pillar in a Spiderman imitation, to win an ill-conceived bet with herself? Because someone was trying to throw her off the building, and she was trying not to go?

'Would you stop dangling over the city?' Frank said, his voice dangerously tight.

'Ma'am, please step away from the edge,' Chris Novosek said with even more authority.

Theresa removed herself to safer ground. 'Yes. Sorry. No, don't come any closer! I want to take another stab at looking for shoe prints. And there's some blood smears on this pillar I'll have to collect.'

She retraced half her steps, then turned back and crouched. This time the rising sun worked for her, outlining every disturbance on the smooth concrete surface. Theresa sketched, marked, approached, tried to photograph as best she could.

'What do you think?' Frank finally asked. 'Murder, accident or suicide?'

'I think it's still a wide-open field. We'll have a lot more answers when we get her tox screen back, find out if she was staggering drunk or as sober as a church lady. But I've got two shoe-prints here without much detail but too much length to belong to Ms. Zebrowski. Which means someone was up here with her.'

'How can you be sure of that?' Novosek demanded.

'I'm not trying to make your life difficult. It could be suicide, or accident, and whoever was here with her is afraid to come forward because they're traumatized or because they think they can be held liable. But between Sam bleeding before she went over the edge and Ghost's insistence that someone pushed her mother, we're going to have to proceed with choice number three. Murder.'

NINE

Ian Bauer didn't hang on to the construction worker as the zip lift ascended, because he was a man and couldn't do that sort of thing, so he let his knees soften and rock with the movement and assured himself that even if he fell flat on his back he still wouldn't go over the edge, as long as he stayed in the center and got nowhere near that thin railing that looked as if it wouldn't hold in a slender six year old. And there was another reason he didn't grab the man's arm. Most people shied away from being touched by a guy who looked like Ian.

He was homely. After forty-seven years this had become the easiest way to describe himself

65

to himself. He wasn't hideously deformed or scarred or discolored, he was simply too tall, too thin, his hair too sparse (and getting sparser, to his dismay) and his eyes sunk too far back into his skull, his skin too pale (and not in a good way, more gray than porcelain), his fingers too long and his lips too wide. He looked like exactly what people expected to find in the dictionary when looking up the word 'pedophile', which seemed doubly ironic to him since he had prosecuted six pedophiles in the course of his career, and they had all resembled soccer dads.

He had done the best he could to deal with this handicap; he kept himself clean, dressed professionally and neatly, was uniformly polite to everyone he met and pretended not to notice the shock in their eyes at their first meeting, or second, or third. At the fourth it began to level out and they got used to him, sometimes enough to shake his hand without flinching. He had a job he enjoyed, a suitable little city loft within walking distance of it, and a few real friends to share the occasional beer or wine. Not bad at all. He was, of course, single. Single and searching.

He tended not to think on his situation much these days, which was why he had plenty of notice left over for how many feet of empty space were accumulating between him and the ground.

'Where are they?' he asked the guy, shouting over the light wind and the whine of the lift machinery.

'Twenty-three.' The worker grinned. A manly

man, with steel-toed boots and a flannel shirt over a stained tee. He had shaggy hair and a dissolute bonhomie that meant, had he been born thirty years earlier, he would have been a hippie. Except for being tall and wiry, the utter opposite of Ian. Making some guy in a suit and tie nervous was probably the most enjoyable thing he'd done all week. Ian didn't begrudge him. Life was hard; you had to get your fun where you could.

The platform slowed to a merciful stop and the worker waved a gracious hand at the nice solid concrete floor. Two men and a woman were present. He recognized the detective, at least. The woman wore a windbreaker with 'Medical Examiner's Office' on the back.

'Patrick,' he said, and approached.

Frank Patrick nodded. 'Don't know yet if it's accident or murder. Or suicide. What are you doing here?'

A good question. Because it was a spring day and he was dying to get away from the pile of briefs for a drive-by shooting didn't seem sufficient. 'I happened to be in the room when the boss got the call. County building, dead woman. He thought I might as well walk the block and a half and take a look.'

The detective shrugged and introduced him to the project manager, whose expression said he had already pegged Bauer for a pedophile, hands down.

'Her car's down there,' said a voice behind them. The worker who had run Bauer up in the lift had not left. 'Sam's car, that piece of shit

67

Camry she drives. It's parked on the grass, just like normal.'

'You go in it?' Frank Patrick asked in a tone that left no doubt as to what the man's answer had better be.

'Hell, no. Just sayin'. You can see it from here.' He jerked a thumb toward the western side of the building, as if he'd be happy to point it out from above.

The detective didn't move.

Bauer watched the woman for a few minutes while Frank Patrick filled him in on what they had learned so far, which didn't seem to be too much, from the victim's extreme injuries to the pathetic image of the child carrying around her mother's tool. She had set up a tripod over what appeared to be a nondescript patch of concrete floor, collecting copious photographs and not, apparently, happy with any of them. When the detective had finished, he moved closer.

'Stop!' the woman said, and held up a hand for emphasis but without even looking up from her viewfinder. He obeyed, and after another few moments she either finished or gave up.

'OK.' She stood and rubbed the back of her neck. 'You guys can come on now. I think I've gotten everything there is to get.'

He went past her, up to the edge, tucking his body behind the pillar in order to feel secure enough to look down. The height was dizzying, but he could just glimpse the dark-red patch on the concrete below. If it was suicide, the woman had really wanted to ensure the outcome. No crippling, no spending eternity on life support.

Just bam, DRT. Dead Right There.

'So she wasn't dressed for work and for some reason had her kid along,' Bauer began, thinking out loud. 'She didn't stay late or come in early. And even if she was working she would have no reason to be on this floor, is that right?'

Novosek nodded. 'All the finishers are done on this floor. They're up on twenty-eight now.'

'Any security? Cameras?'

'No and no. Not until we're enclosed.'

'What about the elevator?' Bauer asked. 'Will it eventually go back down by itself?'

Novosek opened his mouth but the construction worker answered. 'No. And someone's got to have a hand on the control box the whole time. So she either walked up, or someone took it back down afterward. If the first guy here this morning had to walk up twenty-three floors to get it, sure as – well, we would have heard about it.'

'Better get it back down now, Jack,' Novosek told him, quiet but firm. They all waited until the disappointed-looking construction worker left. All but the forensic woman, who pulled out swabs and a plastic vial and collected the blood-stains. She dropped the swabs into a paper box, the tiny box into a paper envelope, taped and initialed the seal. Very little of that made any difference to the blood sample but would make a huge difference when – if – they went to court.

As soon as the lift departed and the top of Jack's head disappeared below the edge of the open floor, Bauer went back to musing aloud: 'In her sneakers, not dancing shoes, so she could

69

have climbed twenty-three floors. But why?'

'She didn't want to make one of her co-workers do it?' the woman suggested.

'She was afraid of the lift?' Frank directed this question to Novosek.

The manager grimaced. 'You don't work high-rises if you have a problem with heights. She wasn't afraid of the lift. If she was afraid of anything, she kept it to herself.'

'Or heights at night,' Bauer went on. 'She came here in her own vehicle, parked it in the usual spot. Doesn't sound like duress. At least not until they got up here.' He stayed next to the pillar. The breeze was light; it might be heavier at times but it wouldn't sweep the victim out into the abyss, not unless she wanted to go. The M.E. woman seemed to have no more fear than the construction workers; she knelt at the edge, popping another dirtied swab into its cardboard box. 'What's your name, anyway?' he asked her.

'Theresa MacLean. How long have you been with the prosecutor's office?'

'Ten years.'

She hid it better than most. Just the tiniest hint of a wrinkle between her eyebrows as she tried to figure out what was wrong with him, with his face and his body. It smoothed as she gave up. 'Odd we haven't met before.'

'We probably have.' He lied, because she would certainly remember the strange-looking something he represented and he would certainly remember those eyes. Perhaps it was only that the late morning sun slanted directly into the irises but the light seemed to penetrate their color and produce a glow of sky blue with a touch of aqua. The rest of her face had the same level of quality and for a moment he had no idea what to say next. And a lawyer was always supposed to know what to say next.

She turned back to her swabs, slipped the box into an envelope and relieved herself of the burden of gazing at him without recoiling. Usually he appreciated that avoidance, but now the melancholy slammed his body as hard as their victim's final stop.

But then she looked up again, spoke to him. 'At the moment, forensically, there isn't much I can tell you. She might have come up here on a drunken lark and fallen. She might have been depressed and jumped. She might have had a fight with her boyfriend and been pushed. Unfortunately every person on the site has access to this floor, as well as any person in the city who could climb the fence and figure out how to use the lift. The larger shoe-prints could have been here yesterday or the day before. Maybe. I have no idea how long they would last up here.'

Somewhere in the middle of her fourth sentence he had prodded his mind to overcome the suddenly vexing problem of coherent speech. 'Things will be a lot simpler if she was good and drunk. Misadventure, and the county and the construction company will be off the hook. Any family members will take accident over suicide and hold off suing either group.'

That little wrinkle came back. He should have just stayed dumb.

'Sorry,' he said. 'That sounds cold. Mostly I

71

would just hate to think a healthy young woman would want to die this much.'

She said, 'I hate to think of making this fall sober. But that's always a toss-up.'

'What is?'

'Is it better to die with your eyes closed, or open?'

'Better not to die at all,' Bauer said. 'I think we should take a look at her car.'

Shit, he thought. There really *had* been a girl? It hadn't been an angel or a demon who looked right up into his face; not a figment of his imagination, but a real child.

Who had now become a real problem.

TEN

Theresa had offered to accompany Frank on his winding trip down twenty-three flights of enclosed concrete steps, but he waved her off; she had her camera and the crime scene kit to carry. And so she wound up with her feet back on solid ground in record time, making conversation with the project manager, that rather unfortunate-looking prosecutor, and the talkative ironworker named Jack.

'We all park on the grass here – that's her Camry, two over from that beat-up blue pickup. That's mine. Some idiot busted out my window last week, that's why the cardboard is in it, but I'm going to get that fixed. We're allowed to park there 'cause it's part of the site, and using a lot down here would take half our pay, seems like.'

Theresa scanned the haphazard rows perched on the lawn of the south-eastern quadrant of the Mall – now a sea of fairly firm mud with only the occasional stubborn blade of new grass clinging to its trampled life. The statue and its water jets called The Fountain of Eternal Life stood only two hundred feet away and had provided no such benefit for Samantha Zebrowski. Future inmates granted windows would have a terrific view. Starting with the public library to the south and pivoting north, they could see the sweeping mall and, beyond it, the Marriott Hotel (tallest building in the city), a sliver of the Justice Center, and then the convention complex and the blue expanse of Lake Erie.

'There's only about twenty cars here,' Theresa said. 'How many people—'

Novosek rubbed his left forearm again. 'Fifty-seven at the moment. Close to a hundred and thirty when we get into the later stages, drywall, tile.'

'How many are women? Of the current fifty-seven.'

'Three,' he said; defensively, as if waiting for her to make something of it. 'Including Sam.'

'I think we should talk to the other two women. Maybe she would have told them things she didn't share with the men.'

'Oh,' he said. 'Sure. They didn't work together, though. Thompson is an ironworker and Missy Green is a pipefitter. They might have gone out after hours, but I never noticed them in a huddle here. She worked mostly with the other finishers and concrete workers.'

'Most of the guys take the bus or the rapid, or have their wives drop them,' Jack went on as if there hadn't been a digression.

'What about after work? Any favorite hangouts?' Theresa asked him.

Pleased, as she expected, at this show of interest, he named two or three bars within walking distance. 'But we're not big drinkers. I know it sort of goes with the persona, but when you've been hauling beams or hanging pipe for eight hours you don't have a lot of energy left over for raising hell. Most guys just want to go home, take a shower, eat more than their body weight in food and put their feet up. Fridays they might feel like partying but on a Monday night there'd be no one there except your hard-core alcoholics.' The watery eyes widened when he noticed the other three people gazing at him. 'Not that we have any of those.'

Prosecutor Bauer glanced at a gaping concrete path that disappeared into the depths of the muddy earth. 'You're going to have underground parking?'

Novosek looked at him, winced, then said: 'The old building had the underground lots. No point wasting a perfectly good excavation and, like Jack said, city parking is a bitch. It will also have an enclosed sally port for secure prisoner transfer.'

A burly kid with blond hair approached Novosek with what looked like a phone book wedged under his arm. 'The slump test was OK.'

'Go ahead, then.' This didn't seem to please the project manager much, though, and the guy didn't move until Novosek looked at him again. 'Go ahead, pour it. And put the book back. Oh great, there *they* are.'

Theresa followed his gaze. Three people, armed with signs and a cooler, stood on the tree lawn between the sidewalk and Rockwell. A fourth person joined them, pointing to the construction site and the cop cars in particular. 'Who are they?' Theresa asked.

'Protestors.'

'Oh, I read about that. The school administration building was a historic landmark, wasn't it?'

'*Was* it,' Novosek said with feeling. 'The old protesters are still fighting about it, petitions, council meetings. The place is *gone*, rubble, and they're still bending the mayor's ear. It was a Walker and Weeks building, like the rest of the group around here – the convention center, the Federal Reserve, the library. All Beaux-Arts.' He gestured as he talked, waving a hand at each of the graceful stone structures which encircled them. 'What? I build things for a living. You think I don't know architecture?'

'No, no,' Theresa assured him. 'I just can't believe they would tear down a Walker and Weeks building.'

'It *is* kind of a pity, but the building needed too many repairs and the county needed a new jail. They already owned the land, so money trumped history.'

'Not for the first time,' Ian Bauer murmured.

'But those aren't them,' Novosek said before he slumped to a stack of concrete blocks and pulled out a small box. 'Those are the new ones. Cigarette?'

'No, thank you,' Theresa said. 'What do you mean, new?'

He sighed again. She got the feeling the man needed a vacation, or at least forty-eight straight hours of sleep. 'Just how I got to thinking of them. The old ones protest our disrespect of the past. The new protestors think we have no respect for the present. This jail has a new design. I mean, *new*, as in never having been done in the history of the world.'

'You're using some new building technology—?'

'No, no. Nothing radical about the actual structure, it's just steel and concrete like anything else. I mean, some eggheads got together and decided that what causes the chronic failure in the rehabilitation of prison inmates is other inmates, and that the most danger to any inmate comes from other inmates. Fighting, shivving, rapes, settling scores left over from the outside – if they're kept away from each other, that kind of stuff can't happen. So they're physically safer when isolated. Then the reason that rehabilitation falls short is that the mopes don't learn skills for a constructive life, they learn skills to become better criminals. The same habits, the same gangs, the same occupations just transfer from outside to inside and back again. The only way to get them to build up enough of their own identity to be able to break away from all that is to give them a vacuum in which they finally have the freedom to think for themselves. I.e., isolation again. I'm quoting, understand. Nobody asked my opinion on the relative merits of social reform programs. I'm just building the building.'

Theresa studied the group, which had now grown to six, spanning race, gender and age from a white-haired grandmotherly type to two men, one black, one white, who looked as if they could work as bouncers or perhaps extras on *The Wire*. Plus a person shaped like a tall barrel with hair to his (her?) waist. All were united in the evil stares they sent in her direction. 'So the designers think the perfect prison is one where each prisoner is kept in solitary confinement for the duration of their sentence?'

'As I said, I'm just building the building. The cells will be set up with two sections: a bedroom and a small exercise area. How they're going to exercise without equipment, I don't know. Supposedly they're trying to design an indestructible treadmill as we speak.'

'Complete isolation,' Ian Bauer mused aloud.

'Complete *physical* isolation. They'll be able to hear each other and will be able to talk all they want. But never physical. Food will be delivered. Books, supplies, and temporary and highly monitored laptops will be brought to the cells. They'll actually have more personal space than ever before but no common space. No cafeteria, no library, no prayer meetings. No exercise yard, which should reduce the number of murders to a fraction right there.'

'Like a kennel,' Theresa said, picturing where she had once had to leave Harry for a brief stay. 'No wonder they're protesting. The concrete block cell with a remotely operated door to an outside area. Shoving in dinner through a slot in the door.'

'Exactly like a kennel. The blacks say the man has been trying to get them back in chains since 1865. The Hispanics say they're treated like dogs everywhere in America and apparently that includes prisons. The whites say it's barbaric to deny any human simple human interaction. I say maybe it's more barbaric to toss a guy into a pit of snarling hyenas, but there's no capital letters at the end of my name. I'm just building the building.'

Theresa ran one thumbnail along her teeth. 'So this patch of land was not a happy place even before Samantha's death.'

Chris Novosek puffed. 'You could say that.'

'These protests ever get violent?'

'Not yet. They have to stay off the property and they do. They have to stay off the mall green proper and they do. They put their vitriol in writing and direct it to the prison commission and the city exec.'

'Never a run in with one of your guys?'

'Nope, got to say that for them. They don't accumulate until after we've started and they disperse before we leave for the day. They concentrate on office workers and yuppies who come to eat their lunch on the mall. They're not stupid, they know enough not to pick a fight with a guy who spends all day lifting very heavy things, and they know no one here is going to sign a petition that might put them out of work, not in this economy. But it won't be long. They're growing in numbers and starting to shout insults now and there.' He didn't sound bitter toward the protesters, he didn't even sound particularly unhappy. But then a shadow crossed his face and he said, 'You think maybe they came in here to kick up their efforts and ran into Sam? Maybe she got caught in the middle?'

'I don't know. But I'm sure Frank will want to check it out.'

The man in question reappeared, red-faced and having shed the jacket. He panted: 'Car is registered in her name. Chief says we don't need a warrant.'

Theresa put an arm around him. 'It's over here. No matter what we find, you are not making that climb again today.'

'You're telling me.'

She rubbed his back. 'Maybe you need to start running again, cuz.'

'Too hard on the knees. I think I need to start drinking again.'

'You stopped?' The group made their uneven way towards the parked cars. Bauer glanced back at them with a frown. He probably thought them unprofessional, but Theresa had dropped caring what other people thought on her fortieth birthday and had never looked back.

Jack led them to the Camry, opening the passenger door with a toss of his shaggy hair.

Theresa ruined this gallant flourish when she asked him to please not touch it. She might want to fingerprint the surface.

Theresa felt torn about the car. If Samantha had come to the building with a boyfriend and that person had then pushed her off the floor, he might have left hairs and fibers behind him in the vehicle which could be picked up with adhesive tape and analyzed. If Samantha had jumped or fallen, then the vehicle and everything in it (excepting a suicide note) became irrelevant. Towing the car to the coroner's office created an expenditure she would have to justify, but impounding it, or worse yet leaving it to be picked up by family members, would eliminate its current integrity.

A thorough search, she decided, dusting the doors and rear-view mirror and then a quick taping of the seats and floors should cover all her bases. She could pick up any loose hairs or fibers and then let the vehicle go, because what she didn't see was blood. No drops on the dirty gray upholstery, no signs of a struggle. Nothing broken or, aside from the collection of stained McDonald's coffee cups littering all four floor mats, out of place. Neatness, apparently, did not count for much in Samantha Zebrowski's life, to judge from the interior of her unlocked Camry. Neither did safe driving practices – she had two outstanding speeding tickets and five parking violations, which Frank detailed for them as his breathing slowly returned to normal.

On the rear passenger side floorboard, tucked under a reusable shopping bag, Theresa found an oversized purse in shiny black vinyl, with large silver-colored rings and clasps. It held a department store of mascara, lip gloss, scratch-off lottery tickets, about fifteen bucks in crumpled bills and loose change, four condoms, two pay stubs and a phone number written in pencil on a scrap of paper. It had been torn from a menu, apparently, since the reverse side read '—*wich with tomato on rye, $7.95.*' She read the number to Frank but slipped the paper into an envelope to process later for fingerprints.

'She had a passenger,' Ian Bauer said. 'Or else the purse would be on the passenger seat, wouldn't it?'

Theresa shook her head. 'She had it tucked underneath the shopping bag. That suggests to me that she didn't want to carry it but didn't want to leave it in plain sight and give any passing thieves a reason to break her window.'

'And then leaves the doors unlocked?'

'Doesn't make sense,' she agreed. 'So perhaps she *was* distracted with a passenger.'

'And if you're about to kill yourself, why worry about your purse at all?'

She grinned. 'You have to understand the long-standing, long-suffering, deeply ingrained relationship between a woman and her purse.'

Bauer flushed as if she had spoken of thong underwear, and Frank said, 'That number comes back to city hall.'

Theresa stopped grinning and blinked at him. 'What? What department?'

'Switchboard. She could have been trying to talk to the mayor or pay her water bill or ask

81

about one of those parking tickets.'

Novosek had been watching them work with a reluctant but dutiful gaze. He wasn't responsible for Samantha Zebrowski's life, Theresa knew, yet he seemed to feel obligated to observe the processes of her death. Such things came with being the boss. He had sent the hovering Jack back to the steel beams as work resumed in every area except the concrete pad and the twenty-third floor.

Theresa shut the door, and she and Frank discussed the release of the vehicle for a moment or two. Frank would come by the coroner's office to get the car keys, which they assumed were in Samantha's pockets. Then he and Angela would go the extra mile and drive the car to the family rather than make Betty Zebrowski pay to have her dead child's vehicle towed.

'You can't get it out of here now?' Novosek had been about as cooperative as possible, but Frank could tell the shock had begun to fade as more practical matters seeped back in, such as how much of the day had been wasted and how that might affect all future stages of construction.

'No keys,' Frank said. 'Plus, we don't have either permission or probable cause to remove it. Why?'

'It's just...' The project manager, as large and tough as he looked, squirmed like a schoolboy. 'When somebody dies on the job, it freaks everyone out. It's probably the same at your place – if a cop gets shot, don't you all get jumpy? I've got to get that blood off that pad, and her car sitting here where everyone can see it—'

'I understand,' Frank said. 'I'll do what I can but it's still going to be a day at least.'

'Yeah, I got it,' Chris Novosek said. 'It's just that here, jumpy can get people hurt.'

ELEVEN

Angela returned. As she and Frank headed up the stairwell she said that the county child advocate had arrived and talked to Betty Zebrowski about funeral arrangements and also about living arrangements, which would not be changing. Mrs Zebrowski could handle shopping, cooking and cleaning for the household. The only thing she couldn't do was climb the steps to the second floor.

The child advocate had also spoken to Ghost about death and stages of grief.

'How'd she take it?'

'As well as can be expected. She seems like a pretty sensible kid, almost too sensible ... I don't know, as she was listening to the caseworker – at times she'd zone out or start to cry, but other times she'd just stare at the woman and I could swear she was thinking to herself, "Yada yada yada."'

Frank tried to control his panting, but by the fifth floor it had grown difficult. 'So you think

83

she might be right about a man pushing her mother over the edge?'

'I don't know. She didn't say anything more about it. Still, how does Samantha, her daughter and a killer all wind up here at the same time? If she's meeting a man, why bring her daughter?'

'Wanted her to meet the new daddy?'

'In the middle of the night?' She didn't even breathe heavy when she said it, damn her, but at last they could stop. Samantha's two fellow finishers were working on the sixth floor, and Frank wanted to talk to them before time, thought or regret could affect their stories.

The guys weren't hard to pick out. They were the only two humans in the vast empty space. One held a long piece of equipment that resembled a lawn edger, and the other carried a simple trowel, but it didn't appear that a lot of work was getting done. Conversation broke off as the cops approached.

Frank introduced himself and his partner, not in a pleasant social way but in the *don't let that courtesy fool you, I will be asking the questions here* tone that he had learned in the academy. 'You're Kyle Cielac and Todd Grisham?'

He waited until they specified who was who. Kyle resembled a high school football hero ten years after graduation, fleshy shoulders and no neck, close-cropped blond hair. Todd had dark good looks of indeterminate origin. But they wore identically wary expressions. In the next few minutes Frank established that the two men had worked with Samantha Zebrowski since the project began, or rather since the project pro-

gressed to the point of needing concrete finishers. A finisher usually worked with the concrete
after it had been poured into the giant rebar-
enhanced slabs that formed the floors of the
skyscraper. They would trim the edges and cut
the grooves into the slab that would keep the
concrete from cracking during the temperature
changes endemic to northern Ohio. They also
followed up with finishing touches and repairs.
One pointed to a slight crack in the corner, too
close to that sparse railing for Frank's comfort,
their ostensible reason for being off on a tête-à-
tête.

They were thirty and twenty-eight respec-
tively, both unmarried with no kids. Kyle had
been in construction one way or another since
high school; you could say it ran in his family.
Todd just needed a job after getting out of the
military. Neither had known Samantha before
this project, neither had dated her, neither knew
who she was dating, if anyone, and neither had a
conflict with her, or knew of one she might have
had with someone else.

None of this struck Frank as plausible. Samantha had been single, hard-bodied and a bit of a
party girl, and neither of these guys wanted to
tap that? He would have thought they might be
more interested in each other than their curvy
co-worker if it hadn't been for their constant
glances toward *his* curvy partner. Though perhaps they were admiring her fashion sense. She
did look good in those stretchy dress pants that
all the female detectives wore these days and a
thin brown sweater that matched her eyes ... but

still. It seemed to him that two single guys should have a lot more to say about one of the few women on the site.

But maybe he was just the cultural dinosaur that Theresa sometimes accused him of being. Maybe they viewed Samantha simply as one more fellow construction worker, no more, no less.

Yeah, right.

The rest of their testimony stayed in line with that of their boss: Samantha had been good at her job, reliable, seemed to care deeply for her mother and daughter, and nothing at all had seemed amiss during her last day on the job.

'And she would have told you if she had a steady boyfriend?'

'We heard about her daughter's math grade, her new sports bra and her mother's pot roast,' Todd said. 'So, yeah.'

Frank rubbed the back of his neck. 'OK. Say she meets a guy, or has a new boyfriend. Would she bring him here?'

The two construction workers exchanged a glance, nodded.

'Probably,' Kyle said. 'She said she drove her kid by, and a girlfriend. She was real proud of the place. This is the biggest job she'd ever been on, did mostly parking lots until now.'

'What about to do something besides marvel at the majesty of the architecture?' Frank asked. 'Might she bring a guy here to have sex in a – different setting?'

They didn't bother to exchange a glance before nodding this time. Todd said, 'That'd be Sam.

86

Uninhibited, you might say. Besides, she lived with her mom, so she always needed someplace to go besides home. According to her. You might want to use that black light thing on the back seat of her car,' he added with a smirk that faded into a much sadder expression of regret, either for a young life cut short or the fact that now he would never know the wonders to be found inside the beat-up Camry.

More questions on the subject of Samantha Zebrowski's sex life garnered no useful information. She had been an upbeat young woman, more or less liked by her co-workers and without any apparent romantic or financial woes. Her mood on the previous day had been utterly normal with no indication of any distress. Suicide, Frank thought, appeared more unlikely with each passing minute. 'And no problems on the job here?'

'No.' They answered in unison, too fast.

'What about you guys? Any problems, conflicts?'

'No.'

He caught the first scent of fear, like the hint of distant smoke. 'Union negotiations? Safety issues?'

'Nothing,' Kyle said, and Todd nodded.

'What *did* you do yesterday?' Angela asked.

'Poured thirty,' Todd said, and Kyle nodded.

Frank said nothing. He was a man and supposed to understand the language of construction as intrinsically as the language of football, or belching.

Angela had no such restriction. 'What does

that mean?'

Kyle said, 'Cement is pumped up through a flexible pipe and poured into the forms with rebar and metal mesh.'

'And then you finish it?'

'Not until it hardens. The pouring, we mostly just help out with the physical labor. They need every hand they can get when we're pouring a floor. Once the stuff is mixed it has to go, but it has to be the right consistency so they do a slump test. If that's not right ... then they have to adjust the mix, and sometimes you can get a blockage in the tubes, and all sorts of stuff can cause a delay.'

'So it's stressful,' Angela surmised.

'Yeah. Well, more for the masons – it's their responsibility. Like I said, we just help out.'

'And Samantha worked on this? No problems?'

'None,' Kyle said, exchanging a look with Todd.

They both had alibis for the evening, more or less: Todd had been living on his brother's couch since the previous year, and so he had a sibling, a sister-in-law, a fourteen-year-old nephew and a ten-year-old niece who liked to use him as a sparring partner to swear he stayed home all night; Kyle had a room-mate with not one but two live-in girlfriends, who took turns sleeping on the couch – don't ask him how *that* worked – so he also had the potential to prove that he had not left his bedroom all night, unless he snuck out his window and managed to climb down five stories of sheer brick wall.

88

Frank kept at them for another twenty minutes, going in every direction possible, without shaking loose one more iota of information regarding Samantha Zebrowski. These two had worked with her for eight hours a day, five days a week, and yet seemed to know no more about her life than the big boss.

Possibly, Samantha had been one of those people who could talk a lot without saying much.

Or, Kyle and Todd had something to hide.

TWELVE

'Anything on the prints?' Frank asked. They stood on opposite sides of the autopsy table where whatever parts of Samantha Zebrowski's body that remained together were now being cut apart. The clothing had been removed and hung to dry, the contents of her pockets spread out on a clean sheet of paper in the examination room, the fingernails (though soaked in blood) scraped and the toothpicks secured in tiny folds of glassine paper. Christine Johnson, pathologist, made the Y incision herself, avoiding the natural rips in the flesh as the body had impacted the concrete slab at a force equal to Samantha's body weight times acceleration due to gravity.

'Nothing. Nothing interesting in the hairs and fibers – a variety of both, but at this point I have

89

no idea what's significant and what's not.'

'Watch your tie, Detective,' Christine murmured as she directed a spray of water at the ruined flesh on the table. Red-stained drops flew over the side and Frank took a step back without any change of expression.

'I liked it better when we could drink coffee in here,' he said, apropos of nothing.

'Me too,' Christine agreed. 'How many stories?'

'Twenty-three,' Theresa told her for the third time. 'Why? Doesn't that seem consistent?'

'Oh, completely consistent.' Christine poked a gloved finger into the pile of still-neat small intestine gathered on Samantha's right side. 'Just hard to picture.'

Frank went on, asking Theresa: 'Nothing so far supports the suicide theory, but then suicides are often careful to act like everything is fine. I can't imagine why else she would drag her kid there in the middle of the night.'

'Ghost insists she went there on her own. Says she's done it before.'

'That stretches coincidence even further, if she just happened to show up right at the moment her mother bites it. Is it possible she didn't see the actual plunge, only found the body?'

'The shaking, the zoning-out, the way the blood drained from her face every time she looked at the concrete slab all suggest post-traumatic stress. But finding the body would be extremely traumatic too, so I don't know. There's so much about kids I don't know, despite having raised one.'

With the shards out of the way, Christina removed the organs which had been sliced and diced by the broken bones, then scooped out what little liquid remained in the peritoneal cavity. 'Toxicology is going to be crap,' she pronounced. 'Gastric and urine is all mixed in with the blood. But I can smell one component.'

'What?' Theresa supplied.

'Alcohol.'

Theresa added to Frank, 'But the blood was still very wet when it seeped into her pants. If Ghost didn't witness the actual death then she arrived shortly after.'

'Which still makes even less sense than arriving with her mother. Unless the girl is telling the absolute truth and she does make a habit of roaming the city in the wee hours. She wouldn't be the first kid in history who had to go and pull their parent out of the bar on a regular basis.' A shadow, or perhaps a memory, seemed to color his face for a moment. 'All we're getting right now is the knee-jerk the-victim-could-do-no-wrong reaction, but perhaps Samantha Zebrowski had a lot more faults than anyone is willing to admit.'

Christina picked up a large metal bowl that in another profession would be used to whisk eggs or mix dough and took it over to the counter. Theresa and Frank followed, watching over her shoulders as she examined and dissected each on a thick polypropylene cutting board. The heart, aside from where it had been slashed by the sternum, had been as strong and healthy as one would expect in a twenty-nine year old. The lungs would have wanted Sam to lay off the cigarettes but were otherwise clear. The eleventh rib had punctured the stomach, leaving only the partially digested residue of some corn product.

'Like tortilla chips?' Theresa suggested.

'Tacos?' Christina suggested.

'Are you guys hungry?' Frank joked.

To which the two women answered 'Yes,' in unison.

Christina returned to the body, theorizing: 'I'll bet it's bar munchies. There's not enough for a full meal, and not much in her intestines. It would fit with the odor of alcohol.'

'So her last meal wasn't even a full one,' Frank said with the first touch of sympathy he'd shown.

'Food only absorbs the alcohol,' Theresa explained.

'I'm not going to ask how you know that, cuz.'

'Tavern on the Mall is right across the street.'

'Didn't that used to be Pat Joyce's? But if she's drunk, then tell me again why we think this is murder, why Sammy here didn't just take it in her pickled little mind to get a look at the city skyline at night. Other than the little matter of how the zip lift got back to the ground, that is?'

'This,' Christina said.

She had flayed back the skin on Samantha Zebrowski's right arm to reveal the pinpricks of broken blood vessels. 'Petechia in an area about three inches round.'

'What's that?' Frank asked.

'It would have been one hell of a bruise, had the ecchymosis not been arrested by this girl's

92

death.'

'She worked in construction,' he pointed out. 'It's a very physical activity.'

'True. But if it had happened on the job it would have been a full bruise by the evening, and the forearm is a common place for someone to grab you when they want you to do something and you resist. Like climb a building in order to fall to your death.'

Frank and Theresa said nothing as Christina examined more beginning-to-bruise areas, and eventually concluded that Samantha had suffered contusions very shortly before her death in six areas: right and left forearms, stomach, breast, and at least two spots on the left side of her face.

'She was beaten,' Theresa said.

Frank said, 'Or she got in a fight with someone. She takes boyfriend up there for a little canoodling high atop the city lights, and they have an argument. She falls, and he sure as hell isn't going to fess up, lose his job and probably go to jail.'

'There's no reason to think he's another construction worker,' Theresa said a bit regretfully. 'She might have met him in a bar just that night. She wants to show off, and he takes it as an invitation to accelerate their relationship a bit faster than she was ready for. She resists, they fight. Though none of this explains how Ghost comes to be there.'

'Maybe she did walk a mile or two to drag Mom out of the bar. Mom decides she's a terrible mother and kid would be better off without her.

93

Or Mom is having too good a time with her new beau, decides to show off her workplace first.' Frank sighed. 'We need someone else who saw her that night besides the kid. Time to pound the pavement.' He'd have to show Samantha's picture to every employee of every bar or restaurant in the area and any others she was known to frequent. They'd have to question every pal and acquaintance for any mention of a romantic interest, any recent friendships. Then, even if they found a likely suspect, they might be left with no way to place him at the scene that night. 'Sure you can't call this one an accident, doc? Maybe a misadventure?'

'Sorry,' Christina said, without sounding sorry at all.

The DNA analyst, Don, stopped in the doorway to the autopsy suite. 'Theresa, there's a kid here.'

Three faces swirled toward him, all struck dumb.

'To see me?' Theresa finally got out.

'No.' Don nodded at the body on the stainless steel table. 'To see her.'

It couldn't be that hard to find her. How many Zebrowskis could there be in the city? He'd check the phone book. Phone books still existed, right? Sometimes time passed so quickly that things disappeared for years before you even realized they were gone. Like phones with dials. Anacin aspirin. Parents.

He went over it again. The Tavern, he figured, was fine. No observant witnesses there. The mall, empty. Construction site: empty, until it wasn't.

He still couldn't wrap his head around the idea of the kid's presence. How did she get there? Where was she while he was on top with Samantha? He had looked down, hadn't seen any movement. No one there, then suddenly she was. Just transported there like—

The car.

Sam's car. What if the demon/angel/child had been in the car, if Sam, that paragon of mother-hood, had left her kid locked in the car while she bar-hopped? What if the grandmother needed a night off and no babysitters were available? Was that why Sam had gone to the car, to make sure the kid still slumbered, clearing the next hour for Mom to get some? Maybe Sam already had the screwdriver on her, or combined the two tasks.

That made a lot more sense. It also made him feel a little sorry for the kid. Some upbringing.

Not sorry enough, however, to forget the fact that the girl remained a witness. The only wit-ness. His angel-demon was a sane and real human, and her presence there a sane and real event. And she now represented a threat to him, sane and very real.

THIRTEEN

Charlie's Bar-be-que had been a west-side staple since long before Damon's birth, back when – according to local tales – he roasted the succulent meat out of the back of an old school bus, parking in whatever lot would tolerate him for a time. Once you located Charlie's and placed your order, you then had to listen to him try to save your soul as you ate, but even the irreligious found this a small price to pay for the best ribs north of the Mason-Dixon line.

The current incarnation of Charlie's had a permanent location, curtains on the windows and Formica on the tables, and a smell that Damon loved more than anything else in the world. He lit into his second slab of ribs; with all the work he'd done that day, he needed a meal that would stick to his. Across the table, Boonie grinned as if reading his mind, halfway through a second slab himself. 'Nothing like honest work to give a man an appetite.'

'Got that,' Damon nodded. Work at the construction site constituted his first foray into 'honest' labor in all his nineteen years. He had never picked up a wrench before but their boss – their real boss, not Chris Novosek or even the plumbing foreman – had greased some palms and suddenly Boonie and Damon were apprentice pipelayers. Even though the 'laying' part didn't seem to fit, since most of the piping ran along the ceiling instead of the floor, and they both – especially Boonie – resented the job title. There was nothing 'apprentice' about either of them. Damon had started out as a runner when he was barely old enough to read and managed a crew that spanned two blocks by the time he was sixteen. Boonie had started at fifteen, but Boonie was some distant cousin of the boss's, so he had preference. His blocks had done well, too, always sold out and never skimmed, and there had been talk of expanding his territory, taking over Marlow's crew while Marlow served three to five. But then the boss got this idea, and boom, they were out of the drug dealing business and into the pipelayers' union. Paying dues and shit, the whole tamale.

Damon finished the ribs, then condescended to notice his coleslaw. After the third bite he slowed down enough to say, 'Didn't get nothing done today, what with that chick and all. Turning up dead. We didn't even get to the first bend at the elevator shaft.'

'Dead chick on our watch, and all you care is how much pipe got into place?'

'Just sayin'. She got nothing to do with us, anyway.'

'I know that and you know that. The cops ain't going to know that, especially if they find our sheets.' Boonie had done five years for aggravated assault. Damon had been to jail twice already, but only for minor possession charges.

'Totally different floors, different jobs. I didn't even know her name. You?'

'Nope. Noticed her ass, though.'

'Only one there worth noticing,' Damon agreed. 'But nothing to do with us. Wish she'd jumped off someone else's site. Blew practically a whole day.'

Boonie watched him dig the last bit of shredded cabbage out of its plastic cup. 'You're likin' this, aren't you?'

'Huh?'

'This workin' and shit. Getting up before dawn every day, punching a time clock. Eating your lunch out of a cooler like some tomato-pickin' illegal. You actually *like* it.'

Damon thought before he spoke. The boss always seemed to, and he studied the boss's habits carefully. Now he thought that, though he would trust Boonie with his life, and there were only three people on earth he would say that about, there were also things, subtle things, that he might want to keep to himself. Such as, he *didn't* really mind working on the site. He found it interesting – connecting one pipe to another, making them capable of holding water without leaking for the next fifty years, fitting each piece into the vast network that would span forty-one floors without any loss of pressure. How the men took a picture on a piece of paper and translated it into a solid structure of steel and concrete. How water and power, two things he had always taken for granted – you turned a knob and they came out – were the lifeblood of the city, living, breathing entities that could be channeled and controlled. All this spoke to a part of him he hadn't known was there. Yeah, he kind of liked it.

What he didn't like was the boss's plan, which seemed highly improbable at best and, well, stupid at worst.

But the one thing he would never admit, not even to his best friend, was any lack of faith in the intelligence of the boss. That way lay annihilation. So now he said, 'It's different, that's all. Maybe I was ready for a change. Got to admit, running a crew is stressful.'

A pause. *'Stressful,'* Boonie said, as if Damon had brought up the latest fashion in slipcovers or perhaps his golf handicap.

'I'm sayin'. Got to watch everybody every minute. Everyone who works for you is looking for a way to skim. Everybody don't work for you is looking for a way to rip you off. Boss is looking out in case *you* skim. Cops looking out to get their cut or run you in just to show they're doin' something. Then there's the drama. Guys dippin' into their own supply, getting all crazy. Fightin' with their ladies. The girls hauling their babies all over the place, whinin' to me about their dude like I'm freakin' Dr Phil or something.'

Boonie shrugged. 'That's the life.'

'I'm just sayin', that's all. Rough.'

'So you'd rather cart pipe around for the man, make practically minimum wage?'

'Didn't say that, did I?' Damon asked as he studied a rib, picked clean.

'Whatever. But on that other thing – we tight,

99

right? We ready?'

'Absolutely,' Damon said. He snapped the rib in half with one twist of his toughened hands and examined the exposed marrow with great interest. 'Hey.'

'What?'

'Think that chick's bones looked like this?'

Boonie laughed so hard he spewed tiny bits of barbecue sauce on to the Formica, wet bits of dark red that glistened like blood.

Ghost sat in the lobby, in the same clothes she'd donned after her shower, rubbing at one reddened eye. She straightened up as Theresa approached, steeling herself for the inevitable confrontation. The kid might not have good grades but she had quite a handle on how the world worked. Theresa's first words did not seem to come as the slightest surprise. 'Ghost, you shouldn't be here.'

'I want to see my mother.'

'This isn't the place for that. You'll see her at the funeral home.'

'Then why can't I see her here too?'

Technically, of course, a reasonable question, so Theresa fell back on the great stonewall: policy. 'Because no one under eighteen is allowed past this room, just like children aren't allowed to vote or drink or see R-rated movies.'

'I thought that was because the people were having sex. In the movies.'

The receptionist giggled. Theresa sank on to the ancient vinyl bench next to the girl, who smelled of strawberry shampoo with the faintest

100

hint of leftover cigarette. 'There's a collection of reasons for all those rules. It's just better for people to remember their loved ones the way they were, and to see them in a peaceful setting like a funeral home, where they can be surrounded by their family and friends for support. We don't let adults in here either, unless we absolutely have to for purposes of identification. That's just the way it is, Ghost.'

The girl didn't seem convinced, so Theresa added, 'And you couldn't see her now anyway, because she's in with the doctors.'

'Are they cutting her up?'

Theresa gulped. She had always believed in honesty being the best policy when it came to children, but now began to reconsider. 'The doctor's name is Christine, and she's looking at your mom really closely, to see if there's any bruises or scratches on the skin or if maybe she had been feeling sick or anything like that. Ghost, how did you get here?'

'I walked.'

'From your house? That must be three miles.'

The girl shrugged. 'I walk a lot.'

'What do you do when you walk?'

'Look for – stuff,' she mumbled, but at least she didn't ask any more questions about the autopsy.

Theresa asked, 'Does your grandmother know where you are?'

'She laid down for a nap. I didn't want to wake her,' she added with patent innocence and the first hint of sneaky and totally normal kid behavior that Theresa had seen from her.

'Ghost, you can't walk all over by yourself like that.'

'Why not?'

'It's not safe.'

The kid fixed her with another one of those looks, the one that said her statement had been belied by the facts. Ghost had, so far, been perfectly safe. It had been the adult who got killed. 'I need to see her,' she started again, with a cloudiness in her eyes that hinted of a storm of sobs behind it. The receptionist watched them as if they appeared on a TV screen. 'It's not fair! I've got to figure out who killed her.'

'I understand, Ghost, but—'

'I have to find the shadow man!'

'The police will do that.'

'No, me!' the girl wailed. 'I have to do it.'

'Why?'

'Because I don't have a father!' Now she did sob, tears squeezing out slowly as if she didn't have many left. 'There's no one but me and Nana and she's in a wheelchair!'

Theresa put an arm around the child and let her cry. She understood it perfectly, the overwhelming need to *do* something, to push back against this assault on her life. That the girl was only eleven didn't dilute that in the least. So she rubbed Ghost's back, pulled a few tissues out of a box on the end table, and said, 'Why don't we go up to the lab and I'll show you the clues we have from your mother's – case?'

The girl sniffled as Theresa wiped her nose. 'Really?'

'Really.'

Ghost sniffled again, thought of something. 'You're a lot like my mom.'

'I am?' Theresa stood up. 'How?'

'She would always make deals with me too, when I wanted something and she didn't want to give it to me. And she would bite her fingernails without biting them *off* when she was thinking hard, like you do. But her hair is darker. Was,' the child corrected herself with heartbreaking precision. 'Was darker.'

They went upstairs.

'It's a first, yes,' Theresa announced to her boss, Leo, as she escorted Ghost into the lab.

They started out with the Cellebrite device, a small system designed to quickly download information from cell phones. The Cellebrite itself was about the size of an electrical meter, but came accompanied by a briefcase filled with no less than one hundred and twenty different cables to fit most of the myriad of digital phones available on the market. The hardest part of the process was figuring out the make and model number of the phone, which often involved taking off the back and removing the battery, in order to find the correct cable. After that Theresa simply plugged the free end of the cable into one end of the device and inserted a jump drive into the other side. The device would then take all the information on the phone and write it to the jump drive, from which it could be viewed, printed, copied or written to CD.

But again, the market supplied an ever-increasing variety of products, so until the phone had been connected to the device Theresa never knew whether it would be possible to download all the phone's information, including ring tones and text messages, or none. Often it would be some combination in-between. She might be able to get the contact list and photographs but not text messages. Or call history but no photos. Or texts but not videos.

'Why not?' Ghost asked.

'Even with the amazing advances in technology – when I was your age no one had ever heard of a cell phone – there's still a lot of hit and miss. We can only do what we can do. It's never –' Theresa sighed – 'as easy as it looks on TV.'

Samantha's phone proved relatively cooperative and Theresa downloaded the call history, contact list and text messages, both incoming and outgoing. She had already reviewed them before the autopsy and knew there were none that seemed distinctly relevant to the crime, and nothing unsuitable for viewing by an eleven-year-old.

Next she settled the child in front of the comparison microscope, adjusting a task chair to the correct height. Then she provided a short introduction to the basics of microscopy, as Ghost stared down the oculars in fascination. They had to slide back and forth a few times so Theresa could adjust the focus, but Ghost showed surprising patience, waiting to see the brightly colored shapes of the hairs and fibers retrieved from her mother's clothing.

'On the left here is a blue fiber from her shirt. See? It's kind of wide and looks like it has a channel running through it.'

'Yeah.'

'Any idea where that might have come from? Her shirt wasn't blue.'

'No.'

'What about your shirt? The one you were wearing – at the time.'

The girl paled a bit, but then said, 'It was blue.'

'So let's compare the fibers from that shirt.' Theresa placed a slide on the other stage, adjusted the focus.

'You have fibers from my shirt?'

'Yes. I took it out of your bathroom, remember? I told you.'

'Oh yeah.'

'That's what we call a reference sample – your shirt, because we know where it came from and we're using it only to try to identify some of the unknown fibers in this case. Now take a look.'

She squinted down the lenses for a while before saying, 'They're not the same. The one from my shirt doesn't have that channel in it, and has little bubbly things through it.'

'Very good. Those bubbly things are probably titanium dioxide, added to make the color brighter. You're right, it doesn't match. So our blue fiber didn't come from your shirt. Do we have anything else that's blue?'

Ghost shrugged.

'What about her car?'

A wrinkle appeared between the girl's eyebrows. 'But that's painted.'

'Yes, you're right, the outside is painted. But the seats are fabric. And the carpeting is composed of fibers. Let's take a look at the carpeting.'

'It's the same!' Ghost said after a moment.

'Yes, it looks the same. We can analyze the samples in this machine here, too, to make sure that they're both made of the same stuff. So that eliminates that blue fiber that we found on your mom because now we're pretty sure where it came from.'

The wrinkle returned. 'But then – how does that tell us who—?'

'It doesn't really tell us anything helpful about what happened to your mom, no. But it tells us what isn't relevant. Then when we find a hair or a fiber we can't explain, maybe that will be a clue to – what happened.'

The girl sighed.

'A lot of this work is like that. It's not always how it is on TV. We have to go through all the pieces that tell us stuff we already know so we know which pieces tell us stuff we *don't* already know.'

Ghost sighed again. 'What if the shadow man didn't leave any fibers?'

'Then he might have left something else. And physical evidence is only part of solving a crime.' She spoke with more confidence than she felt. Samantha's assailant might still be simply a product of a traumatized child's imagination. The bruising on the woman's body supported the theory but didn't clinch it.

'But,' the little girl said, her sad voice barely above a whisper, 'what if we never find him?'

'It's much too early to give up hope, Ghost.

Let's try another slide. Look at this one.'

'That looks strange. What is it?'

'I don't know.' Theresa pulled a long but somewhat flat file box from a cabinet. 'These are slides of all different kinds of fibers and materials. We'll have to look at each one to see if we can find something that looks just like our sample.'

'I thought you would put this stuff into some kind of machine,' the girl grumbled as Theresa set up the first slide.

'Sometimes we can. But sometime you just have to look at it.' She left the girl going through the reference library, placing each tiny glass slide on to the microscope stage with a light touch. The slides were so uniform that the focus did not need to be adjusted with each new one, so Theresa felt free to step away from the extremely expensive piece of equipment just long enough to snag the cup of coffee she so desperately needed. She kept an eye on Ghost from Leo's office.

'What the hell are you doing?' he asked, to her complete lack of surprise. He didn't bother to lower his voice, either, and she saw Ghost glance over at them. 'You know what a big deal a defense attorney would make about you letting a kid into the lab?'

'I wasn't planning to tell them. Besides, she's not touching anything confidential, she's just looking at slides. And what're they going to say, that an eleven year old planted evidence to frame a person unknown to her at this point, one we're not even sure actually exists?' Of course Leo, skinny, bespectacled, paranoid-as-all-get-out Leo, was probably right. Having unauthorized people in the lab was never a good idea. 'The kid has to do something other than sit in her bedroom and contemplate life as an orphan.'

'They have people for that, and those people are called social workers. You are not a social worker.'

'I know.'

'There are other people who have died in the past twenty-four hours. You have gunshot residue samples to run and that gang-banger's clothing has got to be dry by now. I want your report on that before you leave today.'

'Uh-huh.'

He could have simply kicked both of them out, but Leo's style of management had always been to retain all power without ever actually making any decisions. 'She has to go. Now.'

'I know.' Theresa sipped, the hot liquid coursing down her throat, and watched Ghost move on to another slide, the tiny fingers moving the piece of glass around as gently as humanly possible, working with a concentration that pierced Theresa's heart. 'You know about my dad.'

'Yeah,' Leo said. 'But you weren't *that* young.'

'Fourteen. Only three years older. And he wasn't murdered, he died of a brain aneurysm, and I wasn't there when it happened. But I still remember pacing through my house, walking from corner to corner, from the bedroom to the kitchen to the basement ... just wanting to be able to *do* something to fix what had happened or at least to understand it. To find something that would make me comprehend why the day couldn't start over and take a different course. No one had any answers. No one even had any questions.'

The day hadn't started over, which was why her ex-cop grandfather had more or less taken over the role, which was probably why, relatives often sighed, Theresa and Frank had wound up in their respective lines of work.

From the edge of her line of vision her boss watched her. Then he said, 'You can't run a day care here just because you feel sorry for the kid.'

'I know.'

'Get her out of here.'

'All right.'

She returned to the main lab, where Ghost held a slide in her flat palm as if it were a live butterfly. 'I think I found something.'

Theresa promptly decided to ignore Leo a while longer. 'Let's take a look. I think you could be right.' The reference slide had been labeled *asbestos*.

'What's that?' Ghost asked. 'I thought that was bad.'

'It's something to make stuff fire-resistant, so it's not bad in certain conditions. It was probably around the job site, or left on her tools or car from a previous job.'

Eyes on the prize, Ghost asked: 'Will that help us find the shadow man?'

'I don't know yet. It might. Even if it doesn't help us *find* him, it might help us prove he's the shadow man once we do find him.'

The girl had cornflower blue eyes, something like her grandmother's, and she rubbed one of them. Fatigue had begun to catch up. Briskly, Theresa explained that she would drive Ghost home now.

The girl offered some half-hearted protests and then gave up. 'You are going to catch him. Right?'

Theresa had hoped to avoid that question. 'I'm not going to lie to you, Ghost. There are no guarantees. But I can promise that we're going to do our best. We – I am going to do everything I possibly can.'

The girl's expression said it all:

Not. Acceptable.

FOURTEEN

'How's it going?' the boss asked Damon upon his arrival at the motel off of I-90. The boss's name was Leroy Whitman, but no one ever called him that. He sat in a folding chair outside the open door of room twenty-three. The motel had been closed for a year and still didn't have a new owner, which made it a handy place for temporary storage.

'Good. Took seventeen minutes to get here.'

'No cops?'

The boss was large and black and deceptively

110

mild looking, with a moon-like face and short wavy hair that Damon always thought looked more Italian than black. As with all his opinions, Damon kept this one to himself, speaking only of business and only when spoken to. 'Ain't seen any.'

'Good.' The stretched-out plastic weave of the lawn chair strained under the boss's ample girth as he fished a pack of cigarettes out of his shirt pocket, diamonds glinting from thick fingers. He always had at least three other guys with him: his bodyguard, his right-hand man, and a third guy to take care of errands, phone calls, meal runs and enforcement, in order to keep the first two free for the really vital things. 'This will be a very productive piece of undercover work. Maybe I should put somebody on all major construction projects.'

'Don't know if I'm cut out for an honest day's laboring.'

The boss chuckled. 'Some labors be worth it.'

'You think this one will be worth it?'

The boss stilled, and Damon wondered if he'd misspoken. He hadn't meant to question the boss's judgment – just the opposite, he wanted to keep him talking so Damon could listen and learn. Show respect. It was all about respect. 'I mean—'

The man waved around the cigarette to discourage the mosquitoes. 'Sometimes you have to invest without being one-hundred-percent sure that you're going to have a pay day. Maybe having a diagram of all the hallways and doors and plumbing and electrical work in a jail will

111

come in handy some day. Maybe it won't. Maybe this precious metal will make up for the income lost if your crew ain't running so well without you there, 'cause business is down anyway. Maybe it won't. Maybe, as some colleagues of mine suggested, that pretty new building will all fall down before they can cage up a single brother, and maybe it won't. Long as you get paid either way, it's all good, innit?'

'Long as I get out of the way first,' Damon joked, but he wondered about that. His boss was a profit man, not a political one.

'I'm not a political man,' the boss went on, scaring Damon practically out of his skin. 'But when my great-great-great grandaddy, I'm sure, came to this country, he came with a chain around his neck. Like a dog. Put up on a block and sold like a dog. Now they want to put us in kennels, like dogs. Are we going to sit back and let our brothers be treated like dogs?'

'No, sir.'

'No,' said the boss, taking a thoughtful puff, *'suh!'*

Damon considered this all the way back to the construction site. He had been in a group home. He had been in juvenile detention. He had been in jail twice. And between the beatings, the dramas, the constant and at times overpowering fear, he wondered if he wouldn't have preferred the kennel. At least he could have slept like a normal person instead of the hyper-vigilant, hyper-aware animal you had to turn into in order to survive. Especially with his second cell-mate ... Damon still had the occasional nightmare about that guy. So a cage all his own might be better, in its way. He couldn't get out, but at least no one else could get in.

Of course, that all depended on who had the key.

He had crossed the site three times – slowly, unobtrusively, careful to look as if he had a legitimate purpose – and had not found it. Now he stood in, roughly, the center of the southern half of the building, replaying the previous night in his mind. For a purpose, this time, a purpose other than the simple joy of it, other than to create the pleasant stirrings in his chest and groin whenever he flashed back to that body flailing two hundred feet through space.

He had caught up with Samantha at the bar across the street, one of her favorite haunts. She liked to snag a place near the window if she could, so she could down a Cosmo made with cheap vodka and stare at the building, pick up guys with the line, 'You see that skyscraper going up? I'm building that.'

As if.

Usually she had either settled on a catch for the evening or had a circle of two or three other women who needed to pretend to be there to enjoy each other's company when instead they would abandon their own gender in the blink of an eye if something with a penis came along. But for once she sat alone, chin propped by one hand. In a booth – plenty of seats available that time of the night – so he could slide right in across from her. She had just smiled at him, quickly and not sincerely, before turning back to the window. She said nothing, as if he'd merely returned from a trip to the men's room.

He said *hello* and *how are you doing tonight*.

'I've been thinking about my daughter,' she said without preamble, again as if continuing a previous encounter briefly interrupted. 'I don't want her to repeat my life. I don't have any complaints, but still. She needs more opportunities.'

Like he wanted to hear about her kid, but then pretty girls did that. They could spout any sort of crap because they knew you'd hang on their every word no matter how dull or inane it got. He just let her talk, let her stare at the window instead of him.

'I need to start a savings plan. I'm finally making decent money; I could sock some away and move us out to the suburbs. Someplace where she could play outside and have some friends. Get into a decent high school, you know? Get some tutoring.'

'Great idea. This is a high-profile job; it should help you get good gigs from now on.' He didn't glance once at the building that she couldn't take her eyes off of, not wanting to waste this opportunity to gaze at her breasts straining against the material in her top. He imagined touching them. Then he imagined squeezing them. Then he imagined cutting them.

'I thought I had heard of a program where the city bought houses. Gave you a good price, then tore them down trying to rout out the drug dealers, but I called city hall and they had never heard of it. It would just push the dealers out into

114

the suburbs anyway. Stupid idea.'

'Lots of those around.' He moved his gaze to her throat, to the pulsing tubes that swallowed liquid and pushed blood along. He imagined them broken open, disgorging their contents to the open air. Blood was blue until it hit the air, right? Or just really dark red?

'That's why I have to get my kid out of where we are now. There's a drug house next door, and she's got this bad habit of sneaking out. I can't blame her, really – what kid wants to spend her life locked inside? I know she climbs down the tree. She tries to tell us she just left for school early but somehow the door is still locked from the inside. So I can either nail her window shut or move us the hell out of Dodge.' She swallowed another mouthful of that sickly sweet stuff that pretty girls like to drink. 'Anyway, that's what I need to do. Get my life together. I'm going to be thirty next year, unfreakinbelieveable.'

'You look twenty.'

'Really?' That finally got her attention away from the window, as he figured it would. He had only a few no-fail lines, but that was one of them.

'Really.' And when her eyes drifted toward the glass, he leapt. 'You know what? Let's go over and look at it. Take the zip lift to the top floor and be king of all we survey.'

A delighted smile crossed her face, and when she drained the Martini glass she'd been merely nursing all this time he knew he had won.

He slipped an arm around her waist as they

115

crossed the street, but she giggled and knocked him away with one hip. 'I suppose you hoped I'd think that was a chivalrous gesture, protecting my delicate body from traffic.'

'Gave it a shot.' He hadn't thought any such thing, figuring that a grab at her flesh wouldn't need to be disguised as anything but exactly that. But if she wanted to pretend to be a blushing virgin, he'd play along for a while. It would be a short while.

They turned the corner of the fenced area. 'Hang on a sec,' she said, and trotted over to her car.

Was she going to jump in and escape? Had he blown his chance, startled her too much – 'Come on!'

But she didn't get in the car, merely fumbled around inside for a moment and then backed out of it, slamming the door, trotting back. He had to keep from gasping in relief. Her expression, what he could see of it in the dark, once again seemed flush with excitement and the delight of a misbehaving child. She opened the lockbox, retrieved the key, opened the gate. He kept his hands to himself and closed the swinging panel behind them, so that any passer-by would have to really look to realize the chains were undone.

Then he followed her through the benign minefield of the construction site, keeping his impulses under control until they reached the building proper. Then the sight of that tight ass in her snug jeans as she climbed up the high step of the foundation – he spread his fingers over one cheek.

116

'Stop that! Geez, what gave you the impression you could feel me up?'

He laughed again, couldn't help it. 'Gee, I don't know. Maybe the tight pants? The make-up? The fact that you were drinking alone in a bar at nearly three a.m. on a week night? Face it – everything about you gave me the impression that you *live* to be felt up by somebody. Why not me?'

In the near pitch dark her face turned ugly. 'Because I *said* not you. Just because I happen to be a living human being doesn't mean my services are at your disposal, asshole. Forget this, I'm going home.'

She turned away from him, just as she'd knocked him away while crossing the street, but she hadn't hopped in her car and driven away when she had the chance. She thought she could handle him. She still thought she could handle him.

She was wrong.

He grabbed her hair, that long silky stuff, with his left hand and punched her in the face with his right. It stunned her more than hurt her, he thought, because she didn't shut up.

'What the – what do you think you're doing?'

He punched her in the stomach.

That was when she tried to defend herself with that damn screwdriver, which she must have snagged out of her car. Thinking ahead, just in case he didn't slow down with the grab hands. Smart, he guessed, but not smart enough because Samantha Zebrowski was no Lara Croft when it came to hand to hand combat. He snatched the driver from her fingers, tossed it away, and slammed her a good one right in the eye. That took the fight out of her.

That had been right – here. Just south of the elevator pit. Where he should have walked right over it as he left earlier, but he hadn't. Because the angel/demon/child had picked it up.

Shit.

He had to find that kid.

FIFTEEN

Driving Ghost home provided an annotated tour of the city Theresa thought she knew. The eleven-year-old pointed out that the cemetery had a faded headstone that seemed to show a little boy sitting on a bench with a sailor's hat, and there were pretty gardens around the university's medical education center, and a maze of alleys behind all the fancy restaurants on East Fourth where the wait staff would take their breaks, smoke cigarettes, and explain to you what a sous chef was.

But when she walked in to her house she went upstairs without so much as a *hello* to her grandmother. Mrs Zebrowski seemed beyond caring about minor points of courtesy, however. 'I'm just glad you called, I was nearly beside myself. I'd given up worrying about her, she does it so much – shouldn't have done that. It's got to stop. Now with Sam gone, I just can't take it.'

Theresa handed the woman a small brown envelope with Samantha's cell phone, had her sign a receipt, and then sat down at the table with its vinyl tablecloth and napkin holder and box of tissues within Mrs Zebrowski's reach. The kitchen smelled of stuffed cabbage and grief. Neighbors must have stopped by – five Tupperware containers of various sizes sat on the counter and no doubt there were more in the refrigerator. It was at once clichéd and exactly what Theresa loved about human beings: their drive to nurture however possible. No one starved while in mourning. 'Can I make you a cup of tea?'

The woman snorted a laugh. 'Thank you, dear, but I've practically drunk five pots already. And eaten four muffins and who knows how many cookies. Help yourself.'

'No, thank you. I just – I'm not trying to pry, Mrs Zebrowski, but what did happen to Ghost's father? Is he deceased?'

The woman leaned one elbow on the table and said without rancor, 'I don't have any idea.'

'She showed me his picture, told me he was a soldier and killed in a training exercise, but—'

'That wasn't her father.'

Theresa waited.

The old woman rubbed her forehead with one hand, glanced toward the staircase, and then leaned forward. 'I don't have any idea who Ghost's father is. Samantha told Ghost that boy in the picture was her father, except that picture was taken when Samantha was sixteen. The boy, Nathan, *did* go and join the army and *did* get killed, but that happened at least a full year before Ghost came along. Sam loved that kid, too – Nathan. I think losing him, after losing her father –' now the woman rubbed both temples – 'is why my girl turned so wild. Little after eighteen she got pregnant and wouldn't tell me a single thing about who did it. I guess she was ashamed of herself. Maybe ashamed of him, I don't know. Or maybe she thought I'd go after him, make her get married. And he must have been all right with getting off scot free because no man ever came around here looking to help out, that's for sure.'

'So she let Ghost think that Nathan was her father.'

'He must have made a much prettier story than the real guy. She put his name on the birth certificate even though the dates would make it impossible if Ghost ever really looked it up. And Sam really loved him. She wanted Ghost to think she entered the world through love.'

'I can understand that.' Though eleven years of child support would have been of assistance. Especially now, without Sam's income ... But now it couldn't be helped. The only person who had known the man's identity had died.

Ghost was chasing a ghost.

Theresa handed the woman a piece of paper. 'This is my card. I've put my cell phone number on it, too. Call me if there's anything I can do. And please tell Ghost I said good night.'

She slipped out of the house without further

ado. She couldn't possibly tell the little girl where she was headed.

Kyle Cielac could probably commit any crime he wished without leaving evidence; he had no fingerprints. The pads of his digits were worn and pitted with only a patch of ridge detail here or there. When fingerprinted – because the construction company had done that almost at the start, wanting to be sure who they were working with – the inked ovals were pockmarked with white voids. Cement work did that. Sam had rubbed in hand lotion day and night and it hadn't helped. She hadn't had any fingerprints, either.

Good thing they found her while we could still recognize her face, Kyle thought, and his stomach gave an uncomfortable lurch.

'You OK there, pard?' the cop asked him.

'Fine.'

The cop placed his Styrofoam cup of coffee on the table's gleaming wood surface. They always met here, at his temporary office in city hall, but always after hours when the coffee had grown stale enough to grow legs and walk around by itself. 'So you had some trouble at your site today?'

'You could call it that,' Kyle said.

'She's dead,' Todd said. He had a cup in front of him as well, but hadn't touched it. 'Dead. They said she fell twenty-three floors.'

'Smush,' the cop said, and Kyle gritted his teeth.

'He killed her. She figured out how he's doing it and he killed her.'

'Todd, Kobelski is a crook. Novosek is a crook. They are stealing money by using sub-standard concrete from Decker and Stroud in the county's new jail and pocketing the difference between the cheap materials and the wad that the county is spending on this new and stunning facet of the criminal justice system. Thieves. They don't kill people.'

The lawyer said nothing. He often didn't. He didn't even seem to be listening.

'Do you know how much this project is going to cost?' Todd demanded of the cop.

'Eighty-five million, five hundred and thirty thousand. Give or take some odd change.'

'Of that price, one quarter of it is the concrete. One-quarter – over twenty-one million. One quarter of *that* is the equipment and personnel – the trucks, the troughs, my paycheck. The other three-quarters is the materials.'

'Yes.' The cop rubbed his eyes, not even pretending to look interested. He wasn't really a cop but an agent for the State of Ohio's Congressional Task Force on public corruption; Kyle thought of him as a cop because he had the good one/bad one pattern down. Problem was he fulfilled both roles himself, his temper and impatience zinging him so quickly from patronizing empathy to whip-snapping overlord that Kyle had stopped trying to keep up.

'If you could shave ten percent off the cost of the raw materials, you could pocket over one point six *million* dollars.'

'Yes.'

'So if that's not worth killing for,' Todd said,

'what is?'

A momentary silence descended upon their little group.

Kyle sipped. 'He's got a point.'

The cop, state investigator John Finney, said: 'Fine. So help me catch him. How is he faking the slump test?'

'What's that again?' the lawyer asked.

He would know if he hadn't daydreamed through the first half-hour, Kyle thought; wonder what's got him so distracted? Maybe he's not as sure as Finney about the non-lethal tendencies of career thieves. 'Every truckful of concrete is tested for consistency – both the consistency of the mixture and how wet it is, so that it is consistent between loads. A hollow funnel is filled with a sample from the truck and then overturned on a flat surface.'

'You make a sandcastle and then dump it out?'

No one had any idea how complicated, how delicately balanced, and how vitally important that sandcastle was to keeping a building upright instead of collapsing inward, crushing every single occupant in a nightmare of rock and twisted steel – 'Yes. The sample should slip more or less depending on what you want to do with it and what kind of plasticizers are used. If it's too thin, it won't be strong enough. If it's too thick, it might leave gaps and cavities that will also reduce its strength. The inspector—'

'Kobelski,' the cop interjected, 'who is supposed to be working for the state but is actually working for himself. Or rather splitting his take with the supplier, who has to be in on it.'

'—measures how much the concrete stack falls in height, then checks it against the ASTM charts to make sure it's within the acceptable range.'

'Too little slump, the finished floors will have cavities, too much, they'll be weak. Got it,' the lawyer said. 'And you see him do this and it's within the ranges. So your concrete is right but it's still wrong. How?'

'That's the question.'

'No, how do you know?'

'I've been spreading concrete since I was seventeen,' Todd told him.

The lawyer waited. Then: 'That's it? You know it's bad because you have a *feeling*?'

'No, because I work with it, touch it, spread it, see how it sticks to the trowel or doesn't. It's too thin, and I don't care what the slump test says. That building is going to look great, and then it's going to start to crack deep inside the columns and the floors where no one will see it, and then, in about five or ten years, it's going to come down.'

Finney said, 'We have to be able to prove that. Otherwise this is all academic. Can we prove Novosek? Would he have to know the concrete is bad for this to work? He's not a concrete guy.'

Todd said, 'He has to. The man built the Peterson building, for chri— And he's at Kobelski's elbow at every test. He comes up with stuff to keep us busy. No way he doesn't know.'

Kyle drained the lukewarm cup. 'I'm not so sure. He's a steel guy, barely knows slag from fly ash.'

'I believe you, Todd,' the cop said, shifting back to 'good' mode. 'That's why we need you to stay there and find our proof. Otherwise we'll have a pile of rock and twisted steel and how many dead corrections officers.'

'And inmates,' Kyle said.

'What?'

'All the inmates. They'd be killed, too, if the building collapsed. But I expect you don't care much about them, do you?'

'No,' Finney said. 'Not at all. You can, if you want; feel free to worry about those poor misguided children of Jesus all you like, and help us catch the son-of-a-bitch who's going to get them killed. Don't turn and run because some chick fell off a building.'

'Samantha.'

The cop didn't even bother to respond.

'Her name was Samantha.' Kyle felt the unbecoming flush start at his neck and work its way up until his scalp tingled. 'She first picked up a trowel on her seventh birthday. She lived with her mom and her daughter and her dad died of cancer before she got out of grade school. She worked hard and hated coffee and complained about the price of good shampoo. She was a *person.*'

'Were you doing her?' was all the cop wanted to know.

The tingle became a burning and for a moment Kyle considered leaping over the table and beating the shit out of the guy. Considered, decided not to bother. Yes, he would have gladly 'done' Samantha Zebrowski once she learned to seek more than to pick up and fling away guys who were basically a walking pedestal for their penis. Once he knew her well enough to get over her giddiness at working in a thoroughly male milieu. Once he was sure he actually wanted to do *her*, the sentient being, and not just the slim hips and that hair that hung to the middle of her back and seemed to have a life of its own, because when a woman had those attributes it got real hard to sort out your own feelings. 'No.'

'Not yet,' Todd clarified with that weird insight he could sometimes render. 'Point is, she's dead, and there's no way it was an accident.'

'Point is,' the cop said, 'you bail out now, Kobelski might get spooked and change his ways. Then he pockets his money and goes on to sabotage some other building, and you lose three months of work on this guy. I lose three *years*, but don't let that bother you.'

'Did this girl know about the concrete?' the lawyer asked. 'You said she picked up a trowel at seven. Did she notice the consistency?'

'She complained about it,' Kyle said. 'She'd agree with Todd when he first started talking about it. But nothing more, so I don't think she knew. Sam was good at finishing and edging, not mixing.' And she spent too much time focused on those walking pedestals instead of her job.

'So you have no reason to think her death had anything to do with Novosek and Kobelski.' Todd opened his mouth to protest but the lawyer pressed on: 'There could be a thousand other little intrigues going on at that job site, or she simply drank too much and decided to go look at the city lights. Don't wander around the twenty-third floor in the pitch dark and you will be perfectly safe. Help us put this guy behind bars and a lot of other people will be safe as well.'

Kyle eyed him. 'You're sure?'

'I am,' Ian Bauer said.

SIXTEEN

Frank Patrick asked himself, not for the first time, just what the hell he thought he was doing. He hadn't wanted to be up high in this open death-trap of a structure in the broad daylight. He sure didn't want to be there in the pitch dark.

'It *is* pretty,' his partner chose that moment to say. As Theresa had, Angela Sanchez stood right at the edge with nothing to steady her but one hand on a beam, as if that would keep her from falling over if she, for some reason, lost her balance. Or someone pushed her.

'Gorgeous.' Frank tried but failed to keep the tension out of his voice, and waited for his heartbeat to return to normal. This time he had not insisted on climbing the twenty-three floors, even in the cooler night-time temperature, and consented to get on to the zip lift. He had thought that somehow the wall-less elevator would not be so bad at night, that maybe in the dim lighting he could pretend it was a glass one and that there wasn't really nothing at all but a flimsy cable railing between himself and hundreds of feet of empty air. He had thought wrong. 'What do you think? Any potential witnesses?'

'There's more lighted windows than I would have expected.' Angela waved toward Eaton Center and the PNC Bank building – the idiot, she should keep both hands on that concrete column. 'But I don't see much activity. Lights might be kept on for security. This floor would be hidden to anyone on the ground until Sam got right up to the edge. Nothing was happening at the Convention Center last night. And this could have happened in the wee hours, one, two – when even the most dedicated office worker had probably gone home. No witness except our kid. What do you think of her statement?'

'She says it was a man in the dark. She can't describe his height, weight, clothing, or hair color. All were simply described as "dark". So even if she saw a man, it doesn't help us much.'

'"Even if"? You still doubt her?'

'I still have a hard time believing this kid makes a habit of roaming the city at night when her mother and grandmother have her on a pretty short leash.'

'All the more reason.'

'What if Samantha got those bruises earlier in the evening? Picks up the wrong guy, has a tussle, decides she's a horrible mother and goes home to pick up her kid and end it all. At the last minute Mom can't do it, and mercifully – or not – lets the kid witness instead of participate. Kid can't process what's happening, sees a figure in the dark.'

'It's possible,' Angela conceded. They had seen stranger things.

He turned around, headed toward the south-west corner to make it seem like he had a logical reason not to approach the spot where Samantha Zebrowski went over the edge. 'Hotels are twenty-four hours.'

She joined him, then passed again – what was it about people who liked flirting with a two-hundred foot plunge? – to gaze at the twenty-five glittering floors of the Marriott Building. The cool night breeze off the lake lifted her hair and the city lights turned her to a silhouette, framing a tight figure that the other cops still couldn't believe he wasn't tapping.

He was beginning to have a hard time with that himself.

Angela Sanchez had been his partner for three years and two months. Though she did not talk about herself often he knew everything about her, inevitable after such a long acquaintance. He had met her children on only two occasions but had a good idea of their abilities and general attitudes. He knew where Angela had grown up, that her mother still lived in the same house, that her brother had made a lot of money on a dot.com and then lost it all, and the extra-ordinarily subtle signs to announce her monthly period. He knew that her nose wrinkled when she laughed hard and that she had finally used up that bottle of Polo for Women that some ex-boyfriend had given her for Christmas four years ago. He had learned all this in the last three years and two months. He had spent the last two years and nine months of that period telling himself that he was not going to fall for a partner.

Not even if she were beautiful, intelligent, kind, unattached and managed to not be annoying in any significant way. In short, the perfect woman. Perfect for anyone except him. Falling for his partner would not only be professionally inadvisable – not when he planned to take the sergeant's exam the following month – but pathetically cliché and he was not going to do it. Period. His heart might seek but he would not let it find.

Unfortunately, every day it got harder to believe that. Especially at times like this, when her tailored white blouse skimmed over her breasts and down her abdomen and her sleek black hair brushed her shoulder blades as she turned to look at him with that slight smile, the one that made it seem they shared a private joke. And here they were in the dark, with the lights of the city spread before them.

This could have been the night he gave it up. Had they been alone.

'Are you done here?' Chris Novosek asked.

The guy had to be exhausted, Frank knew, but it had been a long day for everyone else, as well as a very short one for Samantha Zebrowski. So he shuffled the question off to his cousin. After all, this little nocturnal jaunt had been her idea. 'Theresa?'

She moved across the interior of the floor, almost invisible in the dark except for the weak beams of a dying flashlight. Unless the killer had carried a lantern along with him, Frank thought, no potential witness would have been able to see Samantha Zebrowski's struggle for life. Even if the Marriott or the PNC Bank buildings were right next door, and certainly not from well over five hundred feet away. They were wasting their time.

Theresa said, gesturing with the tiny Maglite, 'I'd been hoping to see a homeless guy who camps here every night, or a group of friends who makes a habit of leaving the Tavern or maybe the Crown Plaza at a late hour. But it's pretty quiet down here. One question – what's this big hole in the floor? Elevator shaft?'

'Yep,' the project manager answered.

'Pretty big elevator.'

'There will be three passenger elevators plus room for the counterweights, and more in the south bank. Elevators are always a pain ... They take up a lot of space, but the more floors a building has, the more people, so the more elevators. Determining the elevator to floor ratio is one of the hardest parts about planning. Elevators are expensive, so clients always want to keep to the bare minimum and then the second the place is finished the tenants will already be crying about how the elevators take forever and aren't big enough.'

'There's no one perfect balance,' Theresa muttered.

'That's why no two buildings are exactly the same,' Novosek said. 'We keep searching for the perfect design. Haven't found it yet.'

'Still, I don't think these tenants will complain

131

about much.'

'The staff will.'

'What about the elevator we rode up on? Will that be a glass one?'

'The zip lift?' Novosek chuckled to himself as if that were the funniest thing he'd heard in a month. 'No, that's just for construction. It will be disassembled once all the floors are enclosed.'

Theresa went to join Angela at the western edge of the floor, encouraging Frank's partner to move to the opening.

'Hey!' Frank couldn't help calling out. 'At least hang on to the girder.'

'Beam,' Novosek corrected.

'What?'

'The vertical stacks are beams, the horizontal ones are girders.'

Theresa turned from the western view. 'And ironworkers connect the two?'

'They weld the beams together and the girders to the beams, yes.'

'No rivets?'

'Rivets haven't been used since before I was born.'

'And that's what Jack does?'

She was keeping him busy, Frank realized, keeping the project manager occupied so that he and Angela could look around, do their jobs. Investigate. Problem was, even as he drew as close as he dared to Angela, he still couldn't see anything to investigate except the stack of steel beams on the floor behind them, a lone man talking on a cell phone as he meandered up

Rockwell, and the fact that Chris Novosek knew an awful lot of prison lingo for a guy who was only building one. He also seemed to have no problem moving around the site in the pitch dark.

'Crazy Jack? Yeah.'

'He's crazy?'

'Ironworkers are all crazy. Who else is going to walk along an I-beam four hundred feet above the ground? They have a fall harness, but let me tell you something – they'd do it even without a harness. Most of them are descendants of guys who did, back before OSHA. Especially Jack.'

'Why especially Jack?'

'His father died doing exactly that – working without a harness. Fell twenty-eight floors.'

'Wow,' was all Theresa could come up with, apparently. 'And he went into the same line of work?'

'He's not the only one here who's lost someone to the job. Maybe we're all crazy.'

Frank watched the guy on Rockwell reach the security fence along the sidewalk and disappear from view, hoping Theresa had run down, but no such luck. 'What holds up the floors?'

'A cage of rebar and metal mesh spans the girders. That's filled with reinforced concrete.'

'So the beams hold up the building and the girders hold up the floors. What about the walls?'

Novosek moved to the edge with the women, of course, chatting as if they were one foot off the ground instead of hundreds. 'The cladding? Walls just close in the interior. They aren't particularly important to the structure, which is why you have walls of glass if you want. It doesn't make the building any less sturdy.'

Theresa said, 'I see the floor has been edged and grooved. So Samantha would have been done working on this floor?'

'Yes.'

'Can you think of any reason for her to come to this floor in particular?'

He shook his head, gaze turned toward the Terminal Tower and its well-lit peak. 'Not a one.'

'What's that sound?' she asked.

All four people stopped and listened to a soft padding sound that drifted up from below. Frank checked Rockwell again but cell phone guy had not reappeared at the other end of the site. Now he heard a slight clink as well.

Novosek shrugged. 'The wrappings on three or four, probably. We've started enclosing the lower floors so that the interior guys can start work, get going with the plumbing, heating ducts, metal bars on the holding cells.'

'But you're not finished going up yet, are you?'

'Nope. We have five more floors to add. Be forty-one altogether when it's done. Why we couldn't stop at forty and have a nice even number, don't ask me. Forty-one.' This seemed to irritate him almost as much as Samantha Zebrowski's death, but then it *had* been a long day. 'Once the exterior walls go up they're wrapped in aluminum paper, and sometimes the wind catches it and rips it out. Then drywallers hang plastic to keep the dust out of everyone else's spaces while they sand. Ducts have chains and other braces on them and the wind can catch them too. Wind gets to be a bigger problem the higher you go, especially if you're working with anything more lightweight than a hammer. One unexpected gust and your pail or even your hard hat can go over the edge and bean some passer-by, and then the whole project gets sued ... Anyway, don't let little noises scare you. New buildings can make as much noise as old buildings.'

All the same, Frank thought, and tried to listen beyond their voices as his cousin went on.

'But you haven't enclosed the first two floors, just the next three?'

'Lot more steel has to go in there yet, for the sally port and all. Prisoner transport is apparently the most vulnerable area. And the third floor is all medical – even a drug testing lab – and four will be the cafeteria, so there will be ovens, distilled water lines, garbage disposals, counters with outlets out the wazoo, fume hoods. Those two floors will take more work than the rest of the building put together, so we close them in ay-sap.'

Theresa quieted, finally run out of questions.

Frank said, 'I'm going down. There was a guy on the street out there who seems to have disappeared.' He even forced himself back on to that hellish moving platform that would plummet them to the ground.

His cousin hung on to the project manager again.

Angela did not hang on to him.

135

SEVENTEEN

Ghost did not leave the house that night. Her grandmother pleaded with her, bursting into tears – which Nana rarely did, outside something drastic like her daughter dying – and making Ghost feel guilty for thinking about it since Nana couldn't come upstairs to stop her or even check on her. So she promised, pinkie swear, and she couldn't go back on that.

But that didn't mean she couldn't put the time to good use.

She went into her mother's bedroom, at first held up at the doorway by a wave of grief and guilt. She shouldn't be poking through her mother's things, not that her mother had ever minded Ghost coming into her room. When she was a little kid she used to pull her mother's clothes off the hangers to play dress-up, sure that she would look exactly like the beautiful woman one day. Her mother would patiently drag her vanity chair into the closet so that Ghost could hang all the items back up again, waiting for her daughter to decide the work wasn't worth the fun. It took more than a couple of sessions.

Too old for that now, and her pale skin, boring brown hair and shapeless body didn't resemble her mother in any way. She must take after her father. She checked his picture on the mirror again, the stiff smile, blond hair sticking straight up in the style of the time, a loud shirt threatening to come untucked from dress slacks that looked too big. The beginnings of a dimple in one cheek. He shouldn't be too hard to recognize if she saw him. When she saw him.

She also needed to find the shadow man.

Her father could help her. He's the only person who could, who would – he must have loved her mother once. She really needed him right now, which was why it would be the perfect time for him to reappear.

But of course he might really be dead like Nana said and like Mom usually said. Then she might really be on her own, except for Nana and that nice lady Theresa. Theresa was also looking for the shadow man and she had all those microscopes and technology and computers and stuff so she would be able to do it. Ghost knew that from watching TV, when she could coax the remote away from Nana and her reality shows.

So she had better stick close to Theresa. Theresa would find the shadow man and tell the cops and they would come and arrest him and tie him up and put him in a room with bars, where he would never ever get out. Maybe they'd even shoot him. That would be all right with Ghost.

But just in case, she should look for clues on her own, too. So she did a slow pirouette in her mother's bedroom to see what she could see.

The police had brought back her car and handed Nana a brown paper bag with her mother's purse and keys and other things from the car that they had examined. Nana hadn't even looked inside, just asked Ghost to take it upstairs. Now she dumped it out on the floor. Keys – keys. No clue there. A box of cigarettes which had some black powdery stuff all over it. It came off on Ghost's fingers and she wiped them on her shirt. Some papers with the name of the car and the insurance company and other boring stuff like that. Ghost turned to the purse. Her mother had bought it at Payless and loved the big slouchy thing even though the vinyl had worn off in spots. Inside she found two more boxes of cigarettes, two ropes of plastic beads (red and yellow), pieces of gum and a vial of hand sanitizer, four different lip glosses and one ChapStick, two bottles of perfume and one powder compact as well as mascara and a slowly leaking bottle of foundation, which meant Ghost had to wipe her fingers on her shirt again. Her mother's wallet, which held twenty-two dollars and fifteen cents, her driver's license, other plastic cards and a bunch of worn business cards. Some were restaurants, or grilles, or had people's names on them. These were also covered in the black powdery stuff. None sounded familiar to Ghost. She put aside the money to give to Nana and separated out all the restaurant and bar cards. She made a third pile with the lip glosses, which she might want to use some day. Waste not, want not, Nana always said.

That just left her mother's cell phone. Ghost ripped open the Manila envelope and let it slide out. She didn't have a phone of her own but navigated the device with the same facility as any average American child. The last call made came to their house, probably Mom calling Nana about some little thing, which she did about a million times a day. Two prior calls to numbers Ghost didn't recognize, and one before that to a cousin in Pennsylvania. Incoming calls didn't help, either. The last one had been at 12:15 p.m. from a local number and lasted three minutes. Ghost picked up the phone and punched in the number and got 'Dr Bashir's answering service'. She hung up. Of the other two numbers, one didn't answer and the other was the Cleveland Public Library. Ghost gave up on the phone numbers and paged through the rest of the menu.

The last photo taken featured Ghost, and she knew that had been several weeks prior when she spent dinner making funny faces, which amused her mother and annoyed her grandmother. Samantha's text messages on the previous day had all been to and from a childhood friend who had moved to Detroit and centered on the friend's impatience with her husband. Some of the shorthand mystified Ghost but didn't seem relevant to what had happened that morning. Her mother's last few texts did, however. The friend had apparently gotten bored with electronically bashing her spouse and asked: *'Where R U?'*

Samantha responded. *'Tavern of crse. Slim pickins!'*

The friend: *'No1 good?'*

Sam: *'Losers cap L!'*

Friend: *'Go home.'*

Sam: *'Goin 2. Love U.'*

139

Friend: *'Bye.'* The last text had come at 2:28 that morning.

'What are you doing up there?' Nana shouted from below, startling Ghost's entire body into a spasm from head to toe.

She recovered enough to shout, 'Nothing!'

No further inquiry. Nana just wanted to make sure she hadn't snuck out.

So her mother had been in a tavern a few hours before she died. Ghost knew what a tavern was, it was a bar. Her mother liked bars. Nana didn't. Nana would always say a bar wasn't a place where a young lady should be by herself, and Mom would always respond that she went with a bunch of friends and they had fun. Ghost couldn't wait to be old enough to go to bars.

She went into her room to store the lip glosses in her pink vinyl jewelry box and got one of her school notebooks and a pen to write down the unidentified numbers. School would be letting out in two weeks and they would be having tests and things, but she couldn't think about that now. She didn't care much about school in general and wondered if she even had to go now that she didn't have a mother. She probably did. Nana would make her.

But not tomorrow. Tomorrow she needed to retrace her mother's footsteps. She plucked the picture of her mother with her two friends off the vanity mirror. She could show it to people and ask them if they'd seen her the day before. They did that on TV all the time too and always found out something important. After a moment's thought, she took the one of her father as well,

140

sliding them both carefully into her back pocket.

After that she poked through her mother's laundry, even though the items were a day or two old. She didn't find anything but some cellophane from a cigarette wrapper in a pair of jeans and a gum wrapper in a shirt. Nana always used to yell about her mother's habit of leaving such debris in her clothing. 'Disintegrates in the wash and gets all over, or winds up a lump of melted plastic in the dryer.' And her mother would laugh. It occurred to Ghost that she would never hear her mother laugh again and suddenly she was crying, crying in great gasping sobs that choked her until she stopped just long enough to get a breath and start again. Almost more of screams than sobs, animal noises that echoed in her head long after she had fallen into an exhausted sleep, curled up among her mother's dirty clothes at the bottom of her closet.

EIGHTEEN

When they reached the bottom, Frank told Novosek to take Theresa up one floor and wait there. Predictably, his cousin began to argue but Novosek seemed content, either to play her protector or to stay out of the cop stuff, and the lift ascended before Theresa could exit.

With a nod, Frank and Angela separated. She went outside into the relatively well-lit yard, and he moved through the pitch that was the building's interior.

Anyone on the premises would have heard the lift mechanism, of course, but still he tried to move as quietly as possible. He kept his weapon holstered and instead took out his unlit flashlight. Couldn't see a thing, but thought he heard someone. A scrape, a footstep, a soft clank.

He moved toward the sound, promptly grinding one toe into a five-gallon bucket. Only the distant openings to the outside were visible; the entire interior was one big ball of night.

He moved around an encircled area in the center – the bottom of the elevator shaft, he guessed – and caught a flicker of movement. Despite every box, barrel, pipe and beam in the place trying to trip him, he moved closer. The guy was in the south-east quadrant of the first floor, bouncing around with something shiny and accompanied by a steady sound Frank recognized but couldn't place.

Three more steps.

Almost like water running through a pipe, or—

The man crouched, the sound came, he straightened again.

Spray paint.

Frank unclipped his weapon but did not remove it, right hand resting on the butt. With his left he raised the flashlight and flicked it on. 'POLICE! DON'T MOVE!'

The guy didn't listen. In one smooth twist he threw the metal object at Frank and dashed for the south edge.

Frank tried to dash, stumbled over something,

regained his balance, shouted again, picked up some speed and tripped over something large and heavy. Couldn't recover, went down hard on his left shoulder, hoping he wouldn't wind up speared on a piece of rebar or anything else...

'STOP!' he heard Angela shout, but he was too busy turning his face to avoid getting a small cylinder in the eye, and still getting a large object to the kidney. Then he was up and moving again, part of his mind wondering how these workers ever got anything done with all this crap in the way. The man's silhouette stood out clearly against the outside light, finally coming to a stop and raising his arms. It took all the self-control Frank had not to draw down on him, but felt fairly sure that a paint can versus a Glock 40 would not be considered comparable force. Besides, Angela *had* drawn on the guy, and the street lights glinting along the length of her barrel now provided more than enough incentive for immobility. The man stayed completely still – except for his mouth.

'Jeez, guns? Don't you think that's a bit of an overreaction?'

Frank pulled back one of his hands for a cuff, and then the other. 'She saw her partner go down,' he said in what he considered a reasonable tone. 'You're lucky you don't have three to the center mass right now.'

'Yeah, yeah.'

'Anybody else here with you? Tell me straight, or I'll turn my trigger-happy partner loose and whatever happens will be on your head.'

'No. Just me.'

Frank believed him only because he had seen him come in, but then, it was a big site. He'd leave the gun unclipped for now. He marched the guy out to Angela, then went back in to retrieve the paint can, picking it up with two fingers on the edge. His cousin had drilled proper techniques for the preservation of fingerprints into everyone she knew.

Then he scouted the area with the flashlight, listening to Angela collect the guy's vitals: *Name*, Scott Crain. *DOB*: 7/30/84. *Address*—

'Little old to be tagging buildings, aren't you?' Frank called, having found the man's handiwork. 'We Ire Not Dogs. What does that mean?'

'We *Are* Not Dogs.'

'It says Ire.'

'It's dark in there,' Crain said with a pout. 'Do you know what they're going to do in this building? Keep people in cages—'

'It's a *jail*,' Frank heard Angela say in disbelief as he returned to the lift to give Novosek and Theresa the all-clear. Theresa went off to get her camera to photograph the damage and Novosek, without comment, went with her. Frank wondered how foolish it might be to let him, technically a suspect in Sam's murder, serve as Theresa's escort, but at the moment Crain and his allies were the more unknown threat, and Novosek would hardly attack one of the investigating parties while in proximity to other investigating parties.

Still, he didn't like it, watching his cousin's body disappear through the gate in the fence. He didn't like anything about this whole case.

He returned just as Angela asked their prisoner if he knew Samantha Zebrowski. After a pause that lasted one half-second too long, he said no. Angela showed him the picture taken from the dead girl's photo ID.

'I can tell you one thing,' Scott Crain said.

'And that is?'

'She won't be the last.'

He drove past the house, slowly. It hadn't been hard to get the address from the records. All dark, no sign of the kid, although he hadn't really expected her to be waiting for him on the porch holding a sign reading: *I'm the one who saw you. Come and silence me or you'll go to jail forever and ever.*

That's if the kid even existed. He still couldn't be sure she hadn't been some sort of an angel, Samantha's soul incarnate or a truer form of the hopeless demon that bitch had actually been.

Could he really do that? Kill a child? He didn't have anything against little kids, and she might be all right, might grow up to be an easy-going sort and not a frickin' tease like her mother. Though it wouldn't be physically hard: just bash her in the head or strangle her. He could probably choke her with one hand, that tiny little neck.

Or he could take her up the building? Go even higher this time, all the way to the top? Toss her down to the same spot as her mother. The bones would scatter for twenty feet, easy.

Then what kind of angel would come to weep for her? An even smaller one? If she *had* represented Samantha, who would embody the child's soul...? Trying to picture even the question much less the answer made his head swim. But the image of the girl falling backward from the top of the building, plunging into the dark night air, filled his brain with a growing brightness that eventually blinded him, so that he had to step on the brakes to avoid hitting some idiot who stepped out into the street.

He took a better look at his surroundings. People came and went from the drug house next door, but those kind of people would not interfere unless he threatened their trade. The house across the street and slightly south of the kid's place had grass two feet high, three broken windows, and not a trace of internal illumination. Vacant.

Perfect.

He pulled into the drive and up next to the house. Then he got out, locking the vehicle securely, and waited for some response from the place.

Nothing. Perfect again.

It might even be a good place to hide the body, should he choose to go that route. Throwing the girl from the building would be delightful but possibly – what, impractical? Too showy. The cops would go crazy. But if she simply disappeared, well, any one of a million things could have happened. She might have run away. She might have run into the wrong wino during one of her walkabouts. Sam would be written off as a suicide and he'd be free to soar on to his next adventure.

But dropping her over the side of the forty-first floor...

As usual, his romantic side warred with the sensible half. The eternal struggle. Besides, would she really be able to identify him? Would anyone even listen to her? She was just a kid.

It occurred to him that the cops hadn't been walking around with any composite sketches, so obviously she hadn't been able to describe him too well.

He pushed open the gate in the rickety fence; it made no noise, the hinges well-oiled. Ah, my little Ghost. You've made things so easy for me. We're more alike than you might think.

Climbing up the steps to the porch took a lot of the perk out of his attitude, however. For one thing, the steps creaked. For another, the door seemed nowhere near as rickety as the fence, and was locked. He pulled out his knife, tried to fit it into the keyhole and turn. He could do this without making any noise but it also didn't open the door.

Stumped. Whatever else he might be, he had never been a thief. He had no idea how to break into an apparently secure household.

Of course, what self-respecting thief goes in the front door anyway?

He got back down from the porch without alerting the media by stepping on the furthest side of each riser where it connected to the frame. Then he circled the house. No one raised a hue and cry. Not a sound from the drug house, though a glowing dot on the back porch in-dicated a cigarette-smoking sentry. A dog rustled in a yard a few houses over, but it merely whimpered a bit. People in this neighborhood had been trained to mind their own business.

The basement windows were glass block. No love there.

The back door proved as sturdy as the front. He could break one of the panes and open it, but that would alert the grandma and maybe the kid. He wasn't even sure what he planned to do once he got inside and so couldn't decide on a blitz attack or a more stealthy approach.

Then he circled into the north side of the yard, a grassy area about eight feet wide, with a tree. A huge tree with one huge limb that led right on to the half-roof outside the second floor. He had to back all the way up to the neighbor's fence to see it, but the north wall had two windows on the second floor. One of them had been left open. Only an inch or two, but open.

And now he knew why the kid oiled the gate but didn't care that the steps squeaked.

Damn, kid. You really *did* make it easy for me.

Thank you, my little angel, my little demon.

NINETEEN

Theresa called her daughter on the way home, using the voice calling feature on her cell phone so as not to endanger those driving in the other lanes of I-71 as she squinted at tiny digits on the keypad. The phone felt cooperative that night and only made her repeat the name twice. 'Call Rachael. Call Rach-ael.'

Rachael's roommate answered, a sweet girl from Maple Heights who was thinking about pre-med. The prior month she'd been thinking about pre-law, and before the Christmas break, elementary education. The phone must have been moved to her desk as Rachael herself never answered any more, and now, though Kia promised to hand the phone 'right over', she took an inordinate amount of time to move six feet across the room to pick up the receiver. 'Hello.'

The conversation didn't pick up much from there.

Her nineteen-year-old child responded in civil monosyllables, asked how her mother's day had been and courteously listened to a brief description of the construction site. She chuckled dutifully at the description of 'uncle' Frank on the zip lift. With more detailed questioning, Rachael reported that she was fine, healthy, and if she sounded a bit morose it must be due to a history test she had looming at the end of the week. She hung in, letting Theresa decide to end the phone call after ten minutes and put them both out of this unspoken mutual misery.

Theresa didn't tell her how many hours she had spent with a now-orphaned girl, that it had been the kind of workday that made her crave the sound of her daughter's voice, made re-establishing her connections in this world a necessity more vital than food or light. She simply snapped her phone shut.

Her daughter was not angry with her – Rachael never had any problem expressing anger. Nor did she sound depressed; at least, not the sort of occasional depression that touched all teenage girls, with heavy sighs and ominous predictions of a bereft future. She didn't sound evasive or guilty or hurt. But clearly she had something on her mind, and equally clearly she did not want to tell Theresa about it. And Theresa didn't know what to do except follow the parenting maxims: give her space, but leave the lines of communication open. Let her know she can come to you whenever necessary.

Rachael *did* know that, didn't she?

It had been a less than satisfactory evening all around. Scott Crain, urban activist, had explained his cryptic comment by telling Frank and Angela that he had met Samantha Zebrowski at House of Blues, recognized her from the work site, and converted her to their cause. Or at least begun to convert her. It sounded as if she had been converted only so long as he bought the rounds, but of course a psychic autopsy could not be performed without a lot more information so at present no one knew what Samantha's true feelings had been. That had been his only inter-action with the dead woman and none of his cohorts had met her, so far as he knew, and he refused to reveal their names. Not that that mattered, Frank confided to Theresa, because the group had to have a permit to demonstrate at the site. The members of PETI – People for the Ethical Treatment of Inmates – would be listed on their permit application at city hall. Theresa remembered the flyer in Samantha's bedroom and made a mental note to tell Frank about it.

Just before her cousin had guided Scott Crain into the back seat of their police car, he had turned to Theresa, the slanting orange light from the overhead tungsten street lamp giving his eyes a demonic glow.

'Them, I can see. But you're a scientist, sup-posed to be searching for the truth. How can you be a party to this assault on human decency?'

Too surprised to respond, she watched Frank push him into place before she could point out how her part in a murder investigation had noth-ing whatever to do with the social theory sur-rounding the prison design. It wouldn't have mattered anyway. Crain had the flush of a fanatic, and even eminently logical reasons would be only excuses in his mind.

The phone rang again, and Theresa snapped it up lest it be her daughter on the other end, having decided to change tactics and spill.

Alas, the voice was distinctly masculine.

151

'Theresa? I'm sorry to bother you after hours. Your switchboard gave me your phone number. I hope that's all right.'

Ian Bauer. 'Sure,' she said, though the deskmen on night duty had been instructed over and over not to give out people's cell phone numbers, and over and over they thought it terribly funny to do so anyway.

'I just wanted to find out if you got the tox results back yet, and if there had been any surprises at the autopsy.'

'You watch too much TV, counselor.'

He laughed, low and smooth. Without his unfortunate face to distract a person, she realized that he had a lovely voice, deep and mellifluous. It rolled over her like a warm but mysterious fog, strange and new and somehow enticing.

Whoa. Where did *that* come from?

'I know, don't tell me. Lab tests aren't ready by the next commercial break and real CSIs turn the lights on. Anything at the autopsy?'

'Besides a lot of broken bones? No. She was otherwise healthy, not pregnant, and her last meal probably included tortilla chips.'

'Hmm.' He pondered that longer than she expected, then said, 'Tavern on the Mall is right there. They have a taco salad.'

'Did you just run through the menu in your head?'

'It's on my way home. I'm a bachelor and they have half-price appetizers during happy hour, so yeah, I have a file drawer in my head just for menus. But there's plenty of other places she could have gone – Moriarty's, 1890 ... though

152

that would probably be a higher price range than she'd want...'

'She had her car with her, so she could have eaten in Shaker Heights, Lakewood, or at home for all we know. I guess it just doesn't make sense to me that she'd stop by her work site if it were out of her way.'

'Lord knows I never do. Much. But what I also called to tell you is that Samantha Zebrowski had no criminal record beyond some speeding tickets and one DUI last summer that was eventually dropped.'

'Yeah, Frank told me that.'

After a brief pause he went on. 'Also that the job site itself has been largely accident-free. The most serious injury before today required only seven stitches and some antibiotic ointment. The worksite, however, has a lot of enemies. Public meetings regarding the school administration building got hot enough to call in extra security as the history buffs and the "we need jobs" camp butted heads. The county execs received several death threats – not that that's anything new in the world of local politics – and one council member came within a hair's breadth of quitting but, sadly, didn't. Then there's a group called PETI – not PETA, PETI—'

'I'm aware.' She told him of her evening's adventure at the dark construction site.

Again, a longer silence than she would have expected. Then he said, 'I wouldn't be too quick to dismiss them. Two years ago Scott Crain started a group to protest building a casino on Whiskey Island. They went so far as to threaten the developer's family, including his children. They also sent a note to the financier promising an attack on his person.'

'With spray paint?'

'With dynamite. His car exploded outside his office in Lakewood. It barely totaled the car and didn't harm anyone, but if he'd been inside he'd now have years of plastic surgery to pay off. Crain's group did not claim responsibility but neither did anyone else. Friend of mine prosecuted the case but didn't get a conviction.'

'So if a stack of I-beams had been blown up, we might want to look at them. But would Scott Crain throw a young girl off a building? Especially since – here's the rest of the story – he claims to have met her at House of Blues and shown her the light. He says his final cryptic comment meant that PETI would convert all the construction workers, as well as the rest of the city, to their viewpoint.'

'Do you believe him?'

'Don't know. She did have that city hall phone number in her purse. She could have been checking out his credentials.' Theresa took the Southpark mall exit off of 71. 'My best guess is still that Samantha Zebrowski went there for love and found anger. From the condition of her car, parked in its usual spot, I have to believe she went there of her own free will. She was the one who must have known how to get in. She planned to impress the wrong kind of date, and her plan backfired.' She braked at the utterly-impossible-to-get-through-without-stopping light at Howe. 'Unless the person she fought with also

154

worked at the job site. That would open up a whole new list of reasons for her to be there other than looking for love in all the wrong places.'

'Aren't we all?' She sighed, and when an awkward silence ensued she prompted: 'What other reasons?'

'Theft. Corporate espionage. Maybe Crain told the truth and she was scouting out opportunities for sabotage. Or she and a co-worker or -workers were up to something, and there was a falling out.'

'Then where does her daughter fit in?'

'I have no idea.' Ian Bauer remained silent for a few moments as Theresa pulled into her driveway. Then he said, 'OK, but one third possibility before I get off the phone and let you enjoy what's left of your evening. Maybe Samantha Zebrowski didn't intend to meet anyone, simply went out for a bite, drove past her workplace and was struck by a sudden desire to see the city lights from twenty-three floors up. Would someone who sweated at that site all day really want to do that?'

'I would,' Theresa said.

'Me too. OK, so she slips through the gate, somehow has her daughter in tow as well. Then she comes *upon* a co-worker who's engaged in theft, or sabotage, or corporate espionage.'

'And they have to make sure she doesn't tell anyone.'

'But that still leaves the kid. It's just a possibility.' She heard him exhale in a sigh. 'One of many.'

'Maybe we should ask Chris Novosek if he's had any signs of an enemy in his midst.' She turned off her car but stayed in her seat, listening to Ian Bauer's voice in the darkness.

'Speaking of Novosek, that's what else I found out.' He didn't wait for her to ask, 'What?' which she appreciated. 'I checked his record too. One juvie charge, four parking tickets, and three civil suits pending, all three relating to previous building projects.'

'Safety violations?'

She could hear him shaking his head. 'Sexual harassment. All three suits brought by female construction workers on his job sites. I guess our head foreman isn't quite as egalitarian as he likes to let on.'

TWENTY

It had been a number of years since he climbed a tree, but he shimmied up the branch like a squirrel on his way to a really big nut. It groaned and scraped against the roof to remind him that he weighed considerably more than an eleven-year-old girl. Then it snapped up when he step-ped off it on to the shingles, shaking like a devil and causing the tree to release a bunch of the helicopter-like seeds to rain down on him, land-ing on the roof like an impromptu hailstorm. Then when that wave of sound managed not to wake anyone inside (that he could tell) he took some cautious steps forward and slid on those same seeds, knocking one knee into the shingles with a thud that seemed to reverberate through the structure.

Damn, he thought in a rare moment of self-doubt. I suck at this.

He made it to the window as quietly as he could and stayed there for a while, peering through the window. The tree also served as cover, hiding him from anyone who might pass by on the street as well as blocking the light from the pole further up which would have reflected off the glass. As it was he could see into the room well enough to know that it must be the kid's room. A decorated mirror over a sagging set of drawers and stuffed animals on the bed. Though that didn't mean it couldn't be Sam's room. Lots of grown-up girls still kept stuffed animals on their beds. Which told you everything you needed to know about women, really.

He put one hand under the window frame and pushed. It slid upward without a sound.

Good job, kid.

He waited for the night air to flow into the room, for the angel/demon girl to stick her head up from the stuffed animals and shriek like a banshee. Then he waited some more.

Nothing.

He pulled himself through the window, the sound of his pants on the asphalt shingles ringing in the ears. But no cry ensued. One by one he put his feet on the floor. No sound from the rest of the house, and the girl hadn't screamed

157

because there was no girl in the bed. He checked the floor next to it, even crossed to the closet. Nothing.

Unless she had heard him coming. A kid might not do the sensible thing, which would be to call 911 or at least run and wake up her grandmother. She might do the kid thing and hide under her bed.

He crouched down, flipped up the edge of the quilt.

Darker than blindness in that storage space. If he intended to make a habit of this he needed to start carrying a mini flashlight. But if she hid there she managed not to either scream, twitch or breathe, and he didn't think an eleven-year-old would have that kind of self-control. He abandoned the bedroom and went out into the hall.

The second window on the north side let in just enough light to guide him past the bathroom – empty, as well as he could determine – to the other bedroom. This one must be Sam's – what looked like a purse on the vanity, high heels and jeans strewn about, and the odor of stale cigarettes in the air. He took a few steps into the room, checked that bed, both sides of it and underneath – no kid, no grandma.

He went to the top of the stairs, paused. What was he doing here again? If he could have made off with the kid, snapped her neck and then carried her across the street to that empty house, that would help matters. But if he got the grandma involved too, then what would he do?

He should just leave. Go out the way he came

in, and cut his losses while still ahead.

His foot found the top step as if it had floated there, drifting along on a draft of fate.

This isn't smart, he warned himself, but his feet kept finding more steps. They also seemed to find every creak and groan in the wood of those steps as he waited for a light to flick on, for a little girl's cry or the reedy voice of an old lady to say, 'Who are you?' And yet he didn't stop.

The ground floor had more ambient light, what with two large front windows and glowing standby lights from the television, the stereo, the answering machine and the coffee maker. How had thieves ever accomplished anything without standby lights?

The living room occupied the front half of the house, which wasn't saying much. It barely had room for a couch, chair, coffee table and TV stand. A bathroom had been tucked under the stairs and the back of the house held a kitchen and another room. Hanging curtains closed it off from both the kitchen and the living room. He crept up to the gap in the middle.

Nothing too exciting, just the grandma snoring away underneath a triangle dangling over her head. Maybe the kid was in there with her, somewhere under the comforter, who knew. He could take care of both of them, the kitchen must have a ready supply of weapons, but knifing grandma in her bed would be, again, showy. He should probably avoid showy. But it would be easy then, to grab the kid and go. No, if you're going to be showy with the grandma then you might as well do the kid right here.

He debated. The old woman snorted, shifted slightly, snored some more.

As he thought, his gaze fell on the coffee table, and suddenly he remembered the other reason he had come into the house. Under the dark blotches of coffee cups and magazines, the kid's backpack sat propped against one leg.

He promptly forgot about killing the grandma and snatched it up. It might not be the same one, of course, but he felt sure it must be. How many backpacks would the little bitch have, and surely Samantha and the grandma didn't use one. To have it sitting there ready to catch his eye just as he pondered killing Mrs Zebrowski, that had to be a sign. He had been meant to find it, and now that he had he should go. He must have missed the kid; she had already escaped this little palace and taken to the streets. Just like her mother. Going to get hurt, doing that.

He decided to leave via the back door, recalling from his childhood how climbing down a tree had been nothing at all like climbing up it. It had three dead bolts and a knob lock, and he turned these quietly and stealthily. The door scraped against the jamb as he opened it, but he had already figured the grandma for half-deaf and didn't worry about it.

Then he heard a sound from the second floor.

TWENTY-ONE

When Theresa arrived at the construction site at 6:33 the following morning, the sun had just peeked over the horizon, its beams blocked by low, gray clouds so that the site seemed to glow in a sort of unholy dusk.

Frank and Chris Novosek and a stranger waited for her at the edge of the ground floor, wearing identical and grim expressions. She gave Novosek a fresh once-over in light of what Ian Bauer had told her, but if he harbored any lecherous feelings they had been well pushed aside by the morning's events. His face spoke only of pain and deep worry.

The new guy had a few extra pounds on his 5' 10" frame, a trimmed salt-and-pepper beard and a hard hat. He wore a white shirt and tie with his black jeans and a windbreaker he obviously didn't need, since sweat dampened his brow.

Unlike the previous day, no noise existed at the site, no attempt to continue with work as usual. Silence surrounded them instead of men in hard hats. The only sounds – voices, the squeal of tires – came over the fence from another world.

'What's going on?' she asked in lieu of greeting.

Frank said only, 'This way,' and headed into

the interior.

Chris Novosek put a hand on her elbow to help her up the high step on to the foundation, since she carried a camera bag, a fingerprint kit and the small suitcase they used as a basic crime-scene kit. It added about twenty five pounds to her total weight. Concrete dust and other dirt crunched under her shoes.

'This is State Inspector Kobelski,' Novosek told her, adding: 'It's bad. Almost worse than Sam.'

She didn't ask him to explain, preferring to see the body with an open mind. But in another moment she knew exactly what he meant.

In the center of the building sat the bottom of the open shaft that would become the elevator bank. It appeared to measure, to Theresa's un-practiced eye, about thirty feet by fifteen, and at this point consisted of nothing but extra vertical beams with a central empty space plus a sparse collection of rebar sticking up from the base like punji sticks. And speared atop these sticks stretched the body of a man.

He wore worn jeans and a plaid flannel shirt, now punctured in three places. Feet to the north, head to the south. One of the iron rods had gone through his neck and opened his carotid, so that he bled out in spectacular fashion. Nearly every drop of blood that had been in his body now gathered in a sticky pool two feet underneath his body and his skin had turned a blueish pale. This left his body fairly clean and his face unblem-ished, if you didn't notice how he had landed with his head turned to one side and a stick of

162

rebar had entered his left temple, bulging that eye out to twice its usual protuberance. Even so, Theresa instantly recognized their newest victim.

'Kyle Cielac.'

'Yes,' Frank and Novosek answered in unison.

He had stuffed the backpack into a dented garbage can teetering on the curb after searching it, tossing away Ghost's pen, pencil and math homework. How the hell could it not be there? Where would a kid have – he didn't even finish the thought. She could have put it anywhere. A locker at school – did kids that little have lockers? She'd had all night to hide it at home ... When he had been eleven, he had a loose piece of baseboard, an old apple tree and a large flat piece of shale rock in the patchy woods behind their house to hide anything of value from his two tormenting brothers. So who knew how many hidey-holes this kid had. Maybe he should just not worry about it. The kid wouldn't have any idea of its significance. How could she? He slumped against the bumper of his car.

But he hated to leave a job unfinished. Several years before he had been hired to build a small parking garage off the shoreway. Six months in, the market had crashed and the owner had drowned in his own debt. He still drove past the base of the garage, its upstretched beams rusting and pools of rainwater turning the concrete slick with algae, like one picks at a scab. When he started something, he wanted to finish it. Closure, or whatever. Even if the brain tells you it's not necessary, the heart tells you it is.

He pushed off the bumper. Never leave a job unfinished.

'He's wearing Nikes,' Theresa commented. 'Not dressed for work.'

'No,' Novosek said.

'So we have another employee inexplicably hanging around here after hours and winding up dead.' She looked up. 'Any clue as to how? What floor?'

'No,' Novosek said. 'I made sure to get here first today. Kobelski arrived a few minutes after I did – we had a lot of concrete scheduled to pour today, to make up for yesterday.'

'I have to test every truck of concrete that's poured,' Kobelski announced, 'to make sure it's within the correct parameters for the structure. Do you know how many trucks of concrete go into even one of these floors?'

'I've got slightly more immediate questions at the moment,' Frank said, showing admirable, and therefore suspect, restraint. Theresa and Angela both shot him a glance, but he went on. 'How long were you here until you found the body?'

Novosek said, 'About fifteen minutes, just as the guys began to arrive. I made them move back out, sent them home. No one went upstairs, including me.'

'Good job,' she said. The workers probably wouldn't have gotten much done today anyway and it eliminated the problem of trying to keep

164

them out of affected areas. Their project manager was getting good at managing a crime scene. Theresa wondered if he realized that he himself was a suspect.

Frank didn't seem as appreciative. 'I'm going to have to talk to them all.'

'I know,' Novosek said. 'But I didn't think you'd have to do it right away.'

'Yet our state inspector is still here,' Frank observed. Theresa had known the restraint wouldn't last long.

'I thought I might be able to help,' the man said, without taking his gaze from Kyle's body. His eyes seemed to drink it in, the glistening spikes, the scarlet blood. His voice made her think he should cut back on the cigarettes.

'Help how?' Frank pressed.

He finally turned his head, glaring, chest rising an inch. 'I've been on the scene of a number of industrial accidents. This is hardly the first dead construction worker I've seen.'

Which didn't answer the question, but Frank didn't push it. Exaggerating one's jurisdiction was one of the advantages of government work, after all.

Novosek distracted them with: 'I know Kyle left with everyone else about four thirty yesterday. I saw him.'

'Getting into his car, driving away?'

'Walking toward Tower City. I think he takes the rapid. I've never seen him with a car. This place empties out fast at quitting time, and I made sure I was the last one out.' He didn't look at any of them as he spoke, only at the dead man.

165

The moisture in his eyes ebbed, then flowed, then receded again.

Theresa got out her flashlight and examined the elevator pit. It sat approximately three feet below the ground level with no way of getting down to it except to jump, carefully. The bottom pad had gathered a uniform layer of construction dust which told her no one had walked around in it recently. Kyle's killer had not gone to the body to make sure all life had departed, so she could do so without worrying about shoe prints. She began to photograph the pit and the ground floor around it, thoughts about this new death interrupted here and there by yet another round of possible explanations for her daughter's sudden reticence.

Frank, joined by Angela, peppered Chris Novosek with questions to learn everything he knew about Kyle Cielac. Theresa listened as she worked, but none of it sounded particularly useful. Kyle had just been another worker, reliable, apparently competent, complained about no one and no one complained about him. Kobelski stood six feet away from anyone else, distancing himself while observing all, arms crossed as if he were the one in charge of the whole shebang. Theresa, camera cradled against her chest, slid into the pit.

She touched the man's chest, prodded his arms. He felt as cold and stiff as a Popsicle and she guessed he had been dead for most of the night. The killer had not been lax by not double-checking his work; from the clean hands it seemed clear that Kyle had not moved after landing.

He had not brought his free right hand – the left arm had been impaled just above the elbow – to his body to feel his grievous wounds. The spike through his head took out his brain instantly and mercifully, while the heart kept pumping on its own long enough to exsanguinate its host through the hole in the carotid. It was a ghoulish and unreasonable tableau, but if Chris Novosek thought this was bad, he had obviously never seen the results of a small-plane crash, a motorcycle versus car accident, or a person dead for a week in the middle of summer with no air conditioning.

Considering Samantha Zebrowski's death, Theresa took a close look at Kyle Cielac's hands and face. No apparent bruising or other injuries. The fingernails were neatly trimmed, the shirt buttoned, jeans tightly belted. There might be more stuff under the skin, but she would have to wait until the autopsy. Speaking of that, how on earth were they going to get the body off its pincushion without causing further, and significant, damage?

'At least in here we'll be shielded from the rain, when it comes,' Frank said.

She looked up. The shaft continued in a hollow square straight up to the gray clouds. 'Maybe not. And no idea where he came from, huh?'

'Are you going to start talking about mass times acceleration due to gravity again?'

'Nine point eight feet per second squared. If we knew force, we could solve for feet. Or –' she stopped craning her neck – 'we could just go look.'

167

'I knew you'd get to that.'

But before they could gear up for another ascent, voices interrupted. Todd Grisham strode toward them with a uniformed patrol officer, each trying to keep just ahead of the other until they were nearly running. The officer finally called a halt to both of them at a distance of about twenty feet, throwing a beefy arm in front of the construction worker.

'Is it Kyle?' Todd demanded. 'Is he dead?'

'Guysaysheworkshere,' the patrol officer said. 'Needs to see the body. I said you—'

'Let him in,' Frank said.

'Come here,' Angela said, and without so much as a glance at each other they moved around the hole in perfect unison, in order to flank Todd Grisham as he moved forward to view the dead body of his friend and co-worker. Close enough to both watch his reaction and to grab him if he made a sudden move to either touch the body or run away. A signature move of her cousin; Theresa had seen him in action many a time before.

But Todd Grisham did not move, only stared at the dead man and his grisly position until he was nearly as pale as the corpse. It would have been comical, in a cartoon: the wide eyes, the fallen-open mouth, the stammering pleas for information. But his trembling horror stayed all too real.

'What happened?'

'That's what we'd like to know,' Angela said gently. 'When did you last see Kyle?'

She had to repeat the question three times before he could become self-aware enough to answer. 'Yesterday. As we were leaving.'

'And what time was that?'

'About four thirty.'

With everyone's attention on Todd, Theresa watched Chris Novosek as he heard this part of his testimony verified. His expression did not change and he said nothing, only watched his employee's face as if everything – his life, the building project, the murders – depended upon it.

'Where did he go?'

'Dunno. Home, I guess.'

'Where did you go?'

'Home. What happened to him? What was he doing here?'

'Were you home all night?'

'Yeah.'

'Can anyone verify that?'

'I – dunno. My brother and my niece, I guess. What was he doing back *here*?'

'We don't know,' Frank admitted, a touch of silk to his voice. 'Would you have any idea what he might have been doing back here on the job, after hours?'

For the first time Todd tore his gaze from his dead friend and looked at his boss, in fact stared with a desperate and pleading intensity.

Theresa watched Chris Novosek as he gazed back. If his expression contained the ability to either comfort or threaten, she didn't see it.

'No,' Todd said. Then he noticed Kobelski, standing to the side. His eyes grew even wider and what tiny bit of blood remained in his face evanesced.

'Any idea who might have wanted to kill him?' Frank asked. 'Todd?'

'No,' Todd said. Except he continued to say it: 'No, no, no, no, no,' as he turned and broke at a fast walk for the exit. Three of the five other people called his name, to no avail.

'Follow him,' Frank said to the uniformed officer. 'Don't stop him, but I want to see what he does.'

'But the scene—' The officer made a circling motion with his hand that managed to state his concerns in one-half second: he was the contamination officer, responsible for admitting or restricting human beings from the crime scene in order to preserve its integrity, and how was he supposed to do that when he was following Todd Grisham to the nearest receptacle in which to upchuck or the bus station or his home in one of Cleveland's many beautiful suburbs or God knows where?

'I'll take care of it,' Frank snapped. 'Just go. Consider him a suicide risk.'

The cop hustled.

'*Suicide*?' Novosek asked, with a *what else could happen?* tone to his voice.

'It's as good a reason as any to keep an eye on him,' Angela explained. 'And his reaction seemed a bit extreme.'

'His friend is laying there with spikes through him! Isn't *that* a bit extreme?' The man turned away, finally, as if suddenly more disgusted by the investigators than the sight of the body. He walked twenty feet, slumped to a seat on a stack of cardboard boxes and put his face in his hands.

Kobelski didn't move. He didn't seem to want to miss even a second of taking in Kyle Cielac's corpse, not a bolt of the camera flash, not a whiff of the uncertain smell of fresh death when the wind changed directions, not a glimmer of sunlight reflecting off the pool of blood. Theresa would get Frank to kick him out, state ID or no state ID. She might be accustomed to working with an audience, but he had begun to get on her nerves.

'To everyone except ghouls like us,' Frank muttered.

'Both single, both denied even the temptation to ask Samantha Zebrowski out on a date,' Theresa observed. 'You think they're gay?'

'I think we'd better find out,' he said.

'Either way, that kid didn't kill him. Or else he should be on a red carpet somewhere accepting an award.'

'Agreed. But if they're more than just fellow concrete finishers, then he might know what his buddy was doing here last night.'

Theresa nodded. 'OK, two things. I don't think he fell from twenty-three like Sam Zebrowski did.'

Angela raised an eyebrow. Frank said, 'And you're basing that on—?'

'She hit hard enough to crack the slab. Kyle, on the other hand, doesn't even reach the foundation. The bars don't penetrate the back side of his skull or rib cage, just the more fleshy areas in the arm, stomach and thigh. If I could recall everything I learned in college I could probably calculate it out, but Physics 102 was a long time ago. I just don't think he fell quite as far and that's about as scientific as I can be about it. I'm sure we could find an accident reconstructionist somewhere who could help us.'

'And the second thing?'

'What cuts through rebar?'

TWENTY-TWO

The answer turned out to be a short Sawzall-type instrument, as grimy as a used hard hat but as intimidating as a bone saw. They ran three mesh straps around the body and suspended those from a small winch provided by the project manager, and then suited up a game body snatcher in a leather apron, heavy gloves and eye protection. He got a crash course in how to safely cut through the small iron bars without losing a finger and went to work. Novosek could have done it in a quarter of the time, but he resided firmly in the center of their suspect pool and could not be allowed that close to the body. If it were even possible – the man kept coming close to the pit, taking one glance at the manhandled corpse before turning and stalking a few feet away, then feeling somehow sheepish or weak or disloyal and turning back. He'd take a few steps, his face would flush an unbecoming shade of green, and he'd whirl again. Theresa gave up

172

watching him and instead kept the body snatcher's electrical cord from snagging on the rebar.

Frank had finally gotten rid of Kobelski – Theresa didn't know how but they'd had a short and apparently bitter conversation before Kobelski stalked off, throwing, 'I won't forget this!' over his shoulder. Frank gave her a wink, magnificently unconcerned about the retributions of a state concrete inspector.

The fact that Kyle Cielac's body had been so efficiently drained of its lifeblood made the job much less messy ... which was not to say exactly un-messy. Finally the last pinion had been freed and the winch lifted the skewered corpse up and over to the gurney. They left the sawed-off pieces in him, of course, so that the pathologist doing the autopsy could see exactly what had occurred. The body snatcher heaved the tool up to the ground level floor and then heaved himself up as well, his feet scrambling for purchase. Theresa took a step toward him to help, stubbed her toe on one of the sticks and began to fall. Rebar spikes rose up toward her torso, her arms, her eyes—

'Tess!' she heard Frank shout.

She grabbed the two heading for her neck, all her weight suddenly depending on the grip she could maintain on two half-inch thick iron poles, one of which was slick with Kyle Cielac's blood. The latex glove granted some traction and she managed to keep from impaling herself. Heart pounding hard enough to cause a roaring in her ears, she straightened. 'That would have hurt.'

173

'Get out of there,' Angela demanded. 'Here, I'll give you a hand up.'

'Wait.' Theresa inched – very carefully – through the minefield of rebar spikes, crouching where she had enough room. The pool of Kyle Cielac's accumulated blood had partially dried along the edges, hard and cracked like a dry river bed in places while still smooth and glossy red in the center. She stuck her fingers into this pool, methodically patting every inch of it. Chris Novosek watched her with an expression that said that even with the body gone he might still be sick at any moment, and Frank said, 'Eww,' about every fourth pat.

'You're not helping,' she told him.

In the small lake of blood she found four pieces of gravel, five screws, and a crumpled up foil gum wrapper with a piece of chewed gum inside. That she kept. The coating of blood might make it problematic to impossible for DNA analysis, but toothmarks could be interesting as well. She also kept a crumpled Pepsi can and two Styrofoam cups with dried up coffee on the inside and a splash of blood on the outside. One had a distinct mouth print in deep coral colored lipstick. Theresa found that interesting.

Directly under where Kyle Cielac's heart had been, she touched a flat square of plastic. She picked it up and let the blood drain off it.

'Probably his ID card,' Novosek said.

It had been in such a thick part of the puddle that the blood coating it had not dried, only clotted to a gel-like consistency that slid off easily enough, leaving a slick but sufficiently transparent coating behind. 'No,' she told him. 'It's yours.'

'I lost it yesterday,' Novosek told Frank and Angela. 'Spent part of the afternoon looking for it.'

Frank had brought him to the Justice Center, only two blocks but a world away from his own environment. Away from the jackhammers and the ironworkers, it gave him a tiny taste of what jail might be like, in the form of an interrogation room. The blank walls, the suspicious stares, the knowledge that you are cut off from everyone you know and we really might be able to do anything we want to you without interference – at least, any interference that would arrive in time to help. We *have* you, man. What do you think of that? 'You lost your ID card. Really. Because, as you may recall, we spent a lot of time together yesterday, and I distinctly remember it dangling from your chest pocket. Don't you?' he asked his partner.

'Distinctly.' Angela sat next to him at the metal table, hands folded over a Manila file in front of her. 'When did you lose it, Mr Novosek?'

'If I knew that I probably wouldn't have lost it. All I can tell you is that at some point I looked down and it wasn't there, and I didn't have time to retrace my steps. I had too many other things to deal with.'

Frank said, 'Oh, we know. We were there, picking the pieces of Samantha Zebrowski up off a concrete slab.'

Novosek blanched, but only by a shade or two.

Either he was getting used to the memory or self-preservation now crowded out any feelings of regret.

A loud noise blasted in the hallway outside, stopped, and blasted again; probably a nail gun or sander. The county had finally decided to spend a few bucks on fixing the holes in the walls and getting some new paint and the department had been torn up for months. Frank had gotten used to skirting the equipment but now it annoyed him; he didn't want the bustle to make Novosek feel at home.

So he said: 'You don't like having to let girls do a man's job, do you?'

'Oh, *please.*'

'Don't like when these uppity females throw equal rights in your face, just so they can take a job away from a guy who really needs it?'

'That's completely untrue.' Novosek said this calmly but with a clipped manner that belied the anger lurking within him. 'I have always treated the women who work for me exactly like the men. I don't care who it is, what they've got in their pants, what color their skin is, what church they go to. If they do their work right, they're OK by me.'

'That's very nice,' Angela said. 'That's exactly what you should say. Unfortunately that's not exactly what you do, because three times women have sued you for failing to prevent a hostile work environment. One said –' Angela opened the Manila file and made them wait while she located a particular phrase – 'that she was groped and manhandled by three co-workers while on your job.'

'That's true.'

The detectives blinked. 'True?'

'Yes. She was, and I fired the guys. Two were just jerks, but one had a record that Personnel didn't catch, so she's suing everyone from the building owner on down. Just because I got caught in that net doesn't mean it was my fault. I put a stop to it as soon as she told me. I never harassed Sam and I would have taken steps if she had told me one of my guys had.'

'What about the other two cases? One said—'

'I know what they said,' he interrupted, his face growing red. 'You know how many women I've had work for me over the years? The last time I had to go to court I looked it up. Thirty-five. Thirty-three of them were good workers who did a good job, reliable, pretty tough. Two were lazy bitches who saw an opportunity to cash in. In both cases they worked a week or two and next thing I know I get a subpoena. They never made a complaint to me or to the guys they worked with. Their stories are invented out of whole cloth but you know what? You can't find a judge who will simply say, you're making this up. Because it sounds so *believable*, doesn't it? Women in a man's environment, the men will get hostile. Everyone knows construction workers are a bunch of pigs anyway. So no matter how many times they *don't* prove their case, it keeps getting shuffled to another court. And I keep getting subpoenas.'

He sounded pretty convincing, Frank had to admit as plumes of powdered plaster wafted under the door. And it could be the gospel truth. Unfortunately his innocence in sexual harassment cases said absolutely nothing about his innocence of murder. 'Speaking of subpoenas ... our excellent secondary team canvassed your employees yesterday. You probably saw them. They spoke to each and every person who works at your job site.'

'I hope you cops will be so talkative when the county exec asks me why the new jail is behind schedule. He takes the completion date as gospel. I wouldn't be surprised if he killed Sam himself just so he could take back five thousand dollars a day from what he owes me.'

'That's not funny,' Angela pointed out.

'No,' he said, his voice as firm as the beams in his building. 'It isn't.'

'They interviewed each person, at their homes if need be –' Frank went on as if the other two hadn't spoken – 'except for three. Guys named Johnson, Rodriguez, and Stears. One is an ironworker, one a pipefitter, one an electrician.'

'Uh-huh,' Novosek said.

'They couldn't find them. Johnson, Rodriguez and Stears did not have a correct address, phone, or social security number.'

'Hmmph,' was Novosek's only comment.

'Do you have any explanation for that?'

'Only that I am building a building, not a security detail for the President. Guys show up and turn a wrench, that's all I know. I can't do a background investigation of each one, which is how I got that sexual predator on my crew. I give them a form and they fill it out. I'm not going to follow them home to verify their address.'

A long protest for some missing HR information. 'Sam and Kyle both worked in cement.'

Chris Novosek seemed to examine this statement from all angles before agreeing. 'Concrete, yeah.'

'Weird that both dead people at your site worked at the same job, isn't it?'

'It's weird that they're dead at all.'

'How many concrete people do you have?'

'Seven, including Sam, Kyle and Todd. But they're the only finishers.'

'Can you think of any reason Sam would have had asbestos and silica on her clothing when she died?'

'Huh? No. Well, silica, yes – that's used as a strengthener in the cement, so that's around, at least. But there's no asbestos at my site. It's not used in anything any more – obviously.'

'Could it have been left over from the previous building?' Angela asked softly, in what Frank thought of as her sweet voice.

Novosek didn't think at all about that one. 'I don't see how. Most of it was removed before demolition. It's impossible to get it all out, yes, but the entire building was razed and carted away. I can't see how there could be enough around for Sam to have gotten it on her clothes.' A glimmer of faint hope came into his eyes. 'She must have been somewhere else first. She was somewhere else that night.'

Frank dashed it. 'I'm sure she was a couple of someplace elses. But she died at your site.'

Novosek's shoulders slumped.

Frank ping-ponged the subject matter again. 'Kyle Cielac and Todd Grisham.'

'Yeah?'

'They gay?'

Novosek snorted loud enough to echo in the small room. 'No.'

'You sure? Todd seemed awfully broken up this morning. They don't hit on Sam. They don't seem to have girlfriends.'

'Todd had a girlfriend. They broke up a couple weeks ago.'

Angela said, still being soft: 'Yesterday you couldn't possibly know the personal details of your workers' lives. Today you know when a concrete finisher dumped his girl.'

'She dumped him,' Novosek explained. 'Right after Todd gave her a check to pay for breast implants as a six-month anniversary present. The minute that check cleared, he got a Dear John text and now she's shaking her new boobs at some other guy. Believe me, the entire site heard *that* story.'

'OK. What about Kyle?'

He stopped laughing and shrugged his shoulders. 'Kyle liked Sam.'

'You just said—'

'I said nobody harassed Sam, and they certainly didn't. Kyle probably told you he never asked her out, and he probably hadn't. Because he *liked* her. The serious kind of like. I caught him looking at her one day, and that told me everything I needed to know.'

Angela raised one eyebrow. 'From a look?'

'*The* look. The look a guy gives a woman

when he's so crazy hot in love with her that he can't talk about it, so he looks confused and tongue-tied and soft and a little awed to have finally found what he's been searching for, this woman that's going to fill the empty space in his heart, and over it all is this sad sort of aura because the poor dumb mope is one-hundred percent certain that he hasn't got a chance, because that girl is way too good for him and always will be.' He looked at Frank, suddenly. 'You know what it is.'

Frank gulped.

At least Angela didn't notice. She asked why Kyle hadn't simply asked Sam out, then. They were both single.

'They worked together. Makes things awkward if she says no, possibly makes things even more awkward if she says yes. Maybe he wanted to wait until the job was over. Guys like that, they've always got a million reasons to stay miserable instead of getting off their ass and taking a chance.'

Another gaze at Frank.

Just as the cop wished Novosek would keep his keen insight into the male psyche to himself, the man pressed his advantage. 'Can I go now?'

Angela picked up her file, tapped its bottom on the table in time with the hammering in the next room. 'Yes.'

'Is my site cleared? Can I get the guys back to work now?'

'That's a lot of blood to clean up,' Angela said. 'Biohazard, you know.'

Novosek scowled. 'It's going to be a jail. I'm

181

sure that won't be the last blood spilled there.'

The two partners sat for a moment without speaking after he left. Frank pondered ways to monitor the looks on his own face without constant reference to a pocket mirror as Angela said, 'Maybe we're back to a love triangle. Todd's a free man, turns his attentions to Sam. Kyle's tongue is hanging out for her. One of them meets her after hours and things don't go well. The other figures it out, demands a private meeting on neutral ground.'

'Kyle winds up in the elevator pit.'

'Because Todd took revenge on Kyle for killing Sam? Because Kyle tried to take revenge for Todd killing Sam, or Kyle had to be shut up because he knew? Neither of them killed her but Todd made the accusation, so Kyle attacked and Todd defended himself?'

'Only problem is, we had already decided that Todd is our least likely suspect, based on his reaction this morning.'

Angela sighed.

So Frank went back to the project manager and his missing ID badge. Yes, a lot of debris found its way into the elevator pit, but still – an ID badge. And Chris Novosek wouldn't win any awards for his ability to lie. When he was on certain ground, his court cases, the presence of asbestos, he spoke quickly and confidently. But he was much less convincing on the murders of Samantha Zebrowski and Kyle Cielac.

A young black cop with round glasses, a tattoo and two Manila files came in, dropped the files on the table between the two partners then turned to leave.

'Jeff,' Frank said.

'It's the financials on your two vics. There's seven cases ahead of you, but you all asked so prettily I moved you to the front of the line. Plus it's a county property, so I can't say it was all out of the goodness of my big heart—'

'No, I was going to ask – what's that on your neck? The tattoo?'

The kid brightened. 'It's Shelly. My laptop.'

Frank peered. Sure enough, the squarish ink looked like a computer. 'You not only gave your laptop a name, you had it tattooed on your neck?'

'Best girl I've ever had,' Jeff said, solemn as a judge, and left.

'I hear you,' Frank muttered.

'Wait until Shelly crashes and fries her motherboard,' Angela said, paging through one of the files. 'Then he'll be in here with gauze wrapped around his jugular. Look at this.'

Frank leaned over, trying hard to see the piece of paper without getting close enough to smell her shampoo, or perfume or deodorant or whatever it was.

'Kyle had direct deposit.'

'Good planning. It's very handy.'

'Paid every two weeks, roughly the same amounts. Except there's extra deposits. Six hundred dollars, once a month for the past two months.'

'Second job?'

'Could be. What about Sam?'

He scanned the sheets in the other folder.

'Nothing. Just her paycheck and credit-card bill payments. She lived with her mom, so no rent, no utilities.' They read in silence for a few minutes. Then Frank said, 'Wait. Last month she had a deposit – five hundred dollars even. Cash. Not her paycheck.'

'That the only one?'

'Yeah. A hundred bucks less than Kyle ... If it were going to become a monthly thing, she would have been receiving more next week.'

'Could be anything,' Angela pointed out. 'She could have sold something, pawned a piece of jewelry.'

'Then why let it sit in her bank account?'

'Saving up for something?'

'Maybe. You know who else I'd like to check out?'

'Todd Grisham?'

'Yep. And Chris Novosek.'

'We're going to have to be nice to Jeff.'

'Maybe we should bring some flowers for Shelly,' Frank suggested, and refused to acknowledge the flush of pleasure it gave him when his partner chuckled.

Unfortunately, his phone rang and spoiled the mood.

And what he heard when he answered *really* spoiled it.

'What?' Angela asked, watching his face.

He put one hand over the receiver. 'It's Mrs Zebrowski. Ghost is missing. She called upstairs to her this morning, got nothing, finally had a neighbor come over to go up and check. The kid's gone.'

TWENTY-THREE

'I don't think you're supposed to be doing that.'

Theresa looked up. Her helpful guide from the previous day, Jack, stood on the other side of the elevator shaft, hard hat slipping to one side as he cocked his head at her. The sky behind him glowed a malevolent gray, and a hint of thunder rumbled in from the lake.

Theresa sat with her feet dangling over the edge, ninety feet up, stunned for a moment into paralysis by Frank's phone call. Where could the child be? Frank assured her that he had a BOLO – Be On the LookOut – out so that every patrol officer in the city had Ghost at the top of their to-do list, but that didn't comfort her. What did comfort her, and then only very slightly, were two facts: one, that Ghost admittedly made a habit of touring the city unescorted, and two, that surely Kyle's death and Samantha's occurred in some sort of tandem and, as far as she knew, Kyle and Ghost had no connection whatsoever. That helped her swallow her panic long enough to finish her current job and let the officers do theirs. For the moment.

'I'm not supposed to do a lot of things,' she told the ironworker.

'I could've guessed that. I mean, no work in

185

the pit without a safety harness.' He carried a short steel beam perched on his shoulder like a bag of dog food, but when he tossed it down the resulting boom made her realize it had to weigh as much as a fully grown man.

She glanced at the pit, which she really hadn't wanted to do since the bottom of it currently sat nine stories below her, where a white-suited private cleaner bleached down the stain from Kyle Cielac's blood. The distance made her head swim and she sat back on to the relative safety of the open concrete floor. 'That's probably a good plan.'

'Yeah, OSHA thinks so. Probably because eighty-three construction workers died last year in falls. What are you doing?'

'Same thing as with Sam. Trying to figure out what floor Kyle Cielac fell from.' Several of the upper floors had girders across the pit, separating the three elevators into distinct channels. The odds were good that Kyle would have struck at least one or two on his way down. If he were lucky it would have knocked him unconscious, unable to picture the rebar at the bottom of the pit as he plunged helplessly toward it.

The ironworker also watched the crime scene clean-up staff. 'They're lucky it's not a foot deep in crumpled pop cans. Guys love to throw stuff down the elevator pit.'

'Why?'

'Human nature. You know the first thing a guy will do – provided there aren't too many females around – when he finds himself high atop a deep hole?'

'Do I want to?'

'Spit. Or pick up a rock and drop it down. Why do you think people throw coins into wells? It's not to make a wish, it's just to watch them fall. Human nature.'

'Oh. Well, onward and upward.'

'I'll go with you.' Jack strolled across the beam as unthinkingly as a gymnast, except that gymnasts weren't ninety feet above the ground with only punji sticks for a mat.

Her heart beat faster just to watch him. 'But – hey – what about the eighty-three construction workers?'

'They're not me,' he said, grinning. 'Relax, I do this all the time. If I start to slip I'll just grab the beam. It's not like I'm over the –' at the last moment he must have remembered Sam, and the smile faded from his face – 'edge. Getting anywhere? I mean with who the killer is? I have a theory about Sam. I think she may have come here to get the forms.'

'Forms?'

'The temporary forms for the flooring pours. They keep the concrete contained as it's poured so it doesn't spread out too fast, keeps the drying steady. They're made of aluminum so they're easy to move. All I'm saying is we seem to keep getting more shipments of those.'

'You think Sam was stealing them?' She lowered her voice as they entered the stairwell.

'No, I'm saying it's a theory.'

'And brought her daughter along to help carry?' Though it would explain the lateness of the hour.

'It's not really stealing. They have to be thrown out after they get too caked up, so technically they're garbage. You used to be able to make a lot of money in garbage from a site, back in the day.' He pulled a pack of gum out of his torn jeans and chewed thoughtfully.

'Really? Like how?'

A few more chews and he produced an example. 'My dad knew an elevator man who had to do a mod – a modernization – in an existing building, so on every floor they had to install doors around the elevator to keep the tenants from trying to use them. Four months later he had a storage shed in his backyard – made entirely out of doors. I'm telling you, I'm just waiting for the lab floor here to put in the counters – I could really use some leftover countering for my kitchen remodel. A renovation I did once, really old building, all the old escalator motors were taken out, and a buddy of mine made a couple hundred a week selling them for scrap. The company didn't care – the company was *happy* that they didn't have to pay someone to haul it away.' His expression faded. 'Things are different now, though.'

'How?' They approached the tenth floor elevator opening as the zip lift began to groan, its cables quivering. Maybe it was Frank, with news. It would be bad news, if he took the time to deliver it in person.

'Companies have figured out how much that scrap metal is worth. Copper's the highest right now – three dollars a pound, pure profit.'

'Anything else in the habit of disappearing

around here?' Theresa asked as she crouched next to the gaping hole. Actually, bad news or good news, Frank would probably just call. He couldn't know how attached she had gotten to their littlest witness in the past twenty-four hours.

'I ain't no snitch, Miss Forensic Person. And I said, the forms aren't really stealing. They throw them out eventually and the company don't bother recycling it. Not even on a government job, which I think is basically wrong, don't you?'

Just as Theresa noticed a speck of white resting on the center girder, the construction elevator squeaked to a halt. Ian Bauer thanked its operator and stepped off. He wore a suit identical to the one he'd worn the previous day but a different tie, and the fine skin on his cheeks lifted as he saw Theresa. But all he said was, 'I heard about the girl going missing. Finding anything?'

'Missing?' Jack asked. 'Who's missing?'

Theresa didn't get up from her edge of the pit. Stick to business. Focus. 'Not much. I can't figure out what floor he fell from – I went over every one and, unlike Sam, find no evidence of a struggle. They all have footprints all over the place and there's no drops of blood or sign of a weapon. That piece of paper out there is the closest thing to a clue I've found and the breeze may carry it off at any second.'

The prosecutor nodded at Jack, stepped around him and walked two feet out on the girder just as the latter had. 'What is it?'

189

'Safety harness! Eighty-three!'

He blinked. 'What?'

'Get off that thing!'

'Oh!' He retreated. 'Sorry. I wasn't going to touch it.'

'No, you merely violated several OSHA requirements and almost stopped my heart.'

'Sorry,' he said again, but he didn't look very sorry. 'Son of an ironworker. It's sort of ingrained. You think that's something important?'

'I won't know until I look at it.' She straddled the girder, feet on its lower edge, and inched forward.

The construction worker stopped scowling at Ian long enough to look startled. 'Whoa! I'll get you a safety harness, and a hard hat too, if you really want to do it.'

The wind nudged the paper one more millimeter toward the abyss, and Ghost had not been found or else Frank would have called her. 'No time.'

TWENTY-FOUR

Ghost had promised her grandmother she would not go out that night, and she hadn't. She'd waited until the morning. The sun was well up, somewhere behind the clouds, and the humidity kept the air warm. So it should be all right.

Besides, if today proceeded anything like the

previous evening the kitchen would stay bustling with a group of ladies from the surrounding homes. They had brought food and gossip and moral support to commemorate this opportunity to feel sorry for someone other than themselves. Nana said they already had enough food to last them into next month. Ghost couldn't understand why people would think she felt like eating. But they'd keep Nana busy; she probably wouldn't even notice Ghost had gone.

She sped past the Walker house, quiet and docile in the gray daylight, and up to the intersection. Plenty of people now occupied the same path she had taken the night before; dodging them took some time but she didn't have to stop and hide from cars. The city's occupants paid even less attention to her during the day than they did at night.

She stopped first at a place on Huron with black walls and big posters of people playing musical instruments. It sat a few blocks away from the construction site but she had to start somewhere, and it looked friendly enough – a man sat at a table next to the glass front, drinking coffee and reading the paper. So she pushed the glass door open and went in. Aside from the man with the coffee, the only other person stood behind the counter, stacking glasses on a shelf mounted to the wall. Ghost approached, a bit more apprehensive with each step. The glass wall at the front provided the only illumination and the dark walls absorbed more of it the farther back they went. Bars, she thought, looked better at night. During the day they just looked sort of dirty. Kind of like fireworks.

The man behind the counter did sort of a double take when he saw her, and watched her approach as if she were somehow scary, like a large dog that you weren't sure was friendly or not. She climbed up on a bar stool, balancing on her knees on its surface, and placed the photo of her mother on the bar. 'Have you seen this woman? This one here?'

The guy didn't respond at first, but after he stared at Ghost for a moment or two he glanced at the picture. 'Uh, no. She doesn't ring any bells.'

Ghost tried to figure out from his face if this were the truth; not easy, but she thought he seemed more confused than anything else. 'Are you sure?' she pressed, because on TV people, especially in bars, always said no at first and then admitted they did when the detectives asked more questions. 'Did she ever come in here?'

He picked up the photo and held it up, as gingerly as Ghost had moved around glass slides the day before, and held it at eye level as if afraid to take his gaze off of Ghost for even a moment. 'No. Sorry, I don't recognize her and I'm pretty good with faces. What happened – why all the questions? You lose your mother?'

'I'm just trying to retrace her steps.' This only startled him more, and he put the photo down and slid it across the bar to Ghost, as if trying to keep his distance. She had never known adults to act so – *uncertain* – as they had since her mother's death. She held out the other picture. 'What about this man? Have you ever seen him? It's an old picture,' she added as he picked that one up as well. 'He'd be really old now. Like maybe thirty.'

The guy snorted a laugh, as annoying as it was inexplicable. 'No, sorry, kid. I don't know him either. What's going on? Are you supposed to be walking into bars by yourself like this? Aren't you supposed to be in school?'

'It's over for the day,' she said as she climbed down.

The man by the window watched her over his newspaper as she left.

One down.

She continued down Huron toward East Ninth. It would practically be a miracle if she could find where her mother had been just before she died, but worth a try. Like Theresa and the fibers: every bit of information either told you something or told you what you didn't need to worry about. She trusted Theresa to work hard to find her mother's killer, but knew you couldn't count on adults to do everything themselves. And Theresa had a mean boss who made her work on other things when she needed to be working on her mother's stuff. So Ghost had to help.

Armed with this bit of rationalization, she opened the door to a diner, half-full with the lunch crowd, and pulled the photos from her pocket.

He watched the kid enter the restaurant. What the hell was she doing? This kid should be curled up in a ball in her bed at home, and instead she pranced along the city street like a sales rep making cold calls. Pretty funny, actually. He felt oddly proud of her, as if he had had a hand in her creation.

He had, as decided, left the house by the back door the previous night, even locking the knob before pulling it shut behind him which he thought terribly courteous of him. Wouldn't want to leave the old lady unprotected.

The sound from above had not been repeated, and he thought it must be the maple tree branch moving in the wind, knocking on the roof. Or it might be the girl returning through her window-door. Either way, he decided not to find out. If the kid were wide awake she might hear him coming up the steps and start up with the screeches, loud enough to wake the half-deaf grandma, and then he'd have two of them to deal with, which he had finally decided was not a good idea. So he slipped out, rounded the house, went back to his car – miraculously unmolested, maybe the neighborhood was more law-abiding than it looked, or perhaps wise enough to let sleeping dogs lie – and went home, only to find he remained without the screwdriver and the DNA and fingerprints that could send him to the electric chair. Did they still send people to the electric chair? No, no, it was lethal injection now. And people even argued about *that* – stupid. How much nicer could you be? If they really wanted a human method of execution, he mused as he waited for Ghost to emerge from the diner, they'd go back to the guillotine. The quickest, most painless method ever. Little chance of that, though.

She came out shortly, glanced around as the door swung shut behind her. Her gaze brushed over him, came back, paused, and flustered him so that he pulled out his cell phone and pretended to read the display, watching her through his eyelashes. But she continued her look about, then turned and walked away. Without haste and without looking back.

Definitely a real girl, flesh and blood, seen and reacted to by others. Not an angel or a demon, though he knew he would continue to think of her as such because he enjoyed it. A real girl – who had, apparently, not recognized him.

Well, *that* was interesting.

He followed.

TWENTY-FIVE

'What the hell is she doing?' Chris Novosek boomed.

'Evidence,' Ian Bauer began.

'She said—' Jack sputtered.

From her seat on the edge of the pit, Theresa flung one leg over the girder, glanced down – and then she couldn't breathe at all. She gave it a minute, then slowly tried looking again.

'Get out of there! You're not covered by my liability insurance.'

'I'm covered by the M.E's office,' Theresa said

without looking up. 'Don't worry about it. This falls under "other duties as assigned".'

The crime scene clean-up crew had finished disposing of Kyle Cielac's blood pool, using absorbent rags and gallons of non-bleach cleaner that would disinfect the area without oxidizing the rebar and making it rust. Only the dark sheen of the wet concrete let her know where Kyle Cielac had so recently bled out.

Edges of the other floors lined up above it in a concentric pattern. Occasionally workers would shuffle around them in a flicker of color or movement.

How long would it take you to fall such a distance? Long enough to form conscious thought? Long enough to know you were going to die, that no force in the universe could save you?

Like a horse, she thought. Grip with the knees.

'You have no training in moving around on an I-beam.'

'I'm not going to try a backflip, or even a flying dismount.'

She tuned out the rest of what he said. Forensic work involved the ability to focus; not everything could be done in a gleaming, silent laboratory. Often she had to calculate or collect evidence while surrounded by gung-ho cops, irate suspects, grieving families, dangerous traffic and adverse weather conditions. Theresa had learned to let all her surroundings fade into the background. Frank often said she had learned this technique too well.

'This is my site,' Chris Novosek fumed, 'and you're—'

She put both hands on the girder, one palm on each side. The metal was fairly smooth, coated steel with only a few flecks of rust to roughen the surface. They were called I-beams because of their shape. The top horizontal bar of the I became her saddle, and the bottom horizontal bar her stirrups. It was plenty wide enough for her to sit comfortably, her fingers wrapped around each edge, but her feet in their Reeboks didn't feel completely secure. She pushed with her toes and pulled with her hands, scooching herself forward like a very small child, moving two inches at a time and feeling acutely ridiculous to be sliding around on her crotch in front of the three grown men watching her, until her right foot slipped and she stopped and gripped with her knees and her hands and forgot all about caring what she looked like.

The pit swam before her eyes and the wind felt stronger than it should, there in the middle of the building. Her heart beat wildly for a moment or two; when it calmed some she repositioned her feet and went again.

Just another foot.

'She's doing pretty good,' someone said.

'Shut up, Jack.' Chris Novosek spoke with quiet but absolute authority. 'Just shut up.'

Only a few more scooches and she reached the paper just as the breeze strengthened for another attack. First she clicked a few pictures with the heavy and expensive camera dangling from her neck, after placing a small ruler next to the stain and hoping the wind wouldn't pick it up before she could shove the small piece of plastic back into her pocket. She didn't need that flying off and hitting someone either. Even such a small, lightweight item – what was the conventional wisdom? Throw a penny off the Empire State Building and it would have enough momentum to penetrate a man's skull by the time it reached the ground?

Photographing the paper meant looking down, but at least the background shaded into fuzziness beyond the focal length of the shot. Then she pulled one latex glove and a Manila envelope and plucked up the scrap. White, with a blue border forming a corner. The backing felt sticky.

Had Kyle slammed into the girder as he fell? Was he conscious at the time? Who killed people by beating them up and then pushing them off a building? Killed both male and female? But if it wasn't deliberate, how did two different people get in fights on two consecutive days and wind up stumbling off the edge of their own work space? One person she could see, but two? Kyle and Sam walked along the edge every day. Even in the middle of a fist fight, they would have known to stay the hell away from it.

And where did Ghost fit in?

Now she wondered whether to continue to the other side or go back the way she'd come and turned around to gauge which might be the shorter distance. Of course twisting put her body slightly off balance, so that she repeated the clutching *grab on with the hands and grip with the knees until the heart calms down* process again. Then she began the long scooch back. This time Ian Bauer walked around the pit to

198

greet her, latching on to one arm just as Jack latched on to the other, practically pulling her to her feet and then away from the edge. It would have been less nerve-racking to stand up on her own. Helping hands could, at any moment, change direction and push you in instead of pulling you out.

Neither showed any desire to let go until she shook off their hands and said, 'Enough! I can do this.'

Chris Novosek did not offer to help. He had not moved from his spot at a corner of the pit, watching all of them with arms folded over a wide chest. 'Well? Was it worth it?'

'Time will tell,' she said, stowing the envelope in her camera bag. 'OK, onward and upward.'

'You're not done?' Novosek asked.

'Not by a long shot.'

They continued the trudge upward, checking each floor's area around the open pit for signs of a struggle, signs of recent activity, signs of Kyle Cielac's presence. Ian Bauer continued along but Novosek had sent Jack back to work as the rest of the employees had trickled in, and now the site rang with the usual sounds of saws and jack-hammers, the clang of metal on metal. They were becoming as familiar to Theresa as the whirr of a centrifuge and the hum of the bone saw.

Novosek had been angry when he returned from the police station, which came as no surprise to her. Frank often had that effect on people, especially suspects, and plus her wing-walking exercise had not helped. But that had faded into weariness, and he answered any questions easily enough. He even offered to carry her camera bag. She had already called Frank twice. To keep herself from dialing his number a third time, she asked Novosek about the asbestos on Sam's clothing.

'Yeah, the cop told me that. I don't have any idea. There's no asbestos in any of our materials. Was she doing any remodeling at home?'

Theresa shrugged. 'I didn't see any. Why, would that be a likely source?'

'If it's pre-seventies. Paint, insulation, fiberboard, siding, soundproofing tiles all had asbestos at one point or another. People rip out a wall or redo a ceiling, and expose themselves.' He panted only slightly as they reached the eleventh floor, emerging from the twisting concrete tunnel that formed the stairwell. Theresa hoped they would be well lit in the new jail. The building might be only an open skeleton but the stairwells already gave her the creeps.

'What about the silica?'

'That's in the concrete. That's not surprising. It's a plasticizer, added to increase the strength. Buildings this tall, you have to reinforce it all, especially on the columns.'

'Where do you mix the concrete?'

'At the supply depot over off Broadway.'

'Doesn't it start to dry en route?' They reached the open spot where the elevators would go. Boxes of pipe ends, stacks of metal bars, no apparent disturbance to the dust and dirt near the pit.

'That's why the trucks keep mixing on the way here. The trip is taken into account. The mixer needs to rotate a certain amount of times but not over a certain number, and there are counters on each truck. If it's over the limit, we have to send it back. The first load is checked by the inspector to make sure it's within the slump test specs, then we rely on the counters to make sure the other loads are consistent. They get stuck in traffic, we can lose a lot of concrete.' They plunged back into the dim stairwell on their way to twelve. 'We have to pump it up to the floor. The pump can clog or stick. The time factor is still in play. You've got to get it down before it hardens.'

'I know that,' she said, panting a tiny bit herself. 'One time I responded to an industrial accident where guys were pouring a house foundation. The small crane they were using hit a power line and it wrapped around a guy, practically seared him in half. So we're trying to process his body and his co-workers were out there with trowels smoothing the concrete. But they had to. It would have cost too much money just to show respect for the dead.'

'You probably think that's cold.' They moved toward the center of the twelfth floor.

'Not at all. I've learned one thing about the dead – they don't care. Not any more.' She snapped some pictures, catching Ian Bauer in one of them. 'You don't have to accompany me, counselor,' she said as tactfully as she could.

'I know. But I'd cleared my schedule for a complicated homicide trial and then the defendant pled as soon as he got a look at the jury. If I go back to my office, the county prosecutor will have piled five more on my desk since I'm "free", quote unquote.'

'Hence, a day of hooky?'

'Just one, before I return to be enslaved in my tower of legal pads and fluorescent lighting. So I came here, to be enslaved in a different kind of tower. Are we almost at the top?'

'Almost.'

She examined the next ten floors, until the project manager and the prosecutor were red-faced and breathing heavy and not because Theresa's presence got their juices flowing. And, as so often happened, she searched and searched and searched but did not find what she was looking for.

She found nothing to indicate where Kyle Cielac had fallen into the elevator pit. As a method of murder, it was near-perfect.

TWENTY-SIX

She was worried sick about the kid, he could see that. Hiding it pretty well, but Ian Bauer spent most of every day being lied to and had thus become a pretty good judge of the difference between what people said and what they meant. So when she said she needed to get back to the office to observe Kyle Cielac's autopsy, she really asked for a reason to stay downtown.

So he gave her one. 'I thought we could try out your theory.'

'About what?'

'The menu at Tavern on the Green,' he said, trying not to hold his breath as he did so. The overcast sky had turned her eyes gray.

She locked her camera bag and clipboard into the trunk of the county vehicle. 'Oh, Samantha Zebrowski's stomach contents.'

'Yeah ... not the most gastronomically conducive mental image, but it *is* lunchtime and you are hungry.'

She waited, not even bothering to ask.

'Your stomach's growling,' he explained.

She did not seem to find this attention charming.

He had gotten too cutesy, should have just asked her to have lunch with him – but had figured the chances were not good if he didn't tie the idea to her work. Even then, chances were slim. Anorexic slim.

It was pointless, he knew, to even try. The essential illogic of the world had been demonstrated to him since birth but most memorably during his early years of high school. He had wanted to join the basketball team, just once be able to do something from the center instead of the fringes of his society. It made sense. He was a head taller than the next-tallest kid and could dribble with the best of them. But a coach who believed in democracy everywhere except the playing field let the current players vote. And they did not want the school weirdo on the team.

His parents had grown tired of explaining the basic unfairness of life to him, and he went in search of a fresh ear. The parish priest had listened with great sympathy, then told him that everyone had strengths. His task would be to discover his own. He might be a good basketball player but he might be much better at something else, something that hadn't even occurred to him yet.

Ian had accepted the wisdom of that and from then on focused on school work, since textbooks and standardized tests didn't care what you looked like. But still it rankled. Because he *could* play better-than-average basketball. And he could – and would – succeed in a job where he had to convince twelve people not only to look at him, but to listen, to believe, and to act.

So pointless, as a deterrent, did not always work in his case.

'I need to get back to the office—'

Well, it had been worth a try.

'—so I can't linger. But I am starving and my boss considers eating to be only for the weak.'

Success!

They walked around the outside of the site's fence and crossed East Sixth. He left plenty of distance between them, didn't crowd. Among the few late lunchers in the restaurant, she chose a booth next to the window where they had a good view of the building under construction, then told the waitress, very nicely, that they were in a hurry. She even ordered the nachos, which he thought took scientific investigation a bit far. How could you consume a dish that you'd last seen in a dead girl's stomach? But all he asked

204

was, 'What do you make of the asbestos you found on the clothing?'

She stirred her coffee, staring at the building. But then it must be easier to stare at than him. 'It probably came from the site, left over from the destruction of the old building. The silica is used to strengthen the cement, so that's not remarkable either. I also found a few tiny pieces of metal, some in spheres, some in what I guess I'd call chips.'

'Probably slag.'

Now she turned her face to him, and again the now gray-blue eyes sent a small jolt through his nerves. 'What?'

'It's the overspray from welding the joints of the beams and girders. It can spray out from the joint and then has to be chipped off.'

'So it would normally be found all over a construction site?'

'I'm afraid so. What do you make of Kyle's body? I mean, did anything stand out, even without an autopsy? I mean, anything other than the iron spikes, um, driven into him.'

'No, they pretty much grab your attention and hold it.' The waitress fumbled with their plates, and Theresa waited until she left before adding: 'I didn't see any signs of assault as with Samantha. It's so frustrating. It's possible neither one is a purposeful murder. Samantha might have gotten in a fight and fell, or jumped. No struggle with Kyle, but he could have fallen through a simple misstep in the dark. The outside edges of the building are easy to see, but the interior is not. Both of them could have been intoxicated

205

and that screwed up their balance, and they fell. I've seen bigger coincidences.'

'Maybe she fought with Kyle. He blames himself for her death, decides to check out the same way.' Possible, but he didn't really believe it ... and he knew Kyle much better than he could let on at the moment. At some point in the future he would have to explain his lies of omission to this woman, and he did not look forward to it.

'No scrapes or bruises on his knuckles as if he'd beat someone up. But he is a lot heavier than she is, so he could have done damage to her without much to himself. And if he would commit suicide in grief over Samantha – whether he killed her or not – isn't it more likely he'd jump from the same outside edge, try to land on the same concrete pad as she did?'

An orderly mind. If he wasn't careful he'd fall in love right there over the Formica, to the sound of a dropped plate in the kitchen and the smell of fried appetizers.

He shook it off. This was simply an afternoon's diversion, after all.

Pointless.

'So if it wasn't suicide due to either grief or guilt,' she went on, 'then what was Kyle doing there at all?'

Ian looked into the beautiful eyes of this beautiful woman and took a deep and regretful breath, preparing to lie through his teeth and say he had absolutely no idea. Instead he diverged: 'And where does this kid fit in, this little girl? Her presence indicates suicide to me, that Samantha jumped off that building of her own will, but then where did she get all the bruises?'

'I'm not so sure.' She told him about Ghost's visit to the lab the previous day. 'Ghost could have told the complete truth, that she went there on her own. She got to the medical examiner's office from East Thirty-First like it was nothing. Maybe she does roam the city on a regular basis. Is that even legal? I mean, it can't be all right for an eleven year old to be walking around by herself.'

'At that age, curfew begins at sunset, so if she's running around at night that's definitely against the law. In daylight, she has as much right to stroll down the street as you or I.'

'But she couldn't be home alone. So how is it all right to be out alone?'

'Actually, Ohio does not have a minimum legal age for a child to be home alone. They just have to be mature and capable enough to handle any reasonably anticipated problems. Most states consider twelve old enough, whether the law is written or unwritten. Even if we had a law – trying to clamp down on unescorted children would invariably wind up interfering with kids getting to school, and we don't want to do that. It's hard enough to get them to attend as it is,' he said.

Her expression bespoke such misery that he covered her right hand with his own. 'We'll find her.'

She held his gaze, direct and unhappy, for so long that his lungs tightened up. Then she tried to smile, tilted her head in a tiny nod.

He removed his hand. Reluctantly.

'Thanks for not telling me I'm acting like an idiot,' she went on. 'If Frank were here he'd tell me that Ghost isn't my responsibility and I shouldn't get attached.'

'Oh. Detective Patrick.' He used the moment to compose his face into the most casual arrangement he could muster, to school his voice not to betray the slightest untoward interest. 'You two been together long?'

Then he braced himself for the firm *yes, a long time, meaning I'm very taken so don't even think about it you odd-looking thing*, or even the glow of actual happiness which equaled the same result.

'Together? Oh – *together*. No, Frank and I are cousins.'

'Cousins?'

'Cousins. Mothers are sisters?'

'Oh. *Yes*.' He took several gulps of coffee to cover his reaction; he could feel his cheeks flaming from his nose to nape of his neck. OK. Breathe. Regroup. Not the homicide detective. That only leaves the rest of the males in this county to eliminate, and how to do that without turning the conversation too personal too fast? He had gotten her there with the case, but once that was dealt with—

She went on: 'He'd be right, of course. But that hasn't stopped me yet.'

'What's life for,' he said to her, 'if not to get attached?'

The curve of her lips deepened, warming him to his toes.

Then, unsurprisingly, she got back to business.

208

'But even if Ghost got to the building on her own, it still wouldn't disprove suicide. Samantha could have gotten into a fight earlier, which made her feel hopeless and suicidal. But, especially in light of Kyle's death, I'm going with murder – though in that case why didn't the killer notice Ghost? She says she saw him. Why didn't he care about that?'

'Maybe he didn't see her. It's a huge site and she's a little girl.'

'She says he did. What if he knows he left a witness? What if he comes after her?'

'Why would he? It was dark, no one was around. He could have easily killed her then. In fact that would have been even better for him – Samantha killed herself and took her child with her, and the bruises were sustained in the fall.'

She pondered this. It didn't seem to reassure her much.

He asked, 'Are we sure we've gotten every detail from her?'

'Angela took her statement. But she might tell me more. We sort of bonded over my microscope.'

'Because of your father?'

She raised one eyebrow. 'How did you know about him?'

Oops. 'The Plain Dealer profiled you.'

'That was a year or two ago.' After the Torso Killer re-emerged.

'I was cleaning out a file cabinet last week and ran across it,' he stammered, not wishing to confess to Googling her. Way too stalkerish. 'You're right, the little girl does need to be questioned

209

again, more extensively. That almost always produces a new detail or two.'

'I could do that.'

He needed to pick his words carefully with this. 'You could, but – no offense, but have you ever questioned a child witness?'

'I've never questioned any witness. That's not my job.' Theresa crunched a chip, putting him again in mind of Samantha Zebrowski's stomach contents. He put down his fork.

'It's a science unto itself. Children are highly susceptible to suggestion, as I'm sure you know, so you have to keep your questions extremely neutral and open-ended.'

'Don't ask, "Did you see the man?" Just ask, "What did you see?"'

'Yes. With smaller children we have to establish that they know the difference between truth and falsehood, and also that they know the difference between right and wrong. We don't accept testimony from children under five in general, but the maturity of the child is more significant than their actual age. A mature four year old may be much more reliable than an immature seven year old. Anyway, I'm lecturing.'

She used a chip to dig out the last of her cheese. 'No, go on. As I said, I don't usually have anything to do with witnesses in general, certainly not very young ones.'

Sincerely interested or just being nice? He opted for sincere, given how seriously she took her job. 'This girl is old enough to know truth from a lie, but she's been traumatized. It will be difficult finding out exactly what she saw without leading her. If she has bonded with you then you may be the one person who shouldn't question her.'

'Because she'll tell me whatever she thinks I want to hear.'

'Quite possibly. We have child victim assistance counselors at the office who usually take the lead with questioning kids thirteen and under. They can – um, Theresa?'

'What?'

'Isn't that her?' She turned to look behind her and they both sat in shock for a moment as Ghost Zebrowski climbed up on a bar stool and handed a piece of paper to the bemused bartender. He wiped one beefy hand on his pants before accepting it, lips parting in surprise at either the request or the requester.

Without another word Theresa stood up. So of course Ian Bauer followed.

She slid on to the stool next to the child, put a gentle hand on her back and asked what she was doing there. The girl's face lit up when she saw Theresa. 'I'm retracing my mother's last steps. This man says he saw her here.'

'Ghost, where have you been? The whole city's looking for you. Your grandmother is worried sick.'

The girl could not have looked more surprised if Theresa had produced a live rabbit. 'Why?'

The man behind the bar with his single earring and indie-rock T-shirt two sizes too small had already lost patience with this particular set of patrons. 'Look, does she belong to you? We do not really allow unaccompanied minors in here.'

Theresa identified herself and Ian silently flashed his Justice Center I.D. Not that it really meant much, but it calmed the man enough for him to confirm that yes, Samantha had been a familiar face in the restaurant.

'When did you—' Theresa began.

'What about him?' Ghost demanded, holding out another photo. 'Have you seen him?'

Glance, negative shake of the head.

'Are you sure?' the little girl persisted, standing on the stool in a way that apparently worried Theresa.

'He said no, Ghost. Please get down, you're going to fall.'

'I'm not going to fall!'

'Can you get her out of here?' the bartender asked of Theresa, or Ian, or whoever might be most likely to accomplish the removal of this suddenly very noisy small child.

'Ghost, you really can't be questioning—'

'Yes I can!'

Ian stepped up. 'Why don't you come join us in our booth, Ghost, and we can—'

The girl took one look at him, nearly eye-level from her pedestal. Then she leapt to the ground, landing on the linoleum hard enough for him to feel the vibration through his feet, and darted out the front door before the stunned bartender could even set down the photograph of her mother.

'I'm sorry,' Ian said to Theresa. 'I have that effect on children.'

TWENTY-SEVEN

Frank and Angela surveyed the eleven rather plain stories of the National Terminal apartment building, then, as one, turned to the patrol officer.

'You said follow him.' He shrugged. 'I followed. He walked. And walked. Tried someone on his cell phone who didn't pick up. Walked some more. From the site he went down to Public Square and kept going. He went down the hill, down to the Flats, which I don't need to tell you guys is a ghost town these days, right? Do you know how hard it is to tail a guy when there isn't another person on the entire street? Luckily for me he never turned around. He didn't know I was there, he didn't know *he* was there, because he walked around in circles. Back up the hill at the other end of the Flats, wandered over to Lakeside, started to head toward the Square again, somehow wound up here. Went inside.'

A Waterfront Line rapid transit train rattled up the track behind them, its station still looking shiny and new years after the rails had been added, back when the Flats would teem with hundreds of people every weekend. Exactly why did that stop? Frank wondered. Did we all grow up, or did we simply run out of money?

He heard the rumble of a train, or perhaps it was thunder.

'I already checked,' the officer went on. 'He lives here, the building manager says. Fourth floor. It's his official address. So my nature hike wasn't so much necessary, I'm thinking, but ain't all's well that ends well?'

'Good job,' Angela said.

'Thanks ever so much. Kudos mean the world to me, but lunch means even more and mine is two hours overdue. You need anything more from yours truly or can I get out of here before the heavens open?'

'Nope. We can take it from here.'

The officer began the three-block hike back to his patrol car, failing to keep 'I should think so,' completely under his breath.

Frank turned to Angela, who of course still looked fantastic despite the fact that their lunch hour had also not arrived, and they had barely swilled a coffee, taken a potty break or sat down since the discovery of Kyle Cielac's body. Her hair needed brushing and her skin had grown a bit shiny, but she glowed with the thrill of the hunt.

'Shall we pay Mr Grisham a visit at his humble abode?'

He grinned, getting into the spirit himself. 'We shall.'

They bypassed the building manager and went directly to the apartment. No sound until they knocked, then the steady thump of two feet and a dimming behind the peephole. Then a long pause while Todd Grisham debated his options:

214

a) refuse to open the door, or b) pretend he wasn't home.

He opted for c). They heard a rattle of keys as he undid the bolt and opened up.

Angela greeted him in her most calming voice and asked if they could talk about what had happened that morning. Todd, red-eyed, apparently debated a few more options before saying, 'Sure,' and held the door as far as it would go. The two detectives sidled past him, heading for the living room, grayly bright, ahead.

And as soon as they entered that room, Todd Grisham pulled his key from the deadbolt, sped out the door and shut it behind him. As Frank touched the knob, he heard an unsettling *click*.

Todd had locked the deadbolt from the outside – and it was keyed on both sides with no simple latch to turn. A cute tiled hook rack helpfully labeled 'keys' hung on the wall, empty. Todd had taken them all with him, efficiently imprisoning both detectives.

Frank roared out a curse and banged on the door. Then he pulled out his gun.

His partner shouted, 'No! You don't know who's in the hall.'

She was right, of course. With his luck he'd drill some toddler or a granny who chose that moment to stroll by.

Once they cleared the apartment, the partners spent the next few frantic moments ripping apart every kitchen drawer until Angela found a rusty set behind the potato peelers. She muttered, *'Pleasepleaseplease,'* in a whisper as she fit one in and turned.

Frank thought, *I should remember this moment*, the closest he'd ever seen her to discombobulated. Of course he also found himself locked into a pleasant family dwelling like a squirrel in a Haveaheart trap so perhaps this would not be a memory worth keeping after all.

Nothing. She slid in the other key and the tumblers moved.

They spilled into the hallway, leaving the pleasant family dwelling ransacked and unsecured, and headed for the red glowing Exit sign. Todd would not have waited for the elevator, and as they entered the stairwell Frank could swear he heard the guy's panicked footsteps clattering downward, too many floors below them. But he couldn't be sure.

It had been a number of years since he'd been in a foot race, and he hadn't missed it a bit.

Frank hadn't passed any slowly closing doors to other levels, so they had to keep going and assume he would head for the ground floor, assume he would try to get outside. Frank reached level one with Angela on his heels. The stairs continued downward but, guessing that Todd didn't have a car, Frank plunged through the exit door.

It led to a small concrete landing overlooking an outdoor parking lot, through which Todd Grisham now sped. He dodged cars and their grassy medians, heading east. Frank and Angela went down opposite ends of the landing but reached the pavement at the same time, and pursued. Neither of them shouted Todd's name, or told him he should stop, or that they were the

216

police. He knew all that already. He obviously didn't care.

Todd exited the parking lot and sped across West Ninth Street, producing a screech of brakes and a shouted curse. Frank seconded the sentiment as his lungs began to ache. Todd continued up the branch of Lakeside in front of the Marshall apartments.

Frank and his partner looked both ways before pursuing across West Ninth. Catching up to a guy when they knew where he lived was not worth getting creamed by a delivery truck.

The humidity of the impending storm felt like a weight across his shoulders. Frank had already sweat through his shirt and his legs were getting heavy. But besides his dislike for them, what else had not changed about a foot race was the fact that catching the suspect remained secondary to beating your partner to him. That Frank happened to be attracted to his partner did not affect this dynamic in the slightest and only made it worse. Frank would sprawl across a sidewalk on Lakeside dead of a heart attack before he'd let Angela Sanchez pass him up.

Unfortunately it might come to that.

He had a comfortable three-foot lead when they followed Todd into an alley behind the Marshall that would come out by the Blind Pig sports bar – except that recent street renovations closed off the alley with a chain-link fence. And that Todd Grisham was already dropping himself down the other side of said fence.

Frank had only enough breath to mutter, 'Ridiculous,' before charging the fence. But

West Sixth had a spate of traffic along it and Todd also didn't want to get creamed by a truck, delivery or otherwise. So as he perched on the curb, Angela took the opportunity to ask him just what the hell he thought he was doing, pleasing Frank by panting as she did so.

'Where are you going, Todd? Why are you running away from us?'

He ignored them.

Frank gave it a shot – anything to keep from having to scale a chain-link fence. 'We can protect you, Todd. We can keep you safe.'

The young man turned with an eerily genuine smile. 'You'd think so, wouldn't you?'

Then he kept running.

Frank threw himself at the chain links, scrabbling for a toehold.

He took a moment to consider how Kyle's death affected him. He certainly hadn't meant for that to happen – he had thought only of Samantha – but after examining the incident from all angles he concluded that the concrete worker's untimely demise did not change his focus on Sam and her angel/demon child. No one would connect him to Kyle's murder. Theresa had just demonstrated an inability to connect anyone. He had accidentally stumbled on a perfect way to murder, and only felt sorry that he couldn't tell anyone.

Of *course* he couldn't tell anyone. That would be silly.

Besides, who would he tell? Who else would appreciate such an accomplishment? Other than himself. And maybe Theresa.

But Theresa's focus was catching people who killed, not encouraging them to do it.

Yes, but she still might find the technique interesting, or fascinating. Those who have never picked up a brush still enjoy a great painting. And she had a professional interest, after all.

And she'd obviously gotten attached to that angel/demon child ... spinning the both of them right back to him.

He decided not to worry about Kyle's death. All that mattered now were the female satellites whirling around him – the dead Sam, her daughter Ghost, and Theresa.

TWENTY-EIGHT

Several blocks away, Frank's cousin had also involved herself in a foot race.

Theresa had burst out of the Tavern's door and caught only the merest flicker of Ghost's brown hair as she turned the corner into the alley known as Theresa's Court. She pounded up the sidewalk, grateful that she worked in Reeboks instead of heels.

Ghost did not slow but ran as if the shadow man himself were chasing her, through a parking lot and in between two huge buildings, heading for East Ninth. Theresa called her name, but if the child heard it she gave no sign.

Theresa ran, her feet slapping against the concrete. In twenty steps she gained perhaps three feet of the gap between them and decided she needed to work out more. She didn't know if Ian had followed and was not going to risk a look back to find out. She shouted again. Again, no response.

The girl reached the end of the alley, turned to the right, and disappeared.

Theresa piled on the speed, pricks of sweat beginning under her armpits and between her breasts, and avoided colliding with a nicely dressed black lady heading into the CVS store. Ghost passed St John's Cathedral and approached Superior Avenue, thrusting herself into the intersection without pause. Theresa's heart seized, choking off the breath she desperately needed.

'Ghost! STOP!'

What was *wrong* with the kid?

But the light had been with her and she made it to the other side without mishap. It changed just as Theresa reached the intersection and she lost precious seconds looking both ways before crossing against it. She no longer wanted to know why Ghost had been questioning the Tavern bartender. She simply wanted to stop the kid before she got hit by a car.

Happily for the sake of her cardiac health, Ghost suddenly darted to the right and disappeared between two buildings. Theresa followed, pounding up the four short steps and through the brick arch to the small, pretty Key Bank patio. Ghost had already passed up the tables and chairs available for summer use by the local office workers.

Theresa gained another few steps but mentally paused when Ghost made a sharp left. This kid knew downtown Cleveland better than a veteran cab driver. She might disappear into some cubbyhole at any moment and stay there until after dark, and Ghost wandering around here after dark was what Theresa feared the most. The winos might be harmless. The shadow man was not.

'GHOST!'

At least she had to slow up for two cars blocking the tiny alley that Theresa had never known was there, but once she'd darted around the compact vehicles the kid sped out on to Short Vincent. It might have an odd name but it was a real road with real cars, and Theresa almost shut her eyes as she saw a blue metallic object hurtle toward Ghost.

But one blare of the horn later, the car had passed and the kid still stood there, shocked into a pause. By the time she jumped up on to the opposite sidewalk Theresa had nearly reached her. Two more feet and she could feel the heat from the child's body with her outstretched hand.

It took discipline not to grab her by the hair, but she summoned one more burst of speed from her tired legs and grabbed her T-shirt. 'Ghost! Stop!'

The girl struggled at first, clutching at Theresa's hands, but finally halted, breathing too hard for any words. Theresa wasn't ready to chat

221

herself, and simply guided the child to the landscaped area behind the Huntington Building. There they collapsed on a low brick wall under a tree just as a streak of heat lightning lit the sky. She loosened her grip on the kid's T-shirt and took a furtive look around. Two women having a smoke on Huntington's patio were watching them with eagle eyes, waiting for a sign to intervene. A man pulled open the glass doors and went inside. People waiting at the light crossed East Ninth. Ian had not appeared. Provided no more dramatics ensued, they would not be disturbed.

'Why did you run from me?' Theresa panted.

'Not you,' Ghost said, her breathing already returned to normal. The kid was in decent shape, all right. 'Him.'

'Ian? Why?'

Maddeningly, the little girl only shrugged. 'I don't know. He scared me.'

'That's it?'

'Yeah.'

Theresa wiped sweat from her forehead.

'And,' Ghost added, 'I was afraid you'd make me go home again. I was trying to investigate.'

Anger propelled Theresa to one knee in front of the kid, holding both of the thin shoulders in her hands. 'Why did you leave your house without telling your grandmother? You scared her half to death, Ghost. You scared *me*.'

Again, this seemed to genuinely surprise her. 'I thought she'd think I went to school.'

'*School*. Honey – your mother just died yesterday. No one expects you to go to school.'

Ghost nodded judiciously. 'I wasn't really going to go, anyway.'

'You cannot leave your house without telling anyone. Do you understand that? *Never*. Especially now.' Stress took her voice into the upper octaves, reminding her that she really shouldn't be berating a recently bereaved child and that she should hide her anxiety that Ghost herself might be in danger. The kid was traumatized enough without adding in fear for her own safety. Though fear for her own safety might be exactly what she needed. 'And you can't be walking around going into bars—'

'Why not? Why can't I?' Now Ghost's voice rose. 'She was *my* mother!'

'I understand that, and I understand that you want to do something. But it's our job to find out what happened to her, not yours.' Theresa cringed as the words came out in all their lameness. 'I—'

'Did you know about her phone calls? Did you look at her phone?'

'Yes. She called the library, city hall, and her doctor's office to make an appointment for her annual physical. We've identified all her incoming and outgoing phone calls during the past month except for two numbers. Frank is tracking them down right now.'

That she had that information did not mollify the girl. 'The bartender said she had been in there.'

'Good. Let's go see what else he can tell us, and then I'll drive you home.'

'No! I don't want to go home! Why are you

223

always trying to get rid of me?' the girl shouted. Theresa had hoped she'd go for the idea of talking to the bartender, but Ghost was in full-blown meltdown, so agitated that she began to walk in circles. 'I can come here if I want to.'

'It isn't really safe to—'

'I have to!'

Theresa sat down on the low brick wall, modulated her voice, did nothing sudden or threatening and hoped it would calm the child. In her softest voice she asked, 'Why, Ghost?'

'I have to find him!'

'The shadow man?'

In strangled tones, she spit out: 'No, not him – my dad. I have to find *my dad*!'

Then Theresa stood, still moving slowly, and put her arms around the girl as she burst into hopeless sobbing, spasms racking the tiny body. Theresa rubbed her back, feeling every bone, smoothed her hair and let her cry it out.

Ghost didn't roam the streets looking for her mother. She knew where her mother was. Operating on a single cryptic comment by a hard-drinking Sam about 'losing him downtown', Ghost went out at night looking for her father.

Theresa didn't even consider telling the girl that she was right about her mother and grandmother lying to her but not in the way she thought, that the man she thought was her dad couldn't have been. That was not her secret to reveal, and she couldn't see what good it would do anyone if she did.

Then, as the tears began to slow and the breath returned, she set the girl back down and wiped her cheeks with her bare hands, not having a handkerchief or tissues or anything other than her car keys. Like Scarlett O'Hara, Theresa never had a handkerchief when she needed one.

Ghost slumped, saying nothing. After a moment she pulled the second photo out of her pocket, the one of her mother and a boy at the school dance, and stared at it.

'Ghost,' Theresa said, 'I know it isn't the same, but when I was just a little older than you, my father died.'

The girl looked up at her, listening with caution, extending the benefit of the doubt only part way.

Theresa told how she had come home from school with nothing more on her mind than an algebra test and found her mother sobbing as if her heart had been shredded, as indeed it had. He had suffered a brain aneurysm while at work at the steel plant. There had been no period of emergency, no need for her mother to speed to the hospital, too late to do anything but send his supervisor to the house to tell her in person. The next couple of days had passed in a fog inter-rupted only by moments of piercing agony that radiated throughout her body until Theresa thought she would die herself.

Funny how sharing pain seems to lessen it, and yet it always works. The girl stopped crying, contemplating her photo. 'Who took care of you then?'

'My mother. And my Grandpa Joe. He was a police officer. Mom says that's why Frank and I both wound up doing this for a living, trying to take after Grandpa Joe.' Theresa smiled and rubbed the girl's back again. 'He tried to help me get through the months and years, but it was hard. That's why I know it's very hard for you. Sometimes the hardest thing of all was to *let* him help me. But that's what you need to do here, is let us help you find out what happened to your mother.'

Ghost looked up at her, calmer, a glint of determination back in her eye. 'And when you do, will you tell me?'

'Yes.' Any other answer would not be acceptable, and they both knew it. 'But I'll tell you something else that helped me – I started trying to do what my dad would have wanted me to do. You need to do what your mother would have wanted you to, and she would have wanted you to be safe. She didn't want you going places by yourself, did she?'

'No.'

'She would want you to be considerate of your grandmother, wouldn't she?'

Guilty sigh. 'Yes.'

'OK, then. Let's get back before it starts to rain.' She stood up then, as if that settled the matter, and hoped wildly that it had.

They returned to the Tavern, Ghost expertly navigating their path, Theresa making phone calls on the way. Ian Bauer waited at the bar, Ghost's photo and Theresa's purse on the counter next to him.

'I started to follow you, then remembered your purse. By the time I realized you weren't coming right back I'd totally lost you.'

'No problem. Thanks for guarding it. This is Anna Zebrowski, Ghost to her friends.' She indicated the girl she now wore as a belt, since Ghost had her arms wrapped around Theresa's waist and her face buried in the woman's back. 'She's apparently feeling a little shy right now.'

'That's all right. As I said, I have that effect. Our barkeep Michael says Sam was here often and he is sure she came in the night before last, but is very fuzzy on how long she stayed. She drank mostly with a few other women who frequent the place, maybe one or two guys, but he really can't be sure he isn't confusing it with some other night. The women will probably be back on Friday if not sooner, and he will call Frank when they return or if he has any more concrete recollections in the meantime.'

'Thanks.'

The child unbent enough to take her mother's picture back, shooting furtive looks at the prosecutor as she did so.

'What now?' Ian Bauer asked.

'Now I take her home,' Theresa said, one arm across the girl's shoulders, 'and then I need to get to an autopsy.'

TWENTY-NINE

'Really?' was all Christine would say to Theresa as they surveyed the multiple impalements of Kyle Cielac. *'Really?'*

'I don't know why you always act like this is my fault,' Theresa said.

'Spikes?'

'They're not spikes, they're rebar. They're there to reinforce the concrete.'

'I know what rebar is,' the woman snapped, and didn't say another word until Kyle Cielac had been de-pierced, sliced open, and gutted like a fish. The six wounds had been opened and examined. His nails were clean, his hands rough but unbroken. Kyle hadn't smoked, and he'd eaten a healthy amount of grilled fish and potatoes for his last meal. Then the pathologist finally forgave Theresa enough to ask, 'Did you find anything on his clothing?'

'His entire ventral surface was soaked in blood. On the back I found a few hairs that look like his, a cat hair – apparently his room-mate has one – and some sticky little yellow-colored globules.'

'Is that a scientific description?'

'Close enough. I have no idea what they are but they start coming apart when exposed to

228

moisture. They're either some kind of a pigment or dye, or a food item. I ran them through the FTIR and got a bunch o' nothing, so I suspect they're organic. I'll have to talk Oliver into testing via the gas chromatograph.'

'Good luck with that.'

'If I bring him Cheetos, it usually helps.' Theresa watched Christine slice up Kyle's smooth, red-brown liver with what looked like a bread knife. 'The ironworkers all carry these nasty-looking tools. A spud wrench has a monkey wrench at one end but tapers to an ice pick on the other. A sleever bar is just a pry bar that also tapers to an ice pick at the other end. They use them to line up the beams and girders before they weld them together.'

Christine peered at a fatty deposit. 'So you're thinking someone could have stabbed Kyle and then tossed him into a pit in a way that the stab wound would just coincidentally slide over a piece of rebar?'

'No ... it would take some arranging.'

The pathologist removed a sliver of the tissue and dropped it into the quart container of formalin, already half-filled with slivers of other organs. 'That would be tough to do without causing significant damage to the body. He's a good-sized boy.'

'True. Unless there were two of them.'

Christine picked up a wet, red object about the size of a fist and slashed open the coronary arteries in a series of quick stripes, with two or three millimeters between each slice. 'Then, what, they jumped up and down on his back to simulate a fall?'

'Why not?'

'Because that would take a lot of force. Enough to get some subdural hemorrhaging started, and I don't see any.'

'Oh.' Theresa turned back to the steel table. With his torso flayed open and vacated and his scalp pulled back until his skull cap could be sawed off and even one arm and one leg opened and dissected, Kyle Cielac now bore only a passing resemblance to a human being. 'So we're back with him falling into a dark pit in a place with which he should have been intimately familiar, for no discernible reason.'

Christine didn't respond, only used a bigger knife to section the ventricles. 'He had a good heart.'

'Yes.' Theresa gazed at what was left of Kyle Cielac. 'I think he did.'

Damon picked through five elbow joints before he found one he liked, free of any rough edges or dimples. His father, for the brief few months he had been present in Damon's life, had referred to any blemish on a surface as a 'tit' which always made the child have to stifle a laugh. 'You rub that wax out good, boy,' he'd call from the porch as Damon ran a rag over that falling-apart maroon Cadillac that wasn't worth a wash, much less a wax. 'I don't want no tits in it.' It had been the most amusing thing about a not terribly amusing person. He disappeared for good just after Damon's eighth birthday, the best present the boy could have received.

He cleaned the end of the white plastic pipe with the joint cleaner, gave it a minute, then coated it lightly but thoroughly with the plastic PVC glue. Hard to believe the water pipes in a forty-story building were going to be held together with glue, but the foreman didn't think it strange and Damon didn't want to ask. He didn't want to tip the guy off that he had never put two ends of a pipe together before this job.

As it dried he prepped the next, very long section. Boonie and the foreman helped him settle it in place, then, as Damon expected, the foreman wandered off to have his fifteenth cigarette of the day which gave Damon the time and privacy to pull out a piece of white paper, folded over and over again, and add that day's work to that floor's diagram. He sketched quickly, knowing that if an engineer ever checked his work – which would not happen – he would find it remarkably close to scale. Damon's mother had often told him he would be an artist, a Harlem Michelangelo. Hah. He didn't even tag buildings. His talent with the pen or pencil came in handy but didn't give him any particular joy. He just happened to be good at it.

By the time the new jail opened for business, Damon would have provided his boss with a complete set of plans, including all doors, windows, pipes, electrical conduit, stairwells and elevators. Of course a great deal of finishing work would be done after all the plumbing had been completed and Damon no longer had a reason to be on site, but most of that would be cosmetic. The hardware, as he thought of it, would be set in concrete. They might not know the exact location of controls to open and shut certain containment doors or the pass codes to computers or which clerks might be partial to a bribe, but they would know every way of getting in and out of the building, where the main monitoring stations were and which office belonged to the warden. The boss had said that trying to break out of jail was a fool's errand, in his opinion, but that surely that information would be of great value to someone, some day. *Great* value.

Damon had the paper folded and back in his pocket before the foreman returned, and they moved on to the next section. The second and third floors would have more pipe flowing through them than the rest of the building put together, almost, between the cafeteria, the staff kitchen and lunchroom, and the hospital and laboratory.

'What do they need a laboratory for in a jail anyway?' Boonie grumbled. 'They're going to be doing experiments on the prisoners, betcha.'

'Like sewing their feet on to their shoulders, that kind of thing? Mengele shit like that.'

Boonie handed him the jar of pipe cleaner. 'What's Mengele?'

'You know, that Nazi doctor. Don't you ever watch the History Channel?'

'Yeah, in-between Martha Stewart and Oprah. No, not that kind of experiments – be pharmaceutical testing, more like. That's where the money is.'

Damon slid the pipe end into the sleeve joint.

'I don't mind no pharmaceuticals. Might not be so bad in here, if that be the case. 'Cept for us blowing the place up, maybe.'

'Shut up,' Boonie hissed with more than his usual vehemence. 'Five-oh.'

Damon looked up, and sure enough, two guys in suits were crossing the concrete toward them. He schooled his face, kept his shoulders and arms down, took a deep breath to relax his vocal cords. Cool. We're just a couple of workers, doing a job for the man. We're supposed to be here. We're *paid* to be here.

'Hey,' one of the cops said. 'You two are Cooper and Whitson, right?'

'Yep.'

His partner, a chubby dude in cheap pants, asked: 'Did you guys see or speak to Kyle Cielac yesterday?'

'Nope.'

They followed up, easily accepting Damon's monosyllabic answers and Boonie's accompanying nods. Then the first one asked, 'You guys know a Rodriguez?'

'Couple of them,' Boonie said. 'Which in particular?'

'Tyler Rodriguez. Pipefitter.' At their blank stares he added, 'He works here,' as if they were idiots for not figuring that out.

'Don't know him.'

'Me, neither.'

'Rodriguez,' repeated the one with bad taste in clothing. 'Rod-ri-giz.'

'Heard you the first time, man. Don't know him. But it's a big building.'

'So it's possible he could be a pipefitter here and you just don't happen to know him?'

Damon shrugged. Boonie shrugged. And they kept shrugging until the two suits went away, shaking their heads in frustration. Damon watched them go.

Figured. The first true answer he'd given, and the cops didn't believe it. 'What do you make of that?'

'Nothing to do with us,' his partner said. 'That's all I care about.'

'Who's this Rodriguez?'

'We know everybody who lays pipe here. Probably someone who quit the first week. Maybe he don't exist, the boss man just uses the name to round out his payroll.'

'So it looks like he's paying some guy named Rodriguez, but the money's going into his own pocket?'

'Lot of shady stuff go on around a construction job. But the boss white, so he ain't going to end up a client of this fine establishment, once it be finished,' Boonie said, already losing interest in the topic.

'This is not a good day for this to happen, with that other thing comin' up.'

'It is not.'

'They're checking everyone out. So how come they haven't come down on us yet? We've both got paper.'

'They might yet. That's why the situation bears watching. You see her today?'

'Yeah,' Damon said.

'Bears watching.'

'Yeah,' Damon said again. 'I got that.'

Thunder rumbled in the distance, low but persistent.

Chris Novosek paced the marble hallway of the county planning office, cursing slowly and steadily under his breath. He had left the site in the hands of his capable foreman but still chafed at being away, even for an hour, on such a cluster of a day. The copper tubing had been delivered and the guys were installing it as fast as they could, but the day had gotten such a late start with Kyle's death and they couldn't possibly get even half of it done. Not that the copper would necessarily be safer stretched out and bolted in – at three dollars a pound, thieves were breaking open small window units to get the A/C coils – but having to cut each individual pipe would be a lot less tempting than a big stack of it lying there loose. He had even considered hiring his own security guard but the county had some restriction about private security on their property. They wouldn't hire their own, though, because that would be an addition to the contract amount and they had their constituents to answer to. The deals we will make in a down economy, Novosek thought. He should have stayed in residential work. Give him some Gates Mills mansion to build, where the contract is a handshake and the owner doesn't give a damn about much as long as the finished product has more square feet than his neighbor's.

By the time the contract specialist emerged from his office and waved Novosek in, he would have gladly strangled the man and left his body there on the marble floor to cool. But all he said was, 'This had better be good.'

'Good is what it's not.' The man collapsed into his desk chair as if he'd just climbed ten stories. The desk and both extra chairs were piled high with papers and blueprints and Novosek didn't bother to clear one off. He wouldn't be staying that long. 'You get your concrete from Decker and Stroud, right?'

'Yeah.'

'There might be a problem with them.'

Now Novosek wished he had cleared someplace to sit down. 'What?'

'They won the bid with extra points for a minority-owned business.'

'So?'

'So they might lose that rating.'

'How is that possible? I've met Decker; he's as black as the ace of spades. If you'll pardon the expression,' he added to the county worker, who was equally dark.

'That's the result of one tough gene from one single grandparent. Johnson isn't a minority; he's an opportunist. His name is all over the company – along with Stroud, who's Irish – but the actual articles of incorporation are in his wife's name. Who, as long as we're using descriptive language, is as white as pasteurized milk. Apparently Mr Decker has some fraud convictions in his past which would have precluded a business license.'

'How does this affect me?' Novosek's voice hinged on desperate, because he suspected

236

exactly how it affected him.

'It's a nightmare,' the clerk went on as if Chris hadn't spoken. 'The protests over the jail design have not gone away. They haven't even faded. Every civil rights group in the country is weighing in on the topic and the ACLU is recruiting talking heads by the score for the series of lawsuits they're already writing up. The prison superintendent is getting death threats – from people who actually sign their name at the bottom. How does it affect you? At least twenty percent of your subcontracting work has to be a minority-owned business. Concrete is such a huge chunk of the overall that Decker & Stroud alone more than fulfilled that clause. If they're reclassified, you're in violation.'

'Somebody may be in violation, but it's not me! I didn't certify their status, the county did. I didn't solicit a quote from them, you guys did. This isn't my fault.'

'No one's saying it's your fault, Chris,' the man told him with patent patience. 'I'm just saying that the entire contract will have to be reviewed. It's possible you have enough other subcontractors that fit the bill to make it a moot point. It's possible that we still have time to add them on in the finishing work stages. Maybe the exec will reassess the policy. Mostly I just wanted to give you a heads up because there might be some bad press on this.'

'Not for me. This is the county's screw-up, not mine.'

'And you expect them to own up to that? No, they'll let the chips fall where they may, and if some fall on you instead of them, they're not going to worry overmuch. You know how it goes.'

Novosek rubbed his temples, feeling the first rumblings of pain behind his sinuses. 'Great. Whatever. You really could have told me this on the phone. My copper pipe came this morning and thanks to losing half the day with the cops I'm going to have to work everyone on overtime to get it laid before night falls and it disappears to the recycling centers. I knew I should never have built a jail. It's a bad place with bad – I don't know, karma.'

The county employee smiled wearily. 'You superstitious, Novosek?'

'Never used to be. But I'm starting to reassess that policy.'

THIRTY

Nana had been pretty upset. She yelled at Ghost and said she should be locked in her room if only Nana could get up the steps, which made Ghost feel bad. Then Nana burst into tears again, which made her feel even worse.

No one seemed to believe Ghost when she said she thought Nana would simply assume she had gone to school. Apparently a death in the family meant you didn't have to go to school, but Ghost hadn't known that and no one had told her.

School would be out for the summer in another week anyway. Hard to believe that she had been so looking forward to the break, to not having to go to that noisy place full of kids who shoved and shouted. She had been dreaming about summer for the past two months, and now it had become completely unimportant, an abstract, vaguely recalled concept.

Nana had relented enough to make her a toasted cheese sandwich – arguments always seemed to end in food when it came to Nana, along with disappointments, celebrations, debates, bad weather and the kind of day Mom used to call 'getting your ass kicked' – and Ghost had eaten more of it than she had planned. All the walking and running must have worked up some sort of an appetite, which Nana said was good since they now had enough food to feed a small army. She let Ghost leave her sight long enough to go upstairs as a knock at the door promised a delivery of yet more edibles.

After Ghost washed her face, she sat in her own room for a moment or two, felt unable to interest herself in a single item within it, and went back into her mother's.

When she had played dress-up in Sam's clothes, Ghost would go straight for the glittery stuff, tops with bling and frilly, lacy skirts (though her mother didn't have too many of those). A stretchy, sequin-encrusted halter top had always been her favorite. She would pull it over her flat chest and thought she looked as glamorous as someone in a movie. Mom would look at her and say the same thing every time:

239

'You'd better take that off before Nana sees you.'

Someday Ghost would be old enough to wear it. But her mother wouldn't be there.

With some difficulty she swallowed the lump in her throat and dug through the closet looking for the top. When she couldn't find it there she started on the drawers. It suddenly felt very important to find it, or maybe she just didn't know what else to do.

She heard a thump downstairs.

In the vanity drawer she found a tangled collection of bras, pairs of underwear and a white envelope with a clear window in it, like the kind bills come in. She glanced inside, saw green.

Money.

Ghost felt surprised, but not that surprised. Adults always had money, even when they insisted they didn't. But she wouldn't have expected her mother to have that much. The bills added up to four hundred and seventy-five dollars.

She wondered what her mother had planned to do with it. She'd probably been saving up for a new television; the one they had wasn't very big. Ghost had seen huge ones in stores. She stuffed the cash back into the envelope and stood up. She'd give it to Nana.

She had reached the door to the hallway when she heard a man's voice.

The mad dash to intercept/restrain/interview Todd Grisham came to an abrupt end on East Ninth Street.

240

Frank and Angela had made it over the chain-link fence with only minor scrapes and closed the gap to half a block when Todd veered through the stately stone doorways of the Cleveland City Hall. Frank almost stopped dead.

'If he made me run for nothing—' he panted to Angela as they plunged through the glass doors. But he couldn't think of anything bad enough to do to the little twerp before catching sight of him gesticulating wildly to a security guard near the elevator bank. 'Hey!'

They approached, pulling out their shields for the benefit of the guard. As it turned out he couldn't care less. But then a beefy guy with sandy blond hair appeared at Todd's elbow, and he didn't care much either from the way his hand went to his shoulder holster. 'Hold it.'

Frank was still waving his badge. 'We're CPD.'

'Gee, that's impressive. What do you want with my guy?'

Todd's face seemed red and twisted from more than the foot race. 'How do I know you're not working for—'

'*Your* guy?'

Angela spoke. 'We have some questions to ask him about the death of his co-worker at the county jail project.'

Sandy Hair let go of his holster, taking her in like a dog eyes a piece of bacon. 'Do me a favor and consider switching agencies. We could use a girl of your – attributes.'

Frank asked, 'Are you *trying* to lose your left nut?'

241

'And who's going to take it from me?'

'She will,' Frank said, because that was the funny answer, but in truth he'd have happily twisted the guy's flesh off with his own bare hand which now clenched into a ball with the nails poking into his palm—

Angela dealt with the sexism as she always did, by distracting the Neanderthals with a shiny object. 'Kyle Cielac was found murdered this morning.'

And Sandy Hair said *'Shit!'*

He thought the flowers were a masterful touch.

They'd cost $4.50 at the local grocery, but were well worth it. The old lady opened the door without hesitation.

'I'm so sorry about Sam,' he said, with the most sincere expression he could muster. 'I was a friend of hers, and I just wanted to come by and express my condolences.'

He waited for her to invite him in, to float by her on the wave of his destiny, but that didn't happen as immediately as he'd expected. It looked like the woman had been listening to condolences all day long and had about heard enough. She'd opened the door, thanked him for the gift, but then left her wheelchair blocking the space. He tried smiling. It didn't seem to charm her. So he waved the flowers and said, 'I should probably go before it starts to rain. But should I put these in water for you?'

She sighed, and he hoped that fate would kick in and she'd feel that finding one more vase would be more effort than chatting with a stranger for a few moments. With an expert flick of both wrists, she backed the chair into the kitchen and let him pass. He sidled around her. He didn't want to take the chance that she might recognize the lump underneath his open flannel shirt where he had stuck his thirty-eight into his waistband at the small of his back.

He started opening drawers, scanning the table and cabinets as he did so – much easier with the lights on. But he didn't see it.

'Vases are under the sink,' the old lady said. 'How did you know my daughter?'

He opened another drawer. Didn't these people put tools in drawers? He always did. But this kitchen held only dish towels and silverware. He needed a look at the rest of the place. And the basement – tools were in the basement.

'Under the *sink*,' the woman repeated.

'Oh, yeah.'

Stupid! He was thinking like an adult. It was the kid who had the screwdriver. She'd put it in a kid place. Maybe by the TV. He handed the vase to the old lady. She gave him a funny look, but then wheeled to the sink, set the flowers on the counter, and began to fill the vase with water.

He took this opportunity to dart into the living room.

The curtains to the old lady's sleeping area were open now, and a lamp next to her bed illuminated the tidy area. The living room lights also blazed – good for his eyesight but making him plainly visible to the street outside since the blinds had not been lowered. He scanned the area, looked down at where he had found the backpack the night before. The same coffee cups and magazines on the table – and a screwdriver with a black and red handle, the initials SZ carved into the plastic.

Success!

'What are you doing?'

He nearly dropped it. The mother had noted the vacated kitchen and wheeled through the small doorway. Her face, which had been simply weary, now seemed seriously suspicious.

'Um – Sam had borrowed this from me. I'll take it back now, so you don't have to trouble yourself returning it later.' He stuffed it into his back pocket, the sharp end pointing up. The gun shifted as he put pressure on the denim.

'You don't take anything out of this house!' The old lady had a pretty formidable tone when she had a mind to. Fortunately for him, he didn't care. What was she going to do, run him over? 'Let me see that.'

He pulled it out, held it up, put it back in his pocket. 'Just a screwdriver. It's mine. Look, I know you must be exhausted so I'll go. I just wanted to tell you how really sorry I am about Sam.'

Her mouth worked a bit, like a fish out of water, but she must have decided that a screwdriver wasn't worth arguing over and said, 'Fine. Goodbye.'

He took one step. 'I'd just like to say hello to Ghost, if that's all right.' Though it didn't matter if it was or wasn't. He didn't intend to leave the house without the kid this time. 'Express my condolences.'

She immediately wheeled herself – being pretty fast with that thing – in front of the steps. 'She is eleven years old. You don't need to be talking to her.'

'Yes, I do. I want to tell her what her mother meant to me.'

He thought he sounded reasonable, sweet, even, but old ladies have that sixth sense, gathered from a lifetime of observing other people. 'No. Leave *now*.' She spoke through gritted teeth.

He moved toward the front door, but only to pick up the bat.

After another moment, he called: 'Ghost? I'm coming up.'

He repositioned the gun – how did people carry these things all the time, without a holster? The clunky piece of metal constantly slid around and he felt sure he would soon shoot off the end of his spine. So he walked up the steps slowly, keeping his arms wrapped around himself to look as unthreatening as possible. He slowed even more as he reached the top, but saw the girl instantly.

The angel/demon child sat on the floor in her mother's bedroom, eyes huge, little mouth hanging open, two pairs of cheap beads around her neck. She watched him, scared, almost terrified and yet not screaming. Announcing his presence had given him legitimacy. She remained calm enough, waiting for him to explain himself.

'Hello,' he said. 'I'm so glad to meet you. I've waited a long time.'

A perplexed frown, but no screams, no gasps. 'Wh–hy?' she asked.

'Because I'm your father.'

THIRTY-ONE

Sandy Hair turned out to be John Finney, State of Ohio's Congressional Task Force on Public Corruption, working in conjunction with and out of the offices of the Cleveland City Hall. He managed to pronounce every capital as he ushered them into a conference room that doubled as a storage closet, with half of the table given over to cardboard file boxes. The view of the lake, however, stunned, especially now with deep blue waves churning angrily under a gray sky, the clouds pulsing and growing darker by the minute.

'He killed him, man!' Todd said for the third time. 'He knows we're on to him and he killed Kyle!'

'Sit down, Todd.' Finney looked at Frank and Angela. 'What do you have, and why were you chasing our CI?'

Frank tried not to chuckle at the straight-from-TV tone and lingo and plucked off the blue and white 'Visitor' sticker the jerk had made him wear. 'We wanted to ask him about his good, dead buddy. How long has he been your informant, and what is he informing about?'

The agent brought the cops up to speed, in a way to give them as few specifics as possible, while Todd panted and sweated and bemoaned his friend. A glass of water did not calm him. A whiskey sour probably wouldn't have calmed him.

'And you think Novosek killed Kyle?' Frank asked the young man.

'*Duh!*'

'How did he get Kyle there, by himself, at night?'

That stopped the kid. 'I ... don't know.'

Frank took a closer look at the reddened eyes, glazed with perhaps more than grief. 'Are you high, Todd? Did you smoke some—'

'Of course I did! My friend is dead, and who do you think is going to be next? Who?'

'We can protect you,' Finney said automatically.

'You said that, and now where is Kyle? Speared, that's where!'

Frank considered how much stock he felt willing to put in this abject grief and how much to put in this complicated tale of public corruption. 'Why would Kyle have met Novosek, the guy you think is dirty, at the site, alone, late at night?'

Todd said nothing, his knees drawn up to his chest in the worn swivel chair.

'But he'd have met *you*.'

'Me! You think *I* killed Kyle?' His voice squeaked on the last syllable.

'I got two unattached, red-blooded American guys working with a very red-blooded, smokin' hot American girl.'

'*Sam*?' As if he couldn't be sure who Frank might be talking about.

'Maybe you pushed her off that floor because she turned you down. Maybe Kyle did, for the same reason. Maybe one of you figured that out about the other and you—'

'*Sam*? I wouldn't have wasted a minute on that little slut. I like girls with some class.'

'And big boobs,' Frank couldn't help saying, and for the first time in their three years of partnership, Angela kicked him under the table.

'Sorry,' he said to Todd. 'Sorry, dude, I know you've had a rough week. But I have to explore all possibilities and right now it seems a lot more likely that Sam and Kyle's murders are connected than Chris Novosek suddenly taking out all his whistle-blowers. And since you say Sam wasn't part of this sting, I have to look at other motivations.'

Todd took a deep breath, lowered his feet, drank his water and visibly calmed. 'I'm not going back there, that's all I'm saying. No way you're going to get me to go within ten blocks of that building.'

'Then Novosek will know we're on to him,' Finney exploded. 'You know how many years I've worked on this—'

Angela said, 'He can at least take a few days off. He's upset about his friend, so no one will read too much into that. If we can get the murders wrapped up, maybe it won't completely derail your investigation.'

'Unless Novosek really *did* kill Cielac. Then

248

you've got him on murder, but what the hell have I got?'

'My heart bleeds,' Frank said. 'Todd, why do you think Kyle would have gone to the site after dark to meet Novosek?'

'He didn't,' Todd said. 'He went there to meet me.'

He couldn't believe how easy it was. The kid hadn't moved from her spot on the floor, simply stared up at him with a slack jaw. He sat on the bed and made himself speak slowly and quietly. Now and then she'd ask a question and listen raptly to the answer. Which, of course, he had to make up on the spot, but so far he hadn't stumbled. The words flowed out of him as if the crazier and more disconnected he felt, the saner he sounded.

How had he known where to find her? Why, Samantha had told him. She'd run into him at work and decided that Ghost was old enough to meet him. At this the kid straightened her shoulders, as if to show him how mature she had become. Why had Sam told her that Nathan was her father and he got blowed up? Because she knew Nathan would never come back, and she didn't want Ghost to waste her life waiting. Besides, her grandmother hadn't liked him and had insisted Sam stop seeing him. That was what really broke them up. The kid had nodded sagely at this, as if she could easily imagine the old lady downstairs doing exactly that. She must have been a real dragon, that one. No wonder it had taken two blows with the bat to shut her up.

Nana would never let him come to the house, he told the kid, and then he had lost Sam's address. So he was right there in the same city the whole time and couldn't find her, though he'd loved her very much. But he still didn't think he should just pop back into her life, until a man working in a diner told him that a little girl had been looking for her daddy. Then he realized that Ghost wanted to meet him too, and that gave him the courage to try again after all these years.

She swallowed this hook, line and red-and-white bobbin. Why not? It was what she had been waiting to hear all her life. He figured that out halfway through his description of his own place where she – and Nana, he added at her insistence; apparently loyalty trumped prior bad acts – could come and live now. It had a big back yard with a swing set and a dog. Well, a puppy, really. He had just bought the dog a few weeks before, a tiny bundle of fur.

He'd better quit before he added a pony and a bounce house. But it was easy, once he started. Somehow he had instinctively tapped into all the things he had wanted when he was a kid. For several years he had convinced himself that he'd been adopted, and that any day now his real father would pull up and take him away from his worthless foster parents and the two pieces of shit they called his brothers. What he would have wanted this fictional father to say, he now said to the kid. And it worked. She had this dreamy look in her eyes and actually clapped her hands at the thought of the dog.

Time to wrap up. 'I think we should go there now, Ghost. After what happened to your mother, I want you to be safe. It's a nice sturdy house and the dog will protect you. He'll bite anyone who tries to hurt you.'

She couldn't bounce up fast enough. 'OK! Let's tell Nana. She can come too; you can just fold up the wheelchair and then it fits in the trunk. We do it all the time. I can help—'

'Let's not tell Nana just yet. I think she still doesn't like me. But if you come to my house and see how nice it is and then tell her you want to live there, then I think she'll like me.'

'Well—' She seemed to puzzle over this.

'Let's just go out your window. We'll be back before she even knows we're gone.'

She stopped bouncing, stopped smiling, but still not scared: 'How do you know about my window?'

He thought fast. 'Because I've been watching your house at night, ever since your mom died. I didn't want you to be here all alone with no one taking care of you, so I would park across the street and keep watch all night. I saw the window was open and the tree is right there—'

'But it's going to rain. The branches really move a lot when it's windy.'

'It's not raining yet.'

A little uncertainty, but not enough to reject the idea of a new house and a puppy, not to mention the perfect, heroic dad suddenly sweeping back into her life. She gave him a smile again. 'OK.'

'Great.' He stood up. Get her out of the house quietly, into his car. Then they'd head straight for the construction site, wait for everyone to leave for the day. He could already imagine her falling, the scrawny arms, the whipping hair, and he felt a tightening in his groin.

And then it all went horribly wrong.

THIRTY-TWO

Theresa ushered Ian into the Toxicology lab and past the rows of Nalgene jars full of blood, urine and gastric contents. The prosecutor's nose wrinkled slightly and he seemed to keep his gaze averted from the counters.

Oliver, as always, stayed shut up in his lair of compressed gas tanks and the GC-Mass Spec, his thin ponytail trailing down his fleshy back like a dead snake. And, as always, he ignored their presence until Theresa spoke.

She introduced Ian, steeling herself for the reaction. Oliver had a brilliant reputation for his encyclopedic knowledge of chemicals and their compounds, forms and effects. He had an equally vibrant reputation for his utter lack of tact, manners or compassion.

Oliver peered at the prosecutor. Peered, squinted, frowned, opened his mouth and shut it again. But mercifully, all he *said* was, 'Yes?'

'Samantha Zebrowski's toxicology results.'

'Classified.'

'Christine says she sent you an email

permitting release of the info to me.'

'Email is so impersonal. How do I know you didn't hop on your little girlfriend's computer and sent it yourself?'

'Call her, then.' Theresa told him wearily. Oliver subscribed to policy only when he wanted to jerk someone's chain.

'I'll make a note in the file that I am taking your word for it.' Oliver had a hundred and fifty pounds on the pathologist, but still feared her wrath as much as everyone else in the building. He just wouldn't admit it. 'She was drunk. I'd say drunk as a skunk, but that saying certainly evolved only because it rhymes. Or perhaps because they have such an ambling gait, skunks.'

'Drunk?'

'What I said. Blood alcohol level: one point two. Not passed-out falling down drunk, but definitely tipsy. Which might have tipped her right over the edge, hmm?'

Theresa and Ian exchanged a glance. This would not help any prosecution, but might also explain why Samantha chose to climb to the top of an unfinished building in the pitch dark. It was a lark, a bit of fun. Until the mood changed and the beating began.

Theresa asked, 'What about Kyle Cielac?'

'Sober. Yes, I have him done already, only a few hours after the autopsy, because I am extraordinary and because your homey put a Post-it on his bottle saying: "Rush!" That woman is entirely too liberal with her Post-its. Oh, he'd probably had a beer earlier in the evening, maybe even two, a big strapping guy like him, but

BAC was zero point four. I'd say sober as a judge, but I've known too many judges. The skunk simile is probably more accurate.'

'What about those yellow globules I gave you? In a glassine fold?'

With an exaggerated sigh he turned away from them to shuffle through the papers on his desk, muttering dark tidings about organic compounds, Post-it notes, and forensic scientists who thought their samples should take precedence over all others in the county.

Theresa turned to Ian. 'Samantha's state complicates her motivations, doesn't it? She might have been there to enjoy the view, to spice up her sex life with an unusual location, because she thought someone was up to no good at the site and decided to investigate, for all three reasons or no reason at all.'

'Yeah. It doesn't help. But I don't waste a lot of time worrying about motivation. After twenty plus years in this line of work I've come to the conclusion that you never really know why anyone does anything.' A thought seemed to strike him, and he turned to gaze into her eyes for a brief moment. 'Even ourselves.'

Oliver cleared his throat. 'Not to tear you away from the labor-intensive process of making puppy-dog eyes at each other, but speaking of sticky balls – the stuff you gave me is aspartame, citric acid, and potassium citrate.'

Theresa considered this while Ian's phone buzzed. He checked the screen, thanked them both for their time (Theresa somewhat more effusively than Oliver) and left.

'It sounds like artificial flavoring,' she mused to the toxicologist.

He turned back to his desk, signaling that she had gotten all the help she'd be likely to for one day. 'It could be a lot of things – drink mix, box mix, kid's candy – none of which concern me.'

'Thanks, Oliver.'

'Oh, any time, any time. I exist to serve at others' whimsical pleasure. You know, puppy dogs are terribly cute,' he added, turning to glance at Ian Bauer's back moving down the hall, 'until they pee on the rug one too many times.'

'Similes. I'm simply drowning in similes.'

When her new father stood up, the front of his long flannel shirt fell open. Underneath he wore a T-shirt and jeans with a leather belt and a large buckle.

The light caught the buckle.

And glinted back to her in the shape of a star.

He wasn't her father. He was the shadow man.

She looked at him, clearly visible in the ordinary light of an ordinary room in an ordinary house, but she knew who and what he was, and now he knew she knew. The expression on his face changed from benevolent to sneering in the time it took her to draw in enough air to scream.

Then he was upon her.

He clamped one hand over her mouth; it felt like it covered her face up to her eyes just as she needed to breathe in, the force coming as such a blow that it knocked her backward on to the floor. The surface met her spine and her head struck the edge of the bed post. She forgot about breathing and saw stars.

'Shut *up*,' he told her.

He put the hand over her mouth again and then picked her up that way, so that her neck threatened to snap from suspending the weight of her body. Ghost sucked in air through her nose just to grunt in pain. Then she felt his hands on her.

He rubbed thick fingers down her arms and back, then moved to her hips and thighs – *nono-nonono*!

She kicked out. Her shoes might be too big but they had a firm sole and she heard the slightest grunt from him. He used the hand holding her face to give her head a shake and then turn it away from him, crushing the back of her skull into his chest. His other hand slid over the front of her body again. Just as she thought she might suffocate, she realized that he didn't mean to molest her. He was picking her up. He pulled her hips up across one of his and marched her out of the room as if she were a plank of wood.

He plunged awkwardly down the steps, practically breaking her neck. She didn't struggle much, too busy trying to comprehend what had happened, until they got to the bottom and she caught sight of her grandmother sprawled on the living room floor, a trickle of blood from the side of her head.

'*Nana! Nana! Nana!*' Ghost tried to scream, and her body rocked in a frantic thrashing. She had to get to Nana. But the man just held her tighter until her spine felt as if it would snap in half. He dragged her out of the living room and to the back door. There he had to take his hand off her mouth for a moment in order to turn the knob. Maybe her cry startled him as well, because he let her feet slump to the ground, but then he put the hand back on her mouth, kept her head pressed to his shoulder, and dragged her through the side yard to the street.

A few drops of water hit her face, and the wind whipped her hair over her eyes, but she saw a car parked at the curb. She silently flailed her arms and legs. She tried to bite him, but he kept his skin away from her teeth. She tried to grab the gate as they went out and got a handful of splinters for her trouble.

With her vision partially obscured by his large palm, she saw a tall black boy in the next yard, one of the younger Walker kids. He had been looking at the car, but did a double take when he saw Ghost and the man.

'Don't say a word,' the shadow man told him.

'Hey – what – let that kid go,' the boy shouted. Behind him, one of his brothers stepped off the porch.

'Shut up,' the man said, and let go of Ghost's waist to open the passenger door.

'You best be letting go of that kid,' the boy said, with just as much authority and now a gun in his hand to back it up.

The door open, the man switched hands suddenly, clamping Ghost's mouth with his left hand and freeing his right. She could have escaped if she didn't need her head, her body free from the neck down but her skull pinned tightly. She tried to kick him, didn't stop even when his right hand came forward with a large black gun in it.

'Get back,' he said to the Walker boy. 'Don't move.'

The boy threw his free arm out in exaggerated exasperation. 'Well, what is it? Don't move or get back? You see, man –' his gun didn't waver an inch – 'you need to let that girl go before I blow your head off.'

Behind him, his brother also had a gun, and both were pointed right at the shadow man. And at Ghost, too, but that was all right. The man loosened his grip just enough that she could turn and kick him harder than she had ever kicked anything in her life, so hard that she felt the impact reverberate up her skeleton and into her brain.

His grip loosened another tiny bit. She pulled out of it and ran, past the Walkers and their guns, down the street, heading for the narrow over-grown passageway between the two homes second and third from the end, the wind clutching at her body.

Behind her, she heard a shot.

THIRTY-THREE

Frank would have bet that nothing else about the day could surprise him – and would have lost. 'What do you mean, he went there to meet you?'

'He figured out how Kobelski did it. How he faked the slump test,' Todd said, his tone hovering between terrified and miserable.

Frank pictured the barrel-chested, pugnacious state inspector. 'What's a slump test?'

Finney told him to shut up before turning to Todd Grisham. 'How did he do it?'

'I don't know.'

The state agent goggled. And with his coloring, goggling turned into a pretty impressive display of apoplexy. *'What do you mean you don't know?'*

'Before we left for the day Kyle told me to meet him back there at ten. He said he knew how Kobelski faked the test and wanted to show me, so we were both on the same page before we brought it to you. In case anything happened to him.' Todd's voice choked and strangled. 'In case anything *happened* to him. I should have just made him tell me right then and there, but there were so many other guys around and everyone wanted to talk to us about Sam and we were afraid to say anything where someone else might overhear. *I* was afraid.'

'So what happened?' Angela gently prodded.

'We went home. I ate dinner – my sister-in-law's gyros, guaranteed to incapacitate – so I was a little late getting back. It was ten sixteen by my watch, but it's five minutes fast. I went into the site—'

'Past the fence? How did you get in?' Frank asked.

Todd shrugged. 'Gate was open. It has a big honkin' padlock on it, but Novosek keeps the key in a lockbox. Everyone knows the code is the street address number, one three eight zero. Even my niece could figure that one out.'

'Would have been helpful to hear that when we were trying to figure out how Sam Zebrowski got on the property.'

Todd shrugged again, his face lit by a bolt of lightning that appeared over the lake. 'Didn't know you didn't know. So I went in, up to where the I-beams are stacked. I figured Kyle had opened the gate. I listened but didn't hear anything, so I called his name. I probably called three or four times, loud as I could. Sounds crazy but what choice did I have? I wasn't going to wander around and I wasn't going to stand there all night.' Now he not so much shrugged as shuddered. 'The darkness just swallowed up the sound like I wasn't even there. Just consumed it, man, like a living thing waiting there to eat me.'

'Very descriptive, Todd,' Frank told him. 'Let's just stick to facts, OK?'

'This is facts. Because there was something waiting for me to come closer but it wasn't the darkness. It was Novosek.'

'You saw him?'

'I didn't see shit. You think I would have left Kyle lying there all night like – like he was?'

Frank tamped down his impatience, but Finney didn't. 'So what the hell *did* you do?'

'I left. I just turned and walked away, man. I went home and went to bed.' His voice broke. 'I left Kyle stuck there with the life draining out of him.'

'You couldn't see the elevator pit from where you were?'

'No. I never set foot on concrete, never walked more than a foot past the I-beams. The whole place was darkness, man, just one mass of living, breathing darkness.'

Frank got down to practicalities. 'How long were you there?'

'Maybe ten minutes.'

'So from approximately ten sixteen to ten twenty-six p.m.'

'Yes.'

'Did you close or lock the gate behind you?'

'Left it exactly as I found it, man.'

'And you never saw another person the whole time you were there? Heard a scrape, a clink of metal? Glimpsed movement, or a reflection?'

'Nothing but silence. A living, breath—'

Finney cut in. 'So you don't know it was Novosek? You don't even know if Kyle had arrived. He might have been late too.'

Todd examined this statement like a tethered Styrofoam ring tossed into raging seas. 'You think so? Maybe he wasn't even there yet?'

261

'Nah, he probably was bleeding out just like you thought. But how would Novosek have known exactly when to come by and give your buddy a shove? Who else knew you two had this little rendezvous planned?'

'No one.'

'Come on! You must have told someone! Your brother. Sam's mother. Your niece. Your bookie. Someone!'

'Nobody! Nobody else would have even had any idea what I was talking about.'

'Then maybe Kyle. Who would he have confided in? His room-mate? His priest?'

'Nobody. Me. Maybe Sam. You. Why the hell didn't he call you?' Todd suddenly demanded of Finney. 'You've been nagging us to figure out Kobelski's trick. Did he call you?'

'That would have made too much sense.' Finney slumped back in his chair to massage the bridge of his nose. 'I hate working with amateurs. And you have no idea what your partner referred to when he said he had figured it out.'

'He's dead, don't you get that? Dead! Maybe that's a little more important than your concrete fraud case!'

'And you've got absolutely nothing on the guy you think killed him. Not for fraud, not for malicious endangerment, not for murder. You'd better rethink your recollections of last night if you ever want to get any justice for your friend.'

'Stop leading my witness.' Frank stood up. 'He's got one thing right – murder trumps fraud. Todd, you're coming with us. I'm going to put you into protective custody.'

The kid didn't move. 'Do I have to sleep in a jail cell?'

He looked so pathetic that Frank couldn't snap at him, as much as he did not necessarily believe a single word of what they'd been told so far. 'No, I think we can find a more comfortable spot than that.'

Todd Grisham used the edge of the table to pull himself to his feet. It seemed to require a great deal of effort. 'Good.'

Chris Novosek's day, like so many of them lately, did not improve. Getting the guys back to the job had been only partially successful; most of them had begun to enjoy their impromptu day off and didn't feel like picking up the phone when the foreman called. They'd miss out on the overtime – good for him – but a skeleton crew couldn't lay more than half of the pipe, even if they worked until nightfall and didn't get too held up by the rain that had just begun to sprinkle them with drops. He found himself calculating the outlay of overtime versus the monetary loss if the pipe were stolen, and figured out they should knock off around eight p.m.

He had just completed this complicated series of calculations, which only intensified the pain behind his eyes, when the two homicide cops showed up again. Definitely not improving. 'Don't tell me you're here to shut me down again.'

'Nope,' Frank Patrick said. 'Or at least, not as far as we're concerned. We just need you. We don't care what your men do.'

Novosek couldn't stifle a groan. 'What *now*?'

'We're here to arrest you for the murders of Kyle Cielac and Samantha Zebrowski.'

'*What*?'

'You have the right to remain silent. You have the right to an attorney to be with you—'

'Didn't we already go through this once to-day?'

'This is different,' Angela told him.

'*How*?'

'This time we have evidence.'

Damon and Boonie watched the two cops lead off their boss. Their *official* boss.

'The man has troubles,' Boonie said. 'Poor man.'

'Lucky us,' Damon added, gazing at the stacks of copper pipe, which shone like gold in the slanting afternoon light.

Theresa snatched up the phone, punched the blinking red light. 'Ghost?'

'Uh, no. This is Scott. I am not yet a ghost, at least not that I know of.'

The secretary had said it was someone about the Zebrowski case. Theresa swallowed her disappointment and said, 'Yes, Mr Crain. How can I help you?'

Apparently she hadn't swallowed enough. 'For starters you could sound a little less annoyed to hear my voice.'

'I don't have a lot of time to spend on a vandal who fancies himself a social activist. What do you want?'

A pause, as if he were swallowing one or two emotions himself. 'I want to talk to you. As a scientist, you should make yourself completely aware of what our government is planning to do inside that new building, and when you do, I'm sure you'll see that we—'

'As a scientist, I should be doing my job, which is to find out how and why two people died.'

'Well,' he said, 'I could tell you something about that, too.'

'Sure. Go ahead.'

'In person. Can we meet?'

'No. I'm busy and I'm a witness in your case. If you have knowledge relating to the recent murders you should contact the investigating officers.' She reeled off this party line but had a hard time feeling it. Despite herself, she began to feel the intrigue of Scott Crain and his ominous hints.

'Those investigating officers are the same jackbooted Nazis who arrested me, so forgive me if I'd rather talk to you.'

This made a certain amount of sense. Better he talk to her than no one at all. 'OK, I see your point. So go ahead.'

'Come outside. I'm standing by your car.'

'You leave my—'

Click.

He had hung up.

THIRTY-FOUR

'What evidence?' Novosek asked for the fifth time.

Frank dropped into the steel chair in the newly painted room, feeling only a twinge of the weariness catching up with him. Mostly he felt the twin surges of adrenalin as when a horse sees the barn and when the fox corners the rabbit. Victory was within reach. All he had to do now was pull it in.

Similes. His cousin had mentioned something about that, when she'd called.

'Do you know why there's so much corruption in the construction trades, Novosek?' Angela began.

Frank sat back and listened. They had figured letting a female take the lead would throw Novosek off even more. Besides, her silky voice made everything sound more dangerous, somehow. Threatening.

Enticing.

Ready to provide something he hadn't known he was seeking.

Concentrate, dude.

She hadn't waited for an answer. 'Because it's so easy. There are so many different aspects of a project, especially this size. Design. Concrete.

266

Piping. Air-conditioning. Personnel. Supplies.'

'Yeah?' Novosek interrupted. The suspense was getting to him.

'Each and every one of those aspects can be pilfered, kickbacks made for using this supplier instead of that one, and the costs can go up in the months it takes from breaking ground to cutting the ribbon. You can double the price of a box of bolts, because really, who in the county is going to go double-check the price on a box of bolts? How much could it be, a buck? Except that buck is multiplied by two thousand boxes. It adds up. It always has. It always will.'

'I haven't stolen a penny from this job. I don't do that.' The burst of a nail gun up the hall served as an exclamation point.

'I want to believe that, Chris. And I do – in one respect. We checked your financials. You're drawing your salary from the job's operating costs, that's it. At least on paper, you have no un-explained deposits, no offshore bank accounts, no recent homes or cars or boats purchased in your name, or your wife's name, or your kids' names.'

His scowl deepened until it left deep creases in his face. 'You leave my family out of this.'

'However, also on paper, you have three em-ployees named Stan Johnson, Tyler Rodriguez, and Slyman Stears. One is an ironworker, one a pipefitter, one an electrician.'

The scowl flattened out. 'Yeah?'

'The thing is, they seem to exist *only* on paper. None of the workers at your site have ever met them. Their addresses are fake, their phone

267

numbers are fake, their socials belong to a professional golfer in Phoenix, a schoolteacher in Moline and I forget who else. Almost as if someone made them up.'

Novosek's expression got even blanker.

'But they make good money, probably better than the teacher. I don't know about the golfer. Nice salaries that are paid to these men out of the general operating fund, which exists from draws made from the county coffers earmarked for this project. Yes, the men don't seem to exist, but their salaries are real enough. Real checks cashed at real banks. What do you think we're going to see when we check the real security footage of these real banks? I'm guessing we're going to see a real person, because tellers generally don't wait on phantoms.'

Novosek said nothing.

'We've got cops at all three banks pulling the video now,' Angela said. 'Like I said, it's not surprising. Large projects just make it so damn easy to steal. It's the nature of the beast—'

'I didn't steal nothing!' Novosek leaned forward and slapped his hands on the table, sending a small flurry of dust motes into the air – the renovations left every surface on the floor covered in drywall powder. Then he stopped, looking as if he were literally biting his tongue. Angela let the silence drag on.

Finally Novosek said, 'Have you seen my contract with the county on this project?'

Neither detective answered.

He sighed. 'The market crashed. The economy tanked. Real estate, I'm sure I'm not telling you

268

nothin' you don't already know, was the hardest hit. No one had money to build, they didn't have money to renovate, they didn't even have money to continue building what they'd already started. I had to lay off. Then I had to lay off more. I had only been in business for myself for seven years and already I thought I'd have to take my kid out of private school—'

'Things are tough all over,' Angela said in a firm tone Frank hoped she would never have to use on him. 'Is that when you decided to rob your next project?'

'That was when I got desperate enough to make a deal with the devil.' Novosek abandoned the tough-guy slouch to rub both his temples. 'I don't know who the new county exec hired to oversee building contracts, but he got his money's worth because the guy made the most of a buyer's market. The job doesn't come in on time, I pay a penalty – which essentially means I knock something off the price. I don't use enough minority owned businesses, I pay a penalty. I don't use suppliers within the county as long as their prices are within five percent of any out-of-county competitors, I pay a penalty. The price of raw materials goes up less than ten percent, I eat it, or I pay a penalty. I go over budget, I pay a penalty. They could nickel-and-dime me into getting the damn building for free if they really try, and they'll really try. But what the hell was I going to do? I could take the job or I could close up shop.'

'Sounds pretty stressful,' Angela said, without the slightest shred of sympathy in her voice. 'So you suppose that justifies pocketing the salaries of three fake employees?'

'Yes. Because I didn't pocket that money. The job did.'

'Pardon me?'

'That money makes up the shortfalls. Because sometimes the cost of raw materials *does* go up. Sometimes rain or a holiday or a water-main break does delay the work. Because sometimes I do have to pay five percent more than I should have to in order to use an in-county supplier. Sometimes the guys screw something up and it costs time and materials to fix it. Sometimes things go wrong. That's called *life*.'

'So you're somehow conning money out of the county for the ultimate good of the county?'

'For the good of me and my guys, who are just trying to make an honest day's wage for an honest day's work without getting strangled by some bullshit fine print.'

Angela did not look convinced, though Frank knew she actually liked the guy. She was a sucker for a working-class hero, which only made what he had to do next more uncomfortable. 'A real Robin Hood, that's you. But whether it's stealing or simply good money management, that's between you and your God and your county auditors. Because my partner and I aren't here to talk about embezzlement. We're here to talk about murder.'

The passion Novosek had shown while explaining his management style faded abruptly. The dust motes settled down. 'What about it?'

'We know about the concrete. We know Kyle

knew too. Is that why you killed him?'

Novosek's jaw actually loosened and hung open for a moment or two. 'You ... What...? You got to be kidding me. You think I killed Kyle Cielac over the minority-owned-business clause? What the hell would he have to do with that? What—'

Angela recovered faster than Frank. 'No, Mr Novosek, we're not here about business clauses. We're here because we think you killed Kyle Cielac to keep him from telling state investigators how you, your concrete supplier Decker and Stroud, and Inspector Kobelski conspired to replace the required concrete with a substandard mix and pocket the difference in the cost. That's what we think.'

Chris Novosek continued to gape at them.

Then he said, slowly and clearly: 'What the hell are you talking about?'

THIRTY-FIVE

Damon and Boonie gave Jack a friendly nod as they left the site. Best to have someone to remember that they had left along with everyone else, nothing suspicious, everyone hustling to get gone before the clouds really opened up, but they couldn't be sure the ironworker would even recall them. Every guy on the site seemed frustrated, frazzled and worried. Two deaths in two days. Come to work, get sent home, come back to work, sent home again. They'd no sooner start a section before some cop came and chased them out and were no longer in the mindset to use the time off as a mini-vacation; the time off represented lost wages and a backlog of tasks that would make the next day even more hectic. Not to mention someone seemed to be out to get them: home-grown terrorists, fanatical civil rights activists, or just some particularly pissed-off ghost. Or worse, maybe one of them. Each man on the job no longer wished to turn his back on the same guys he'd been hauling I-beams, eating lunch or laying pipe with for the past few months.

For Damon and Boonie, however, things seemed to get better every minute. A white guy now sat in a holding cell instead of them. They appeared to be two honest laborers, victims of a string of bad luck. And the fears of their co-workers would keep each of them far away from the site once the sun went down, leaving them all the time and freedom necessary to relieve their beleaguered boss of his pile of expensive copper pipe. It hadn't been their purpose in this under-cover assignment, but, as the boss explained, a smart man always has one eye out for opportunity. And the boss was a smart man.

They walked away from the site without looking back, heading for Tower City where they could get a bite to eat, rest a while, and wait for the sun to go down.

* * *

'Get off my hood.'

Scott Crain twisted his face up to illustrate what he thought of her desire to preserve a '95 Ford Tempo as if it were an Italian sports car, but he slid off the fender obediently enough. 'Who's this?'

'This is my bodyguard,' she said of her co-worker Don, who stood at her shoulder. 'What, some guy I don't know with a documented history of violence tells me to meet him in the parking lot, you think I'm going to come alone?'

Truth be told, Don was a bit slender for protection work, but then so was Scott Crain. And Don had three inches on him, easy.

'Hurry up,' she added, glancing at the third-floor windows. She had given the secretary desperate and pleading instructions that if Ghost called back, she was to open the pane and shriek. 'I'm expecting a phone call.'

Crain continued to glare at Don, who, despite his generally peaceable attitude, hovered just in front of her in a convincingly intimidating manner. He even went so far as to say, 'She's not going anywhere without me,' which she thought was taking the role a bit far but she liked it. So she added to Crain: 'Don is our DNA analyst.'

Receiving another scientist to preach to didn't placate the man as much as she expected, but finally he shrugged and consented to speak his piece. 'Those Nazis didn't believe that I had actually spoken to Sam, the woman who died. But I did, and she did agree with us that the jail design is barbaric. She needed the money – she's supporting her mom – so she couldn't afford to

273

quit on principle. But she was going to get us a copy of the blueprints. We should be able to get a set through a public records request but the planning department won't give them up. "Security reasons," they tell us. The prints are kept in the manager's office but often they get sloppy and leave copies at the various stations. It depends on what stage the work is at.'

'And did she? Get you the plans?'

'No, but I thought maybe that's what she was doing when she died. She was looking for a copy of the blueprints, and somebody caught her. Maybe the project manager. I can't imagine one of those no-neck construction types giving a crap if she had the plans or not.'

Theresa considered this. It was as likely as any other explanation – provided Crain could be believed – but many more facts would be required first. Where in the building were the blueprints kept? Any on the twenty-third floor? And where did Kyle fit in? 'Thank you. I'll let my jack-booted Nazi cousin know about this and we'll check it out.'

'That's it?'

'What else would you like me to do?'

'Have dinner with me.' A crack of distant thunder emphasized the point, as if the man had a supernatural ability to his flair for the dramatic.

'No. Thank you. I appreciate it, but—'

'No,' Don said, and put an arm around her shoulders as they walked away.

'You're good at this,' she told him.

He glanced back at their unusual interviewee.

'Guarding your body is something I take very seriously, girl, and don't you forget it. When you leave for the day you have a deskman walk you out and you check your car first. That man has a look in his eyes that makes my arm hair get stiff.'

The work day had ended for most people, and for the shadow man as well. Without anything else to distract him he went back to the problem of the kid. He couldn't believe he'd gotten past the dragon grandma, soft-sold the kid into coming along, then even though that went to hell and he had to drag her he'd *still* almost had her in the car ... and then those gang-bangers next door had to interfere. They *shot* at him. Who the hell had invited them to the party? That's what he got for hanging out in such a crappy neighborhood.

He'd shot back, thought for sure he'd hit one of them but the guy just stood there as if he was the one protected by destiny. Even as he jumped in his car and took off, the guy hadn't budged, gun still extended.

A bit embarrassing, but otherwise he didn't worry about it. They were unlikely to call the cops. People in their line of work didn't call cops.

Then he'd sped up the street to where he lost sight of Ghost, but she'd darted into a maze of back yards mined with trees and bushes and old appliances and he didn't dare leave his own vehicle, with the engine running and the doors open, long enough to go look for her. He'd

275

circled and circled the streets to no avail. The angel/demon was now a drone somewhere in the hive of the city. She had nowhere to go, no grandma, and the afternoon had probably soured her on the daddy fantasy. The only person she knew, that he knew she knew, was that forensic bitch. But how would the kid find her?

A drone in the hive of the city. And the only thing that would draw her out was a really pretty flower.

And to draw out the forensic bitch?

A really pretty dead body.

He walked to his car, hoping the rain would hold off.

THIRTY-SIX

Frank and Angela took turns laying out Novosek's system for cheating the taxpayers of Cuyahoga County out of approximately one point six million dollars. The money is budgeted for a certain quality of concrete and paid to the supplier. The supplier supplies a lesser mix with cheaper materials. The inspector pretends that the cheaper mix is the more expensive mix, and the supplier kicks back their shares of the one point six million. Very nice, until six or ten years from now when the building falls in on itself. A lot of people then will have a lot of questions, but each of the three parties can point his finger at the other two, and nothing will be proven. 'Just like the Big Dig,' Frank finished up. 'No one will go to jail. You'll all just keep working. A few people might die, but it will be some scumbag criminal instead of an innocent mom on her way to the airport.'

'You're crazy,' Novosek said, but the indignation seemed to sit on the surface with a whole lot of fast thinking going on behind it. 'If you think I would ever put up something I thought might fall down, you're crazy. I put two or three years of my life in to a project like this. You think I'd let that all be for nothing?'

'You want something to drink? Maybe Gatorade?'

As Frank had hoped it would, this threw Novosek off so badly he couldn't even keep up the indignation. *'What?'*

'You like Gatorade, right? The powdered kind, maybe, that you can pour into a bottle of water, mix it up yourself. Handy.'

For a large man, Novosek could sit very still.

'Know why it's called that?' Angela put in. 'A Florida Gators coach asked a professor there at the university what to do about players getting so dehydrated during games.'

''Cause it's so freakin' hot down there,' Frank explained.

'So he invented this drink to replace the glucose and electrolytes the boys would lose while playing. Can't stand the stuff myself. Except for fruit punch.'

'Fruit punch is too girly,' Frank said. 'Chris

277

here goes for the original lemon lime. You know how I know that – I mean, other than I saw you drinking it? Because you left a smear of powdered citric acid and potassium citrate on the back of Kyle Cielac's shirt when you shoved him down that elevator shaft. Did you remember the rebar sticking up at the bottom? Or did you just think he'd make the same sickening every-bone-in-the-body-broken crunch like Sam Zebrowski?'

Novosek began to look as green as his favorite drink. But all he said was, 'Lots of people drink Gatorade.'

'They do,' Angela said, nodding. 'They do. But not everyone's ID tag is found next to the victim—'

'I told you, I lost that.'

'—with the victim's fingerprint on it.'

Now their suspect looked flat-out ready to puke.

He made one last attempt: 'I told you, I lost it earlier in the day. Maybe Kyle found it—'

'Lanyards,' Frank interrupted.

'Huh?'

'They're so popular now. I'm not crazy about them myself; I have the little retractable thingy that clips to my belt, see? Angela wears hers –' his partner held up her ID tag, suspended around her neck by a dark blue strap labeled 'Cleveland Police Department' – 'but she's a girl so it looks OK on her. I noticed you and most of your em-ployees wear them. County regulations, right?'

Novosek said nothing, but his gaze never left Frank's face. He didn't even seem to be breathing.

'But they're a safety hazard, really. The FOP protested when they were first proposed, but who the hell listens to unions any more, am I right? We work with guys all day long who don't really like us, so what's to keep them from using these handy little ID badge holders to choke the living shit out of us? So the manufacturer put in a breakaway. So if I do this –' he reached out and jerked Angela's lanyard from around her neck, eliciting an annoyed bleat from his partner – 'the plastic ends come apart and her lovely neck is saved. It's the same for your guys – way too many tools and cables and beams around that could catch that lanyard and do some serious harm. The lanyard we found in the pit – your lanyard – hadn't dropped out of your pocket or worn through the strap. The breakaway had pulled apart, and I'm betting that happened when you pushed Kyle Cielac to his death. He scrabbled for something to hang on to, for something to save him from that abyss, and all he got was your ID badge. He grabbed for you, and you let him fall.'

Novosek's eyes grew moist, but he scrabbled for a hold as well. 'You can't prove that.'

'Pretty much, yeah. Because if you had lost that ID badge any other way, catching it on a tool or a box, you would have felt the jerk to your neck. It wouldn't have been lost because you would have immediately realized that it had broken. And there wouldn't be a pristine imprint of Kyle Cielac's fingerprints on it.'

The moist eyes widened.

'Kind of interesting, the interaction of finger-prints and blood. A fingerprint is a little raised impression of oil and sweat. That ID badge landed in the pit, and then Kyle Cielac landed on top of those rebar spikes and began to bleed.'

Chris Novosek blanched, apparently picturing this.

'The blood flowed over this print, flooding the little valleys between these mountains of oil and sweat. And then, since it had an unrestrained area to spread out in, the blood kept going. The flood of red cells receded and the mountain ridges stuck out again, like Mount Ararat. You get sort of a reverse image of a bloody finger-print, but still unique to Kyle Cielac's thumb. Kind of cool, in its microscopic way. I only know all that, of course, because my cousin just explained it to me over the phone.'

Novosek shrugged himself back to life. 'Cousin? That girl's your cousin?'

'Between the breakaway snapping and the pristine, fresh print, there's no way I'm going to believe – and there's no way a jury is going to believe – that you didn't push Kyle Cielac down that hole. The only question left is why. Because of Sam, or because he knew about your one point six million in concrete?'

'Why, Chris?' Angela added softly.

And then they watched the man break.

'Neither! I didn't mean to push him! I just went back there to look at the pipes – there's something funny about the guys doing it, and I can't figure out what it is – and yes, to keep an eye on the place. I thought maybe the killer

280

would come back, I thought maybe that protester would come back – I don't know what I thought. But suddenly Kyle popped up in front of my flashlight, scared the crap out of me, and he starts talking about the concrete and how Kobelski switched out the whole book, that was how he did it, and how could I do something like that, risk lives just to make a few more bucks. He was hot and I – I had no friggin' idea what he was talking about, only that I've had one problem after another on this job until I go home every night just wanting to shoot myself. I just wanted him to *shut up* – and I pushed him. I didn't mean to hurt him, I just wanted him to remember that *I* am the boss.' He dropped his face to his hands; a muffled sob escaped. 'I had no idea the elevator pit was right there. It was darker than hell and I had nothing but a little flashlight. How could I have known?'

'So he fell,' Angela finished for him.

The project manager wiped away tears with two angry swipes. 'I didn't know what happened at first; it was as if the darkness just swept him away. He grabbed my badge, I stepped forward, waving around this light that's practically no brighter than a candle, and then I saw the hole. I couldn't see the bottom.'

'Then what did you do?'

'I went out to my car and drove away. Next thing I know I'm in the parking lot of my old high school – I have no idea why, I haven't been there since I graduated, but I couldn't go home, I could never have kept this from my wife. I finally snuck in about three, changed clothes, went and drank coffee at Denny's and tried to figure out how to act when I got to the site that morning.'

'OK,' Frank said. Maybe he hadn't mean to kill Kyle Cielac, or maybe he couldn't admit that to himself. Not yet. Now to wrap up details before the lawyers descended. 'Two questions. You said Kyle said Kobelski switched the book. What book?'

Novosek dried his eyes. 'I didn't know what he meant at the time, it just sounded like gibberish – but if you are serious about this concrete thing, then he must have meant the ASTM spec book.'

Give me a drug deal gone bad, Frank thought to himself, I am sick to death of people using terms I don't understand. 'What?'

'The concrete is tested at the site before it's poured. We have to do a slump test, where a sample from the truck is poured into a metal container—'

'Yeah, I got that part.'

'And the inspector, Kobelski, checks the slump diameter against the ASTM specs. They're kept in a book near the main drafting table, south-west corner of the building.'

'This book locked up?' Angela asked.

'No, it looks like a skinny, beat-up phone book. If someone took it we'd just get another one.'

'That's how he did it,' Frank said. 'He didn't have to fake the test, because he'd already faked the regs. Can't wait to tell Mr County Special Investigator about that one.'

Novosek swore, low but with feeling.

'What's the matter?'

'Those bastards sold me crappy concrete! That building would have – is going to – cave in in a few years and whose reputation will be ruined? Mine, that's who! If I get my hands around that little runt's neck – I'm going to have to rip out the floors ... hell, I might have to take it down to the dirt and start over – oh, *shit*!'

'Time out, Chris, time out. I'm sure it's very bad but it's also no longer your problem, since you'll be in jail for murder. But first, my second question – if you didn't know about the concrete, why did you kill Samantha Zebrowski?'

Chris Novosek gazed at him, a man so pummeled by current events that he could barely spit out another word. Yet he managed to ask, in dazed, bewildered voice: 'Sam? Why would I kill *Sam*?'

THIRTY-SEVEN

Theresa had identified the fingerprint and the powder on the shirt. She had tried to find a phone number for Ghost's mother, without success. Eventually she would run out of reasons to stick around waiting for a little girl to call again and have to go home. She could tell the night receptionist and deskmen that, this time, it was OK to give out her cell phone number. But first she decided to take another look at the asbestos from Samantha Zebrowski's shirt. Maybe she could help Frank sew up the case against Novosek even more tightly.

But first she tried Rachael again, hitting the speed dial almost absently. Asbestos fibers came in several varieties—

'Hi, Mom!'

'Hi ... wow ... you sound like you're in a good mood.'

'Well, yeah, I guess. I'm about ready for that history test, I know my dates and everything. Oh, and I'm going to Kia's house this weekend, by the way. She says she's got a pool and a cute brother, so how can I resist, right?'

'Sounds like a plan.'

Her daughter chattered on, about the price of doing laundry, that they had tuna salad in the cafeteria, that she had gotten her period, that Sartre, in her opinion, had been vastly overrated, to the point that Theresa began to wonder if her daughter had begun to experiment with more than just hairstyles while at college. The thought made her deeply unhappy, but as she listened even more closely, she had to admit that Rachael sounded utterly sensible and utterly sober. She just sounded like, well, like Rachael.

'—and then Jenna said – oh wait, Mom, I got a click. I'll talk to you later, OK?'

Theresa said *sure* and *love you* and slowly snapped the phone shut. Maybe she had just been reading too much into the whole thing. Teenage girls were moody, everyone – but everyone – knew that. Some moods lasted longer than others. There would be other inexplicable phases and unexplained silences and that was just part of life. Rachael was a person. She had a right to her secrets. Just keep the door always open—

Period.

Since when did a girl sound so perfectly OK with getting her period, especially when she faced a weekend of swimming near a handsome boy?

Theresa tried not to follow that chain of thought to its logical conclusion and failed miserably.

When the girl had been worried she might not get it at all.

Theresa's desk phone rang. She ignored it.

Secrets were inevitable. Life was inevitable. What mattered that her daughter was her daughter and she was relatively safe and relatively happy. And the lines of communication, though slightly clogged, were still open.

Right.

The desk phone rang again. She snatched it up and all but barked her name. The night receptionist said, 'You still here?'

'Since I just picked up the phone, I'd say that's – yes, I'm here.'

'Good. 'Cause there's a girl in the lobby for you.'

Boonie unlocked the back of the van, feeling damp. He couldn't tell if the rain had arrived in a thin mist or if the humidity made him sweat more than usual. Copper was not a lightweight metal and even narrow pipes got heavy when

285

you carried enough of them. He and Damon had filled the van from side to side but they didn't want to overload it until the rusted frame fell apart or until the sagging rear end attracted attention, so Boonie went to make a delivery and Damon remained behind to stage another load at the entrance to the parking area. They had plenty of time. As suspected, no one had returned to the site. Their co-workers were scared, and the cops – 'I'm not complaining, mind,' Damon had told Boonie 'It's just, two murders in two days here. You'd think they'd kind of want to keep an eye on the place.'

'They done,' Boonie had panted. Inside the van, he'd grab one end of the pipes and slide them down to the floor between his feet, keeping the noise of the process to a minimum. The street lights, safety lights and full moon provided more than they needed to work. 'Once they take their pictures and move the body and pick up their little things with little tweezers, once they take down that yellow tape, they're done. They don't come back. They go on to the next one.' Sometimes you had to explain these things to Damon. Not a bad guy, but sometimes he just didn't seem to know nothing about how the world worked. 'Besides, nobody wants to be around a huge pile of metal spikes in the middle of a thunderstorm. No one's gonna be out and about tonight at all.'

'Like I said –' Damon had also panted, to Boonie's pleasure – 'I ain't complaining.'

Twenty minutes later Boonie moved the pipe a second time, wishing they could take them

286

straight to the salvage yard instead of eventually having to move the entire load again. This wouldn't have occurred to the boss, who sat on his lawn chair throne next to the open doorway. Or maybe it did.

The boss's errand boy helped Boonie move the pipe; the second-in-command and the body-guard flanked the lawn chair. No one said anything; nothing needed to be said. When the cargo van stood vacant once again, Boonie hopped in the driver's seat and went back down-town, to commit more felony theft within sight of the Cleveland Police Department. The idea gave him a chuckle.

He parked the van next to the growing pile of copper pipe on the outside of the site fence. Cops doing a spot check might notice it, but with the gate shut they probably wouldn't get out of the car to investigate. People were used to seeing stuff piled around a construction site and be-sides, like the boss said, every investment re-quired some risk.

He shut off the van, unlocked the back door and slipped inside the gate. No way would he start loading that stuff by himself. Too noisy and his back was already hurting.

The place was crazy dark. The moon had gone behind a cloud, or one of the security lights had burnt out; he felt sure it had been light enough to see the debris chip piles, like the one he had just tripped over, when he left. And quiet; the most silent he had ever known the place to be. No movement, no wind, not even a car driving by outside the fence. Boonie felt a tiny frisson of –

not fear, exactly, more like worry – brush over the back of his neck.

He stepped around the I-beams and up on to the foundation. He had to pick his way even more carefully there, feeling around with his feet before each step without letting on that he was doing so. He pictured Damon sitting at ease, eyes adjusted to the dark, watching him stumble around with his hands stretched out like he was blind or something. The idea made Boonie cut loose with a curse, adding, 'Where you at?'

No response. The breeze picked up, carrying the scent of concrete dust and a faint, metallic odor that seemed both familiar and strange at once. Boonie reached the cache of copper pipe, accidentally kicking one free so that it rang out with a startled clap. He cursed again, and finally risked a quiet shout: 'D! Where you at?'

No answer.

Maybe Damon had gone to take a leak. Maybe he'd walked over to Prospect to chat up some ladies. Maybe he'd gone to Michael Symon's place on Fourth to have a steak, who the hell knew. Boonie moved off to his right, avoiding the more well-lit east side of the site. One thing was for sure: he was not loading that pipe by his own damn self. He would hunt up his partner first.

He stubbed his other toe on a gangbox and nearly fell over the slag crate, but made it back to the edge of the foundation, albeit on the south corner now. Still no sound.

Boonie stepped down the short embankment of gravel and sand and chunks of concrete, beginning to chafe at the waste of time. He wanted to get the next two loads done and get out of there, get some sleep before they had to come back the next morning. He looked forward to that, acting all innocent: 'Man, the copper pipe got stolen? Shit!' Of course with murders and the boss being arrested, maybe no one would even notice the pipe, which would be even funnier. The idea lifted his spirits until he plunged into the particularly dark valley between the I-beams and the crane and tripped over something.

He seemed to have both tripped and slipped at the same time, and just as this began to ruin his mood the rest of his mind put two and two together – a pliable object surrounded by a pool of liquid – and came up with horror.

'*Damon*!'

Had to be him, the long shirt he always wore over his tee, the Ralph Lauren cologne he practically bathed in. The more Boonie patted and prodded, trying to revive his friend, the more the body crackled like a bag of broken chips and his own hands grew slick with blood. He tried to turn him over, but each limb and part moved on its own and he gave up. At the end he simply crouched, rocking on his feet in time to the wind's keening wail. Once he realized the sound was coming from him, he shut up. He had to tell the boss. The boss would know what to do.

He got halfway back to the van before it occurred to him to look up.

THIRTY-EIGHT

'She's totally worn out,' Theresa told Ian over the phone. 'She's soaking wet from the rain and I think she ran here – all the way from East Thirty-First. What is that, two, three miles?'

'At least. What's her mental state?'

'Not much better. She's nearly hysterical, keeps sobbing about the shadow man being her father and he hurt Nana. The guy was in her *house*, Ian.'

'Her *father*? And what about Mrs Zebrowski?'

'I called Dispatch, they're sending an ambulance.'

'Well, that's best of course – just remember that in Ghost's state, we have to take any statements with a healthy grain of salt. Have you heard back from Dispatch?'

'Not yet. I only just called them, before I called you. I can't get a hold of Frank – he's in the middle of interrogating Chris Novosek. Otherwise I'd call him.'

'Of course,' he said with a sharper tone, then added, 'At least she's safe.'

'No, Ian, she's not. Because if Chris Novosek killed Sam and Kyle, then who attacked Ghost and her grandmother? Novosek has been under police observation all day and in custody for the past two hours.'

'Maybe he has a partner?' Ian mused aloud.

Theresa held the cell phone between shoulder and cheek as she rummaged in the trace evidence department closet for her emergency sweater, a fuzzy red cardigan. It smelled a bit like disinfectant but she wrapped it around the trembling child, now curled up in her desk chair. Ghost was too exhausted to eat, drink, or even talk. It had taken all her strength to reach the medical examiner's office and what little reserve she had left she used to beg Theresa to send help to Nana. After that she'd collapsed into an unresponsive ball of trembling flesh.

'I don't know, Theresa,' Ian Bauer said. 'But keeping her safe is the top priority. After that we have to get a complete description from her. A composite sketch is probably all we need to break this whole case.'

'Exactly.' She sighed and moved out of earshot. 'And we have to hurry. He knows she can identify him, which means he needs to kill her. He already killed two able-bodied adults, why would he stop at a child? Ian – can you get an artist? I don't know who to call.'

'OK, OK. Look – bring her here.'

'Where?'

'My apartment. The police department victim advocate areas are a disaster right now and all the noise and dust will make it impossible for an already traumatized child to concentrate. I will get the artist to come here – with luck Becky will be on call – and I can take Ghost's statement. By the time we're done with that, maybe your

291

cousin will have gotten some more details out of Novosek and we can figure out where to go from there.'

'That sounds like a plan.'

'With luck the grandmother will go to a hospital instead of the morgue and we can take the girl there, have a doctor check her out at the same time. Ready for the address?'

Theresa repeated it back to him, slid the phone into her purse and very gently pulled the nearly comatose girl to her feet. 'Come on, Ghost. We're going.'

Frank knew the crumbling feeling in his stomach was his case coming apart, showering his budding ulcers with shards of flying debris. 'You're trying to tell us you didn't kill Samantha Zebrowski?'

'Of course not! Why would I kill Sam? I didn't even mean to kill Kyle!'

Angela said, 'You expect us to believe that two different people killed two different victims on two consecutive days at the same location, in the same manner?'

'I don't know what you can believe or can not believe, but I never laid a finger on Sam. Why would I?'

'That's what we've been trying to figure out.'

Novosek spoke with great patience, 'The night Sam died, I left work at the usual time. I even saw her heading to her car. I was home in time for *Live on Five*. I never left the house until I came to work the next morning.'

'And who can verify that?' Frank tried to put a

sneer into it but the pains in his stomach made his voice squeak and ruined the effect. 'Your wife?'

'Yeah, my wife. And my neighbor, because I went out and helped him push his lawnmower into his garage when it quit on him at the tree lawn. The sun had just gone down. And my wife's sister, who's staying with us for the week. And her son, who's sleeping on the couch in the living room without a word of complaint because he stays up all night watching pay-per-view because he knows I won't get the bill until after he's gone.'

'Take the remote to bed with you,' Angela said automatically. 'So you're telling us you killed Kyle but not Sam.'

'For the fifteenth time,' Novosek said through the fingers over his face, *I did not kill Sam.* I did not push her. I did not see her. I was not there that night.'

'You had no motive to kill Sam?'

'None. I – I cared for Sam.'

'Then why did you pay her off?' She slapped two photocopies on to the surface in front of him. 'You withdrew a thousand dollars from your paycheck in the middle of last month. My ex, he used to take the same amount out in cash every time he got paid. Walking-around money, he called it. For lunch, parking, a magazine, cigarettes. You do the same – five hundred dollars, every two weeks.'

'I said it was for increased costs—'

'Not the company. This is your personal mad money. Five hundred dollars, every two weeks. I

293

went back six months. All of a sudden, last month –' she pointed to an entry on the bank statement – 'you take out a thousand. Next check, back to five hundred. Five hundred. Five hundred. Then a thousand, exactly a month after the first. Five hundred. Five hundred.'

He had had enough. 'So?'

'After that first double amount, what turns up in Sam Zebrowski's bank account?' She pointed to another entry. 'Five hundred. Exactly. Something about that number you like? Nice and round, maybe? I'm almost convinced you didn't know about this concrete problem, Chris. I really am. But there's this one little detail that doesn't fit.'

'It's got nothing to do with the concrete.'

'Then what?'

He really crashed then, elbows on the table, letting his face fall forward into both hands. 'I gave it to Sam for the kid. To help out.'

'For Ghost? Why?'

'Because she's mine.' He sat back, let his hands drop. 'I'm her father.'

THIRTY-NINE

Boonie didn't mean to go running back to the boss like some sniveling bitch, but he couldn't help it. He'd beaten guys before and seen plenty of blood. He'd come upon men dead of gunshots and knife wounds. He wasn't some young'un. But he had never before stumbled over a body he wasn't expecting to see, the body of someone he knew, of someone he'd come up with and who was practically his best friend in the whole world. No, it'd be all right to be a little freaked out about something like that.

All the same, he tried to straighten up as he walked up to the motel, and gave it to the boss crisp and concise, even with the rain now dripping in his eyes. At least he thought he sounded crisp. Maybe not so concise.

'*What*?'

'He dead. Damon's dead, he was tossed off that tower just like the other two were. There weren't nobody there when I left, I *know*, just Damon. He might still be there, up on the floors, I don't know.'

'Then let's go get him,' the boss said, and pulled his not inconsiderable bulk out of the worn lawn chair. 'Lee, lock up here. You, come wit' me.'

Boonie had half-hoped, half-feared the man

would say that. 'He might still be there, I don't know, sick one like that might stay and be rubbin' on himself. But I don't know—' He threw himself into the driver's seat, and it was a measure of his agitation that his speech did not even slow down when the boss's bodyguard threw him back out of it, took it for himself and let Boonie get in the empty back space where he would have to sit on the floor. 'He might be gone by now.'

'We'll look anyway,' the boss said, in a voice that almost sounded kind.

'Might have a piece, too. I'm thinking about that, and Damon wasn't no bitch.' Actually Boonie had had his doubts about that lately, what with Damon's surprising contentment with a paying job, but now that the boy was dead he would defend his memory with extreme prejudice. 'And he worked out, weren't no weakling. Would have been really tough to pick him up and carry him around and Damon wouldn't have gone with the fool, not unless he had a piece.'

'You're sure he wasn't shot?'

'No. It weren't no rip-off,' Boonie said, remembering the way Damon's bones grated against each other when he tried to turn his friend over. His stomach roiled and he bit down on the taste of bile in his mouth. This might be the worst hour of his life but he would retain the presence of mind not to upchuck in front of the boss. 'Cops might be there.'

The boss turned around and looked back at him, having to peer down over the back of the front seat since Boonie was on the floor, the convolutions of the corrugated floor biting into his buttocks, knees drawn up to his chin. He hadn't sat in that position since he'd been in grade school and straightened out his legs before the boss noticed. Damon might be dead, but *he* wasn't, and a man had to think of these things.

'Are you proposin' that we let this messed up mope get away with killin' one of our own?'

'No, *suh*,' Boonie said.

'If the cops are there, that's one thing,' the boss told him calmly, turning back around to stare out the windshield. 'If they're not, then apprehendin' this dangerous animal falls to us. And we will not fail.'

Boonie felt comforted, in a small but firm way. He had not run away from his murdered friend – he had simply kept the boss in the loop, like any good soldier. Damon, he knew, would have understood.

Ian had not been kidding when he said he walked past the construction site every day on his way to the Justice Center – he lived at the Chesterfield, no more than a quarter of a mile from the Rockwell address. Theresa didn't know where to leave her car; in frustration she parked it in front of the channel nineteen building with the visitor's lot empty at that time on a week night. She guided Ghost out of the passenger seat, then braced her knees and picked the kid up, draping her across the front of her body with the skinny arms around her neck. Ghost didn't protest; she let her head rest on Theresa's shoulder, the arms tightening just enough to break Theresa's heart.

It wasn't easy – skinny or not Ghost was still eleven years old and had to weigh at least sixty-five pounds. Theresa's knees protested just a bit at stepping on and off the curbs as they crossed Chester, but she wasn't about to let go. She had known this child less than forty-eight hours, but might be the only person she had left in the world.

The streets were empty and a little wet from the misting rain. A lone figure shuffled along further up Chester, and she heard a car door slam somewhere. Even with the weather keeping people in, it saddened her how downtown Cleveland had become so deserted. Only a block away there used to be a lounge called The Theatrical, a Midwestern version of Sardis. Anyone who was anyone drank there, from mobsters to politicians to *Press* reporters getting out of work. More deals had been struck—

'Theresa!' A voice broke her reverie. 'You've got to get to the site. Someone else has been killed, one of the pipefitters.'

She stopped, stared. 'Another murder? But Frank—'

'He's there, too. Come on, we'll take my car.'

Ghost's head snapped up. 'Theresa, NO!'

Theresa tottered under her sudden agitation. 'What?'

'He's the shadow man!'

Theresa's heart seemed to seize, and pricks of icy sweat broke out on her skin.

He smiled.

FORTY

Frank left Chris Novosek in a holding cell, then rejoined his partner at their desks. She paged through Todd Grisham's statement, turning each sheet with a desultory flick. Frank slumped into his chair and took a sip of cold coffee before dropping the Styrofoam cup into his wastebasket. The impact forced drops of the liquid upward, leaving a spray pattern on his lower desk drawer, a perfect illustration of his mood. Scattered and dark brown.

Angela sat back as well. She didn't often show her weariness but made an exception tonight. 'I'm lost.'

'Have you tried Hare Krishna?'

'We got one murder sewn up, but we're back to square one on the other. And I don't even have a front runner. I just can't see Todd. I've never been able to figure out where Scott Crain and his protesters figure in – potentially violent but not likely. Then there's our corrupt concrete inspector, likely but not violent. Your phone's blinking.'

'Huh?'

She nodded at the electronic device on his blotter.

He picked it up, checked the screen. 'Theresa called. How much you want to bet this kid's disappeared again?'

'Don't think it. You think she's really been roaming the city looking for her father?'

'We're all searching for something. That's what keeps us moving into new territory, building ever higher buildings. Hoping we'll find it. It's what makes us human. Angela...'

She turned another page of the statement. 'Hmm?'

'Would you like to have dinner with me?'

As Theresa neared the Federal Reserve building, her thighs began to quake. 'I don't think I can make it.'

'Put her down,' he said. The steel barrel bit into her spine, just to let her know who remained in charge. Just as it had when a homeless man had come out of the alley off Chester, and when an occupied taxi had crossed East Ninth in front of them. Besides that, the streets belonged to them and the gun at her back eased up a bit. He didn't touch her otherwise. He didn't have to.

At his suggestion Ghost wailed and tightened her arms around Theresa's neck. Theresa instinctively squeezed back.

'Shut up, you stupid brat. You want to make this poor lady carry you all over the city?' The gun pressed harder. 'Put her down. You, kid, you try to run and I'll shoot you, and then I shoot her. Same deal goes for you, forensic bitch. Got it?'

The child's body slid to the ground, but she never let go of Theresa enough to think about running. Her arms wrapped around Theresa's waist, face buried in her rib cage. It made walking with her almost as clunky as carrying her had been, but Theresa wasn't in any hurry. 'Where are we going?'

'Where do you *think*?' Jack told her.

The sky lit up in a brilliant blue light, and thunder boomed so loud it seemed to quake the very ground under her feet.

Ian Bauer came through the Chesterfield's two front doors. He thought Theresa should have been there by now, but then he didn't know how long it might have taken her to convince Ghost to come, or what her driving habits might be like. He hadn't told her his apartment number and the deskman said no one had come in for the past hour. Maybe she wasn't sure of the building. But the Chesterfield had been there for so many years ... Too many, from the state of the electrical system...

No cars at the curb, none in the street. He checked his cell phone, no calls. A bolt of lightning cracked the sky in two and the resulting thunder followed too closely behind for comfort. Crap.

He braved the raindrops to pace the sidewalk to the south. He would wait. He would wait for Theresa MacLean for the next ten years, yes, OK, but he meant that right now she might not know where to park—

As he pivoted, a lump in the shadows caught his eye. It sat against the building to the right of the front door.

He picked it up without thinking. A wet brown leather purse with plenty of outside pockets, and

301

a chiffon scarf tied to one buckle. Theresa's purse, the one he had hung on to at the Tavern. What the hell was it doing on the sidewalk outside his apartment?

He looked up and down the street again, panic beginning to swell within him. But East Twelfth remained as empty and silent as before.

The gate facing the Mall stood open, about a foot. Theresa pushed it, reluctantly, wondering if she could slam it back on Jack without getting herself and Ghost shot. Most likely not.

'Keep walking.'

'It's dark in here. Where am I going?'

'Turn to the left. Keep walking.' He let a few feet lapse between them; behind the fence he didn't need to touch her back with the gun. This didn't help, as now she couldn't snatch the gun away if something distracted him. As if she could have pulled that off anyway. Crouching Tiger she was not, especially in the slick mud.

Ghost continued to cling, her soft whimpers muffled by Theresa's shirt and flesh. It made travel over the uneven ground difficult but that was good. Every extra second made it more likely that Ian might notice the delay in her arrival, or Frank might call back and then come looking when she didn't answer. But would either of them figure out where to search for her? Her heart, beating wildly, sunk further at the possibilities. No, she and Ghost were most likely on their own, exhausted, unarmed, and at the mercy of a madman. She wiped soaked tendrils of hair out of her face.

Think.

'You left asbestos on Sam's clothing,' she told Jack. 'I should have figured it out when you mentioned your kitchen remodel. You're redoing your counters?'

'Going to look great when it's done. Step up on the platform, there.' He directed them on to the raised foundation that would eventually become a parking garage on the west side of the building. To her left, the fence that shielded them from the Mall and, farther away, the Marriott; to her right, the shifting, murky depths of the interior of the building.

'Where are we going?'

'Didn't you ever want to see the city at night? I mean from forty stories up.'

'I've seen it. We're getting on the zip lift?' She stopped at the edge of it.

He giggled, and the sound raised the hairs on her arms. 'Unless you want to walk all the way up.'

A chance to get a few steps of higher ground while he wearied, plenty of dark turns and corners? 'Yes.'

'Well, I don't. Get on.'

'I'm not riding on this,' she said. Ghost whined a protest as well.

'Fine, then I'll just shoot my little angel/demon here. See, the fates have turned me into an omnivore. Meaning I'll push, I'll stab, I'll pull the trigger. It's all the same to me.'

Theresa put one foot on the small wooden deck and bent down to lift up Ghost.

'Wait a minute. Wait, wait, wait.'

She straightened.

'I have asbestos in my kitchen?'

Grab at any straw. 'Yes. It must have been on your clothing and transferred to her. You should get a chest X-ray, have yourself checked for exposure.'

He appeared to think about it and for a moment a shoot of hope sprung up in her heart. But then he shrugged. 'Not surprising, it was built in the sixties. Go on, get up. Get back against the railing.'

Theresa stepped to the opposite edge, trying not to think that in another minute that edge would be a hundred or more feet off the ground, and slid Ghost down until her feet reached the decking. She took the little girl's hand and wrapped it around the thin railing post which held the cable railings, then stood in front of her, facing Jack.

He had the gun in his right hand, pointed at her, with the left awkwardly crossed in front of his body to reach the lift controls. She could see him clearly enough in the ambient light from the Mall and the mall lights. With a jerk, the platform began to rise, bringing them closer to the errant flashes of lightning.

She let her knees soften, rock with the movement as she planned her next move. She might not be a black belt and she might not be a trained police officer, but if she didn't do something soon, he would kill her. And then he would kill Ghost. Her heart pounded against her ribs hard enough to hurt and she knew if she thought about it for even another split second, she wouldn't do it.

So Theresa stepped forward with her left foot, grabbed his gun hand with her left hand and punched at his face with her right, and brought her right foot forward to kick him in the groin as hard as she could. Her plan wasn't to incapacitate him or even wrench the gun away and shoot him. Her plan was to push him over the side of those flimsy cable railings and let him plummet to the earth just as Sam and Kyle had.

'You going to call her back?' Angela asked him.

'In a minute. Answer the question first.'

'About getting something to eat?' she murmured, paging through one of the many Manila folders on her desk.

'No,' he said so firmly that she stopped paging and looked up at him. 'Would you like to have dinner with me?'

Perhaps the careful enunciation tipped her off, but she seemed to know exactly what he was really asking and somehow it didn't surprise her as much as he had thought it might. But neither did she jump at the chance.

Finally she opened her lips to answer. But just as she said, 'Yes,' his phone rang.

He glanced at the display, sighing in irritation. His cousin's timing had never been worse. But instead of Theresa's voice, Frank found himself listening in disbelief to Ian Bauer's panicked tones.

FORTY-ONE

If she had been a black belt, it might have worked.

Unfortunately she didn't catch either the gun or the gun hand, just his wrist, leaving him free to fire the weapon over her shoulder towards Ghost. And the kick landed on his thigh just above the knee, painful but not nearly painful enough. In a flurried instant he grabbed her in a bear hug and pushed her down on the railing so she could get a good look at the huge amount of empty space, sufficiently off balance that all he had to do was pull up on her feet and she would fall into that inky, bottomless—

She could hear Ghost screaming.

The lift shook as it came to a sudden halt. Without Jack's hand on the controls it had automatically shut off.

Her neck landed across the cable, and with Jack's weight on her back it probably would have sliced her throat open had her hand not been in the way. She clung to the string with all the strength five fingers could produce and tried to breathe with both her hand and the gun jammed into her neck.

'Very cute,' Jack breathed into her ear. 'Do that again and I'll shoot the kid in both knees and let her lay there for a while before I toss her over. Got that?'

She sucked in some air, but not enough.

'Do you got that?'

'Yes,' she squeaked.

He hauled her up by her hair, then let her slide into a disorganized, gasping heap in the opposite corner. He returned to the lift controls. Ghost threw herself into Theresa's arms just as the platform began to rise again. The wind grew stronger the higher they went.

'Why?' Theresa rasped.

'Why what?' Jack snapped at her.

'Why are you doing this?' She spoke as loudly as her aching throat could manage to be heard over the machinery and the brisk wind.

'What did I tell you? The first instinct when you get to a high place is to throw something off.'

'But a person?'

Jack still had a good grip on the gun and held it loosely pointed toward her. 'Have you ever killed anyone?'

'No!'

He seemed to give this serious thought. It made the calm tone of his voice sound even crazier when he said, 'Well, then, I really don't think you'd understand.'

She took a deep breath. Physical force had proven pathetically inadequate. Try talking. 'Was Sam the first person you killed?'

He smiled, which made him look indescribably creepy. 'The first is always so special.'

'Why Sam?'

'Why *not* Sam? If you had – that's right, you'd never seen her alive. She shook her ass at me every day for months now, but when I decide to take the bait she slaps my hand.'

'What do you mean?' Perhaps he liked talking about it, or he just thought it would accomplish the impossible and frighten her even more than she already was.

'Let's see, Reader's Digest Version ... She'd smile and flick her hair, but then the whistle would blow and she'd disappear. I'm speaking figuratively, of course, we don't really have a whistle. But she loved this place. I'd see her stand by the edge and look out, get that breeze to blow her hair back like she was in some kind of shampoo commercial, that sun kissing her skin, and she'd look out at the city like she had a freakin' diamond tiara on her head and it all belonged to her. She'd do it when no one else was around, but when you work up high, you see everything. People think we're nuts, but we see *everything*. Like God.'

The lift came to a stop. 'Please watch your step,' Jack told them as he backed on to the thirty-first floor. 'Keep hand and arms inside the car and remember, if you don't do what I tell you, I'll shoot you a couple times in not very comfortable places. Are we on the same page?'

Theresa didn't answer, too busy trying to climb to her feet with shaking legs and Ghost still wrapped around her waist.

'Kid? You listening?'

Theresa said that the child could hear him and stepped carefully off the lift. At least it stopped

308

the rain from pelting their faces. Jack directed them toward the north stairwell. 'It's no fun if you don't go all the way to the top, don't you think?'

The stairwell. Higher ground with dark corners. Maybe she still had a chance.

Keep him talking. 'So you convinced her to come here with you?'

'But then she got persnickety, somehow palmed a screwdriver that must have been rattling around in that Camry. When we got inside the building, the bitch stabbed me.'

'In the side. You told me it was a spud wrench.' Theresa and Ghost started up the steps, feeling each riser. 'Very clever, getting an alibi out there in case I decided to test the smear of blood on the lift.'

'I'm a clever dude. And I wasn't lying, we gash ourselves with wrenches and sleever bars all the time. So then I brought her up to twenty-three – she was struggling with me so I just gave up and stopped there.'

They reached the first landing, and the turn. If she turned and kicked him now, she and Ghost could dash across the floor – to where? The lift was one floor down. If they jumped—

'She kept fighting me, the idiot. I didn't have a gun then – I mean, not with me. But she wasn't anywhere near as tough as she thought she was, and too skinny to hold that much booze.'

—they'd have to hit a five-foot square platform that was ten feet below them and approximately three hundred feet off the ground. Theresa didn't think it was possible to feel any more terrified, but at the image a fresh wave of sweat pricked out of her pores.

And her alternative would be...?

She turned the corner, the darkest point in the stairwell.

Suddenly a flash of light blinded her, too long for lightning, and for one surging moment she thought help had arrived. Frank had come, or Ian, and—

No. Jack held a mini-flashlight in his free hand, aiming it right at her eyes. She could only see the outline of his legs, too far away from her for any chance of a strike. 'Keep going.'

'She's exhausted.'

'I don't care.'

'I'm exhausted. We can only move so fast.'

'I bet you'd find a mysterious store of energy if I shoot at your ankles. But that's OK, take your time. No one knows we're here. We've got all night, and I'm kind of enjoying this.'

Theresa moved up the next few steps, with nearly all of Ghost's body weight hanging off her waist. The thirty-second floor opened to her left, but if she ran for it Jack would fire before she got five feet. On top of that it had no floor, only a rebar and metal mesh framework stretched between the girders and she wasn't even sure it would hold her weight. Another flash of electrical discharge showed her a small crate and some scattered tools perched on a central X formed by the girders – much too far away for her to reach. With no weapon and no escape route, only one plan came to mind: somehow she had to get Jack over the edge of the building. She would probably have to get shot to accomplish this, but she had some chance of surviving a gunshot. She would not survive a three-hundred-foot fall.

First she had to get free to move.

'Ghost, let go of me. I'll hold your hand. Hang on to my hand.' She pulled the girl's arms from her waist as they walked, gently removing them and placing Ghost's right hand in her left. She squeezed, as a note of encouragement, and the girl clung tightly enough to cut off the circulation to her digits. Jack's flashlight provided just enough light to see the steps in front of them.

'I don't want to fall.' Ghost's voice sounded too tight to allow tears. 'Please.'

'You won't fall. I won't let you.' Theresa raised her voice a notch. 'So Samantha struggled with you. Because she didn't want to see the city lights in your company, or because she knew what you planned to do?'

Jack answered from behind her, the light trained unerringly on her plodding body. 'She had no idea what I planned because I had no idea what I planned. The bitch just thought she was too good for me, is all. A drunk slut, and she was too good for me.'

'Maybe it wasn't that. Maybe you frightened her.'

'Gee, that's nice of you to say. Keep going, we've got another flight.'

'Maybe Sam could feel what you were planning to do, even if you couldn't. She didn't reject you. You scared her.'

'With good reason, as it turns out. Just a few

more steps, dear, come on.'

The risers ended and she had no where to go but the thirty-third floor, consisting of the same girders-and-meshwork she had seen below, and she stopped, preferring to keep her feet on the solid concrete of the stairwell.

They were at the top. The rain and air currents whipped at them with ferocious energy; what she'd felt on the zip lift had just been a taste. Beyond the edge the city spread around them, a glittering panorama of structures and textures, human sounds and even the crashing lake drowned out by gusts of wind. Drops of water pelted her skin like darts.

'Keep going,' Jack said.

'Where? There's no floor. That mesh isn't going to hold me.'

'Don't know till you try.' Much closer to her than she had realized, he pushed her forward with one violent shove.

Her body flew out on to the open floor, pulling Ghost with her.

The rebar and mesh patchwork forming the floor sank underneath her feet with a sickening lurch, but she did not fall through. Too late she realized it would have been better if she had – only ten feet of space to the next floor, a floor that Jack wouldn't be on—

'See? There's wooden braces under the mesh. What do you think keeps the concrete from dripping out when we pour it? Honestly, Theresa, for a scientist sometimes I wonder about you. Turn left. I want to show you where little Sam landed.'

'I know where she landed. I scraped her flesh off the concrete.'

'Temper, temper,' he muttered. 'You're not going to get into heaven with that attitude.'

She and Ghost staggered across the wet spongy floor, perched out in the open atop a three-hundred-foot lightning rod. Twenty feet to the edge and she had no idea what to do. She saw nothing around to use as a weapon, no loose tools, nothing but her own body and her wit.

Hah. They were doomed.

And she would never find out what had been bothering Rachael.

'Why did you follow Ghost home? Why did you tell her you were her father?' Theresa had a good guess, but anything to keep him talking. She had to practically shout over the weather.

'I needed the screwdriver back. I know about DNA too, you know. But I also needed to know if she could identify me. She shows up on the site. She shows up at my bar. I couldn't take the chance that I'd run into her some day and have her scream holy hell.'

'Who would listen to her anyway? She's just a little girl.' Theresa squeezed the kid's hand, to let her know that she didn't mean it, though she doubted Ghost cared much by this point. Their steps had slowed until they were barely moving, and yet the edge came closer. 'She doesn't even know your name. Let her go.'

Ghost's hand tightened on hers, in a spasm of fear, but whether for herself or for Theresa's sake, she could not know.

'Stop,' he said. She and Ghost were five feet

from the edge. 'Turn around.'

She did, slowly, carefully on the uneven and shifting ground, switching Ghost's hand from her left to her right. Lightning flashed, illuminating the man in shades of black and bluish white.

'This is the fun part,' Jack told her.

FORTY-TWO

Angela watched, eyes widening, as Frank listened to Ian Bauer. The attorney's rising tones were easily audible, and she didn't look away until her desk phone rang.

Then she interrupted her partner's frantic questioning of the man to say: 'Report of shots fired in the vicinity of the construction site. Maybe it's thunder.'

'I don't think so,' Frank said.

Boonie, the boss and the boss's bodyguard pulled up to the fence.

'Wait,' Boonie said, kneeling up and peeking over the front seat like some little kid.

'What?'

'I closed that gate when I left.'

'So maybe the guy left it open when *he* left. I don't see no cop cars.'

'Oh,' Boonie said, feeling foolish. The shock of Damon's death was wearing off – death came often in their line of work, you couldn't let personal grief get in the way of thinking straight – and he didn't want to act the bitch in front of the boss. So he straightened up and opened the van door, led the way into the site. Truth be told, he wasn't afraid of the killer, not with the boss and his bodyguard in tow; they would have four pieces between them, and of course Boonie had his own. Whoever killed Damon would be a piece of Swiss cheese two seconds after they met.

But running into the cops with a dead body, two convicted felons and a load of stolen copper pipe *did* worry him. So he stopped dead, his body already soaked, when he heard the sirens. They hadn't even reached Damon's body, were standing out in the open area to the south of the building with only a backhoe and a pile of beams for cover. It didn't seem like enough, not from the killer, not from the cops. Boonie's heart began to thud against the inside of his ribs.

'Well *that* –' the boss had stopped as well – 'changes things.'

Just then they heard a gunshot and a woman's scream. Boonie jumped. 'There's someone up there.'

The boss scanned the dark building; no signs of movement. 'You got any women working with you?'

'No.'

'Then this is not our problem.' He turned and headed back toward the gate.

'But—' Boonie protested, picturing his friend's twisted body, what little he could see of it in the dark fleshed out by what he felt with his hands as he'd tried to figure out what had happened. 'What about Damon?'

The boss looked at him with what seemed like contempt. 'He dead. He don't care.'

Boonie knew this to be true; he had walked away from the dead and wounded before without hesitation. This was different. He took one step before guilt and shame crashed in on him. The boss had turned to go without waiting for his response, and that only added a sheen of humiliation with the next step.

But he moved his feet a third time. Damon *was* dead. And he'd been a soldier.

After that, it got easier, and he had nearly caught up to the boss by the time they reached the gate.

But suddenly, through the rain, bright lights blinded them and a few voices shouted, 'Freeze!'

And Boonie's steps became of lead once more.

This was it. Out of time, out of space, the wind and rain assaulting her as if it wanted to throw her to the ground every bit as much as Jack did. Even if help arrived, it would never reach them in time. The zip lift would not return on its own so any rescuers would have to walk up thirty-three floors, and she and Ghost would be dead by then.

'So what now?' Theresa challenged, with all the pluck she could muster as her feet sank a few inches into the mesh, Ghost trembling by her side. 'You threw Sam off because you were fighting with her. We're not fighting. You're not close enough to touch me. So what's your plan? You have one murder under your belt and suddenly you're an expert?'

'I didn't say it was only one.'

'You didn't kill Kyle. Novosek killed Kyle.'

'Did he really? Somebody being on somebody's take, I suppose – never mind, don't tell me. But the interesting thing about being on the edge, Theresa? It only takes a little push to topple something over.'

'But—'

'Technically I should do you first, get you out of the way. The kid might run in the meantime, of course, but where's she going to go? But I think it would be so much more fun to watch your face as she falls.' In one quick move he stepped up to Ghost and grabbed her shoulder, gun still trained on Theresa.

She didn't think, couldn't think. She just jumped, propelled her body toward his and pummeled into his torso. A blast of sound split the night air as the gun went off, and somewhere at the back of her mind she wondered if anyone would be able to distinguish it from a crack of thunder. The sound felt as if it split Theresa's left eardrum, but she could still hear his frenzied breathing as he fell across a girder with her on top of him, a sharp grunt of pain as the steel beam caught him in the spine.

Ghost screamed.

The gun flew out of his hand, landing in the next section of mesh flooring. Theresa put one knee in Jack's chest to propel herself closer to it.

317

But he reached around with an ironworker's hand and peeled her off him as if she were a piece of wet newspaper, tossing her closer to the precipice and away from the gun. Then he grunted, rolled over and began a scrabbling dash to get it.

He was also between them and the exit.

That left only one way down. And again, if she thought about it for even a second, she'd never find the courage to try.

Still in a crouch, she grabbed Ghost by her shirt front and said, 'Get on my back!'

The girl said something, some kind of protest, but Theresa didn't listen. She swung the child behind her and pulled her arms around her neck, leaving the kid to figure out where to wrap her legs. Then she stood, the mesh sinking even deeper under their combined weight, and staggered the two feet to the edge of the building.

She didn't know what Jack was doing, didn't take the time to look.

Three hundred feet below the ground tilted dizzily, and the street lights blurred in the rain.

'Hang on,' she told Ghost – unnecessarily, the girl now squeezed her neck tight enough to choke her, her clunky shoes digging into Theresa's stomach – and climbed over the side, now slick with rain.

FORTY-THREE

The city might have been glittering all around her like a deep and beautiful jewel, but gravity, that dark Satan, was trying to kill her. Theresa could feel the pull of the earth, steady and inexorable and growing stronger by the minute.

You're going to fall. Your hands are going to slip right off this wet steel.

You can't do this!

Jack is going to lean over that edge and fire a bullet directly into the top of your skull. Or Ghost's.

Beams are vertical. Girders are horizontal. One big crystal structure of right angles. And all around it, a vacuum.

Theresa couldn't tell if her limbs trembled from fear or exhaustion as she clung to the beam, wrapping her arms and legs around it just as Ghost wrapped her arms and legs around her. The I-beam felt much less pliable and much less welcoming. It wasn't the concrete-encased column she had leaned on the day before but a bare steel beam, slippery in the rain. Better because she could get her arms and legs all the way around it; worse because the I-beam was shaped exactly as it sounded, not a solid square but with hollows on each side. The cross hatches of the I gave her hands something to grab on to, but it was a thin, sharp something that bit into her palms without giving her fingers much traction. Her feet pulled her close to the steel as her knees bowed out, but her hands felt as if they had every pound of hers plus all of Ghost's weight hanging from them.

You're going to fall.

She needed to slide around to the other side of the beam, to the inside of the building, out of Jack's line of fire. Then Ghost's arms and her own face could get some space in the hollow of the I, but then the hatches would then bite into her shoulders and she doubted she could make herself loosen her grip long enough to get some leeway to shuffle her body around. She didn't need to let go long enough to slide or shimmy downward – the slick metal, her lack of strength and the force of gravity took care of that for her. She had no idea how far or how fast she had moved, but the beam slipped by. She wished she had gloves.

You're going to fall. And if you fall, Ghost falls.

She needed to tell Ghost to loosen the arms around her neck before pressure on her carotids made her lose consciousness. At least the rain kept her awake. It drove into her like the swiping paw of a huge animal, not a steady force from one side but a random series of blows that changed direction faster than thought.

She needed to scream, to let Frank or Ian or anyone in the vicinity know that she needed help. As if they could possibly reach her in time. As if they could even hear her over the weather.

She needed to formulate a plan for what to do if they, by some miracle, reached the next floor, since she had nowhere to go and could not possibly make it to the stairwell or the zip lift before Jack pounded down the steps to meet her.

He hadn't fired. Why hadn't he fired?

Most likely because he was already on his way down the steps.

The metal beam felt cold enough to numb her skin, and yet it didn't because they hurt plenty—

You're going to fa—

Look, a voice in her head suddenly roared, *you have worked out every day since you were twenty years old. What was that all for?*

You can do this.

Just then her foot touched the outside girder of the thirty-first floor.

One toe slipped off the solid foundation of the next floor's outer girder but the other one left Theresa secure enough to pull herself around to the inside of the beam. Suddenly she and Ghost were not hanging off the side of the building in a driving thunderstorm any more but safe in the dark but much more secure interior of wire mesh and narrow girder and merely soaked through every stitch of clothing she wore. She could have fallen to her knees and wept with gratitude.

Except that Jack would be upon them any second.

After she pried her hands from the beam she

had to pry Ghost's arms from her neck. This proved difficult for the child but Theresa's gasps convinced where words could not. Then she grabbed the girl's hand and ran for the zip lift, as fast as they could across the malleable, spongy mesh floor. Theresa breathed like a freight train but made no attempt to quiet her lungs. It wasn't like Jack didn't know where they were.

They tripped over the first girder they encountered, then the second. The interior of the building held only the dimmest haze of ambient light in between the flashes of lightning. Theresa tried to watch the stairwell entrance as she ran but lost track of it in the shadows.

Ghost cried out as she fell over a small stack of tools near the center of the floor just as Theresa saw a figure appear from the murk of the stairwell. It could have been the figure in a dream, nothing but a darker patch of dark against the wall, but Theresa knew he would prove all too real. He had less distance to cross to reach them as they had to go in order to reach the lift. They'd never make it. He would catch them again and push them over the edge. Ghost first. He'd promised to throw her first.

'Ghost. Run and jump into the zip lift – the elevator. Press the lower button on that box and it will take you down. You can do it.'

The little girl fell again. Theresa yanked her up. 'Run!'

A gentle push toward the lift, but then Ghost stopped dead. In a flash of light she saw Jack come straight for them from forty feet away.

Theresa dropped to the uneven ground, hands

322

rooting through the items there. A five gallon bucket, a safety harness—

'No,' Ghost said. 'I'm not leaving you.'

Theresa thought she hadn't heard correctly over the howl of the wind. She stared at the vague outline of the girl. 'Ghost, please – it will be just like climbing down the tree outside your window. You can do it.'

'No. He made me leave Nana and I'm not leaving you!'

They didn't have time to argue, and besides, Theresa knew determination when she heard it. Twenty feet.

'OK, then I need your help. Find something I can use as a weapon, OK? I'll look here. You look over there. But hide if he comes near you.' She aimed the child toward the darker areas to the south, away from Jack, and gave her a push. *Please run. Please. Let the lightning hold off, let her hide.*

Ghost moved away.

Fifteen feet.

Theresa tried the handle of the five-gallon bucket but to her surprise it lifted easily, so light that it would simply bounce off the man if she hit him with it. The harness – maybe she could use the long strap as a bullwhip—

Right. She was no more Indiana Jones than she was Crouching Tiger.

Ten feet.

Then something small and warm took her right hand and pressed something cold and hard into its palm.

Ghost had found her a weapon.

A spud wrench is essentially a wrench with the other end honed to an ice-pick-like point. The middle is smooth and gave her wet hand no traction. Theresa held it against the back of her damp thigh, gripping the wrench end with two fingers sticking through the opening, figuring that even supposing she could hold on to it she'd probably break a couple of digits.

'Who the hell do you think—' Jack said as he rushed her, hands reaching for her neck even though one still held the gun.

She swung the harness toward his face, stepped up closer instead of retreating and brought the spud wrench up and into his abdomen with all the force her stiff, exhausted hand could muster. Holding it at the end didn't give her a lot of control, but otherwise it would have simply slipped through her palm.

His body went rigid and for a moment she could feel the heat from it searing her, the smell of beer on his breath and even the brush of his shaggy hair against her cheek.

Then the gun went off.

For the second time that night her eardrums were split by the sonic boom of a bullet.

No sharp pains in her body, no sudden sucking feeling of perforated organs. But *Ghost*! Had he hit Ghost?

Lightning flashed, and in its ghostly illumination they were face to face. The side lighting turned his gaunt face to a series of craters and peaks, hair plastered in wet snakes, the face of a monster. Or a shadow man.

Then he fell on to her, and she felt a new

wetness on the hand that still held the spud wrench. She couldn't hold him and without warning her body pivoted so that he toppled across a girder between the mesh and the wrench slid out of him. She dropped it, but remembered to reach down and follow his arm to where the gun should be.

And wasn't.

A quick scrambling pat-down of the area located the firearm as Jack moaned and tried to curl into a fetal position. Theresa tossed the gun – not smart, but she had pretty much used up all disciplined thought for one night – and went looking for Ghost.

True to her word, the girl hadn't moved, just fallen back across the mesh and girders and five-gallon bucket.

She's been shot she's been shot she's been – Theresa's frantic hands scanned the girl's body, searching for a gaping hole of ruined flesh, burnt by gunpowder.

But she found nothing, and Ghost's arms closed around her neck.

FORTY-FOUR

Ian Bauer held Theresa MacLean, and he thought that nothing had ever felt better in his entire life. She had even let him drape her in a blanket he pilfered from the ER, though they were both soaked to the skin with rain that, thanks to the robust air conditioning, felt as if it were turning to ice on their clothes.

Yes, she had been through a grueling and traumatic experience. Yes, she might have her head on his shoulder, her hair brushing the bottom of his jaw, only to keep herself from falling over in sheer physical exhaustion. She had refused to let go of Ghost even after help arrived, staggered into the hospital with the child still wrapped in her arms, releasing her only so that nurses could put the kid in dry clothes and stop her teeth from chattering. But even so, he told himself, women didn't stay long in the arms of men they despised. Certainly not for the entire fifteen minutes they'd been standing at the glass window to one of the emergency rooms watching the hospital staff work on Ghost's grandmother.

Nana Zebrowski had turned out to be tougher than anyone, including Jack, would have guessed and had escaped with a medium-strength

326

concussion. By the time Theresa reached the hospital she'd already begun agitating to leave, alert enough to semi-confirm Novosek's story of his affair with a very young Samantha, back when she had been working a summer job in his former boss's office. 'I never really knew, but that makes sense,' Betty Zebrowski conceded. 'I could have handled her getting pregnant by a schoolmate. I couldn't have stood an affair with a married man. She probably thought I'd kick her out. My poor baby,' she'd told Frank, her eyes filling with tears.

'I don't know how Jack found out about Ghost's obsession with finding her father,' Theresa murmured. 'Somehow he did, and he used it to get close to her. But she recognized his belt buckle – a large star behind a steer's head.'

Frank approached them. He gave Ian the usual skeevy look to let him know he didn't approve of his cousin's choice of moral support, but Ian couldn't blame him. He was, after all, a pretty odd-looking duck. No doubt about it.

It had never bothered him less.

Without preamble, Frank told them: 'Kobelski will be picked up by Finney, since we were kind enough to give him the written evidence in the form of a fake ASTM specs book. And do we get a word of thanks from the Super Special State Investigator?' He didn't bother to answer himself.

Ian sighed. 'I'd better call him.' He slowly removed himself from Theresa's side. The frigid emergency room air sucked into his wet clothes, right where her body had been, but somehow his skin stayed warmed by a heat that welled up from the center of his being.

It felt good.

Frank waited until Ian had been forced around the corner by a team of doctors and nurses wielding a crash cart, and then turned to his cousin. 'I know you, Tess. That puppy-dog adoration is going to be fun for about a week and then it's going to get on your nerves.'

Theresa rubbed one eye, elongating a tiny smear of mascara the rain had left behind. 'Maybe. But you know what? I spent sixteen years married to a man who never, ever, not once even considered putting me first. So a little adoration might be just what I'm looking for.'

He studied her for a moment, then shook his head and used one thumb to rub off the mascara. 'I get it. We're all searching for something. Problem is it doesn't always work out to be what we expected.'

A nurse brought Ghost in, hair still damp but wrapped in two child-sized hospital gowns with pink kitties on them. As soon as she saw her grandmother she hurtled herself across the room and up on to the bed before any of the nurses could begin to react. Mrs Zebrowski winced, winced again as the little girl snuggled into the area under her arm and wedged one temple into the older woman's shoulder, but then the lines in her face relaxed into a beatific smile. She laid one cheek on the child's hair and closed her eyes.

Ghost also screwed her eyes shut, so tight it

seemed that she might be afraid to open them – not surprising, after what she'd been through. One fist clenched her grandmother's blanket, and if she heard the nurses speaking to her, she ignored them.

'For example,' Frank said, putting an arm around Theresa's shoulders, 'Ghost found her father, but just in time for him to go to jail.'

She said, 'Maybe it won't be for long, if he can convince a jury that Kyle's death was manslaughter and not murder.'

'I guess Nana and a team of social workers can decide when and how to break it to Ghost. Maybe – maybe we should just let her keep believing her father really was Sam's prom date.'

'No.' Theresa gazed through the glass. 'She deserves the truth. She searched too long and too hard to get it.'

As if she'd heard her, Ghost's eyes flew open, staring directly at Theresa. The hand unclenched slightly. The corners of her mouth turned up, and her lips formed two words.

Thank you.

Theresa pressed her hand to the window, feeling the cool glass against her skin.

BIBLIOGRAPHY

Ballon, Hilary and Kenneth T. Jackson, Editors. *Robert Moses and the Modern City; the Transformation of New York*. W.W. Norton & Co: New York, 2007.

Ingle, Bob and Sandy McClure. *The Soprano State: New Jersey's Culture of Corruption*. St Martin's Press: New York, 2008.

Saliga, Pauline A., Ed. *The Sky's the Limit: A Century of Chicago Skyscrapers*. Rizzoli: New York, 1990.

Bowe, John, Marissa Bowe and Sabia Streeter, Eds. *Gig*. Crown: New York, 2000.